PRAISE FOR
THE LIEUTENANT

"The beauty and stupidity of military service are on full display, as well the yearnings and failings of young men practicing leadership and preparing warriors for the battle. Dubus's nuanced interiority and patient pacing changed the art of American military storytelling. *The Lieutenant* has been a secret for far too long. Read it."

—ANTHONY SWOFFORD, author of *Jarhead*

"At first a local study of power and of characters desperate to place their faith in corrupted and corrupting human institutions, the notes struck by the novel's end resonate out, leaving us questioning the structure of our own relationship to power, and what, precisely, it is we put our faith in."

—PHIL KLAY, author of *Missionaries*

THE LIEUTENANT

THE LIEUTENANT

A NOVEL

Andre Dubus

AFTERWORD BY
ANDRE DUBUS III

BOSTON
GODINE NONPAREIL
2023

Published in 2023 by
GODINE
Boston, Massachusetts

First published in 1967 by The Dial Press

The author wishes to thank the Writers' Workshop at the State University of
Iowa, Florence Unash, and Captain C.E. Gonzales, USMC (Ret.)

Grateful acknowledgment is made for permission to reprint material from
published sources: Sands Music, Inc.: for lyrics from "Time After Time."
Lyrics and music by Sammy Cahn and Juie Styne. Copyright © 1947 by Sands
Music Corp. Copyright © 1974 by Sinatra Songs, Inc., assigned to Sands
Music Corp., 10153½ Riverside Drive, #107, Toluca Lake, CA 91602.

LIBRARY OF CONGRESS CATALOGING-IN-PUBLICATION DATA
Names: Dubus, Andre, 1936-1999, author. | Dubus, Andre, III, 1959- writer
  of afterword.
Title: The lieutenant : a novel / Andre Dubus ; afterword by Andre Dubus III.
Description: Boston : Godine Nonpareil, 2023. | "First published in 1967 by
  The Dial Press"—Title page verso.
Identifiers: LCCN 2022038896 (print) | LCCN 2022038897 (ebook) | ISBN
  9781567927610 (paperback) | ISBN 9781567927627 (ebook)
Subjects: LCSH: United States. Marine Corps—Fiction. | LCGFT: Military
  fiction. | Novels.
Classification: LCC PS3554.U265 L5 2023 (print) | LCC PS3554.U265 (ebook)
  | DDC 813/.54—dc23/eng/20221027
LC record available at https://lccn.loc.gov/2022038896
LC ebook record available at https://lccn.loc.gov/2022038897

First Printing, 2023
Printed in the United States of America

For Pat
she steered well

An if we live, we live to tread on kings;
If die, brave death, when princes die with us!
—King Henry IV, Part I

CONTENTS

Chapter One

EVEN AFTER HE had been aboard for nearly six months Dan Tierney did not feel that he was part of the ship: an aircraft carrier, the USS *Vanguard*, which weighed seventy thousand tons and had a flight deck a thousand feet long. He viewed it with awe at times, but more often with scorn. He was a first lieutenant, executive officer of the Marine Detachment, and in his fourth year of service; he had come to the *Vanguard* from land, after a year's tour he would return to land, and one of the only pleasures he drew from sea duty was the honor, the prestige, of being chosen to represent the Marine Corps aboard the largest ship in the Pacific. It was an enviable tour of duty for a young officer. Senior officers had assured him, again and again, that this tour would advance his career: he would profit, they told him, each time a promotion board studied his record, that chronological list of functions assigned him during his professional years.

Dan believed this was true, because seagoing Marines are considered elite: traditionally they are at least six feet tall, firm-muscled and sunburned, the kind who stare at you like your manhood's conscience from recruiting posters. In the *Vanguard* Detachment there were short ones, and some who only needed to shave three or four times a week, and one or two with acne. And Dan himself was by no means six feet tall; he was three inches under that and slender (*lean but hard*, he thought, and it was true: he exercised daily); he had dark bright eyes, sometimes appearing black, and black hair which the officers' barber cut very short each week.

If upon first reporting aboard he was somewhat disillusioned by several beardless or acned or puny Marines, he was soon cheered by what he recognized as the essence of his profession: their spirit. They reminded him of his college baseball team and, with a couple of exceptions, he loved them all. So besides the honor attached to his duty, he had that too: serving with troops he admired more than any he had ever known. He was proud of them, and loyal— the pride and loyalty becoming steadily more intense, sustaining him in loneliness and the frustration of sea duty spent largely below decks, among seemingly labyrinthine passageways where strange levers and pipes and switches confronted him daily with his own alienation—and once in a bar at Yokosuka a plump ensign had sung the "Marines' Hymn" to the tune of "Clementine" and Dan had knocked him off his bar stool. The ensign rose quickly, angered even more by the cause of the blow than by the blow itself, but other officers had moved between them.

Midway through the *Vanguard*'s seven-month cruise in the Western Pacific, she pulled out of Yokosuka on a bright November day, leaving Dan's commanding officer in the Naval hospital ashore. He was Captain Raymond Schneider, who had joined the Marines in 1947 when he was eighteen, and had gone into the Korean War as a corporal, a squad leader in an infantry platoon. He was commissioned during the war and now, in 1956, was in his tenth year of duty. Since he had led a squad and then a platoon in combat, he gave Dan the experience which he himself no longer needed: he stayed in the background and let Dan run the Detachment. Dan kept him informed daily, asked for advice and sometimes gave it, and after serving with Captain Schneider for only a month Dan looked on him as a father. He could never forget that while he had been a sophomore, breaking up with his first college girl friend, Captain Schneider had been a corporal in the Chosin Reservoir. Dan had missed the war: on the day it ended he had been a second lieutenant, firing on the rifle range at Quantico, Virginia.

On that first day at sea out of Yokosuka, Dan wrote to his girl in California. Sitting at the desk in his stateroom, he could hardly feel the motion of the sea, for the *Vanguard* was, to him, more like a hotel than a ship: air-conditioned, and it rarely dipped except those times when they had left the breakwater at San Francisco and once when they pulled out of Kobe to run from a typhoon. It had dipped a little then. And sometimes, making a sharp turn into the wind for planes, it shuddered a bit.

He told Khristy that Captain Schneider had a serious ear infection, was in the Naval hospital in Yokosuka where a specialist could treat him, and he would join the ship when it reached Iwakuni. This, Dan wrote her, meant that he would have command of the troops for the next two weeks at sea; for the first time in his career, all the responsibility would be his.

When eight bells sounded next morning, Dan was on his way to the Marine barracks (the Navy referred to their own living quarters as spaces, but the Marines stubbornly called theirs a barracks). The troops were finishing the morning clean-up, and as Dan went down the ladder someone called them to attention. He moved through them, toward his office, and told them to carry on.

The barracks was two large rooms: a long one which they used for a classroom, containing the Corporal of the Guard's desk, rifles stored in racks along two bulkheads and, in stands centered at one side of the room, American and Marine Corps flags. The other room was the berthing area; it was separated from the classroom by a bulkhead with a doorless curtained entrance. Dan's office was at one side of the classroom and, adjacent to the office, was the First Sergeant's stateroom. The office was small, had three desks, and four standing people would crowd it. First Sergeant Tolleson was drinking coffee at his desk; he rose—a man of Dan's height, slender and paunchless after nineteen and a half years of service—and told Dan good morning, then said:

"Unit punishment sheet's on the Lieutenant's desk."

Dan picked it up: in a short paragraph written in

language taken from an example in the *Manual for Courts-Martial* it told that Private First Class Theodore C. Freeman had been disrespectful to a corporal during the morning clean-up: . . . *on or about 14 November 1956 use disrespectful language to Corporal Bradley R.* McKITTRICK *1464203* USMC, *to wit, "Fuck you and the horse you rode in on, Mac" or words to that effect.*

"What the hell got into Freeman?" Dan said.

"Well sir, I guess he figures the Captain's orderly don't have to buff the decks."

"Maybe. Was McKittrick harassing him?"

"No sir, I don't think so. McKittrick's a corporal irregardless, sir."

Dan nodded and read the unit punishment sheet again. Pfc Freeman was one of those who had to shave only every other day and he could use an electric razor for that. He was very slender, had an almost girlishly pretty face, and the troops often teased him, calling him Teddy-Baby; but he was a conscientious sentry, he wore the uniform well and, Dan recalled, he was an expert rifleman. Above all, he had spirit and pride and he had told Dan in a counseling interview that he wasn't sure whether he was a career Marine or not—sometimes he thought he'd like to be— but before he made up his mind he wanted to become a corporal and see what sort of NCO he would be. Because of that, Dan had made him an orderly for the *Vanguard*'s Captain. The duty was considered an honor. Dan knew that Freeman was a parade field Marine, and could probably be a competent seagoing NCO; but it was doubtful that Freeman would ever have the drive required of an infantry leader. Still, Dan hoped that by assuming shipboard responsibilities, Freeman could gain some of those tough qualities he lacked.

This was Freeman's first official offense and Dan was disappointed; but he was also relieved because the case was a simple one, and he repeated the old joke:

"Let the wheels of justice begin to spin; bring the guilty bastard in."

Tolleson grinned.

"Aye aye sir," he said, and went out.

Dan sat at his desk and opened the *Manual for Courts-Martial* to Article Thirty-one; Freeman marched in and reported in a high, tense voice and stood at attention, First Sergeant Tolleson stood at ease behind him, and the office door was closed. Dan knew the troops would be listening from the classroom benches on the other side of the door. This was his first office hours in three and a half years of service and he didn't know if the troops were aware of that, but he thought they probably were, and he was nervous.

It was the performance that bothered him. There were several ways to handle office hours: you could try to be understanding and therapeutic; or you could be as detached as a civil judge; or you could try to scare them. Dan preferred the last; he thought that a man sent to his commanding officer should go through an experience which would send him fearfully and rapidly back to an obedient way of life. And the Marines sitting in guard school should resolve never to do anything that would bring them before Lieutenant Tierney's desk.

So he was preparing himself for the performance, not the sentence. There were only four sentences he could give at office hours: two weeks' restriction to the barracks (a meaningless punishment at sea); two weeks of extra duty; seven days of confinement in the brig; or, because they were on a ship, the only place in the armed forces where this punishment was still used, three days in the brig on bread and water. That was the sentence he had chosen when he first read the unit punishment sheet. Bread-and-water had an aura of the old and traditional. He had heard about it from Staff NCO's when they spoke of the days before military justice had been revised (and ruined, they believed), the days when any company commander, on land or sea, could put a man on bread and water: —*had a CO once, any time a shadow passed his door he locked him up—those days, you went to see the Old Man, you brought your shaving gear with you 'cause you knew you wasn't coming back*— Hearing these stories he had always thought of the Old Corps when officers wore Sam Browne belts and riding boots and carried swagger sticks. Only the swagger sticks had remained and now the new Commandant had publicly belittled them and you didn't see them anymore; Dan carried his, though. He was afraid the Corps might evolve into something totally different from his concept of it: already it had jet planes (he didn't mind propeller planes; he recalled that Lieutenant Cunningham was the first Marine pilot; that Marines had first used dive-bombing in the Banana Wars) and missiles and technicians and administrators who hadn't worn a haversack in years; in the face of this, no tradition should be allowed to die—if the swagger stick went, the blue uniform might go next and Lord knew what would follow.

Now, looking up at Freeman, he had already forgotten the insult to Corporal McKittrick and was ready to avenge those honored and colorful dead of past wars and skirmishes and musketry from wooden ships.

He read Article Thirty-one aloud.

"That means you don't have to say anything that might incriminate you. Do you understand that?"

"Yes, sir."

"All right. Initial here."

Dan turned the unit punishment sheet toward him and started to give him a ballpoint pen but stopped, for it was a blue one and official documents had to be signed in black ink. He opened his drawer, got a black one, and handed it to Freeman, the pen for an instant joining their hands. Leaning over, Freeman slowly wrote his initials in the place Dan had shown him; then he stood at attention again and Dan read the charge aloud.

"Is it true?" Dan said.

"Yes, sir."

"Why?"

"Sir?"

"*Why* is it true? What gave you the idea you could talk back to one of my corporals?"

"No excuse, sir."

Dan paused, looking at him: Freeman's fists were clenched at his sides, his jaws pressed together, and his eyes stared blinking at the bulkhead. Dan watched his eyes: sometimes you raised your voice at a Marine and his eyes were suddenly angry or sullen or hating, but Freeman's eyes—seeming younger than ever now—were as fearful as a child's, and the anger which Dan had so recently generated began to fade. He quickly reminded himself that the Marine Detachment was the only truly disciplined unit on the ship.

"Is that all you've got to say? No excuse?"

"Yes, sir."

"Well, you're Goddamn right about that, lad. You're a United States Marine. You know what that means? It means I discipline, it means devotion to duty, it means you do as you're Goddamn told. Do you know that?"

"Yes, sir."

"Then act like it, Goddammit. You told me you wanted to be a corporal, *didn't* you! Well how in the hell are you going to be a corporal if you can't be a Pfc! Can you answer me that?"

"No, sir."

"You can't. Well neither can I, Freeman. You figure that one out. You go down to that brig for three days and eat bread and water and you think about it. You think about what made you join the only military organization in the United States. You figure out why you wanted to be with the best. And you better come out of there squared away."

"Yes, sir."

"One other thing, Freeman. I made you the Captain's orderly, *did*n't I. And there's maybe twenty Marines out there who want that job. No night watches. Prestige. Helps you get promoted around here. You want to keep that job?"

"Yes, sir."

"Then *don't let me down again*, Freeman. Now get out of here."

For an instant Freeman stood stiffly; then he about-faced and marched toward the door; Tolleson opened it for him and followed him out. Dan went to the door.

The troops were crowded onto benches in the class-room, pretending to listen to a corporal who was explaining the special orders for each post. Some looked furtively at Dan or turned to glance at Freeman standing at the Corporal of the Guard's desk at the rear of the classroom: he stood at parade rest, staring at the bulk-head inches from his face. Tolleson was talking to the Corporal of the Guard, who nodded and rose and went through the curtains into the berthing area. He came back with a Marine wearing a duty belt and carrying a nightstick. He was a prisoner chaser and he would take Freeman to the brig.

Dan smoked a cigarette, giving the chaser time to get Freeman out of the barracks, then he went through the classroom, into the berthing area, and inspected the bunks and deck. He stopped at Freeman's bunk. It was an upper bunk and on a shelf at its foot was an eight-by-ten photograph of his girl. Her hair was long and a wave fell over her forehead above her right eye; it was red hair, though it looked brown in the picture. Dan knew this because Tolleson had told him; Tolleson had also told him that she had a job in Oakland and Freeman was sleeping with her. Ever since learning that, Dan had always stopped to look at her picture.

She knew how to pose. At the instant the picture was taken, she must have been thinking of Freeman—or whomever she originally took the picture for—and you could not look at her face without believing in her fidelity and promise, and when Dan turned from the picture he desperately wanted a woman to look at him that way, to speak to him, and he hoped the mail plane would come soon and there would be a long letter from Khristy; he would not even open it until he was in his stateroom, where he would be alone. For three and a half months, now, he had been faithful to Khristy.

He finished inspecting the berthing area and the head, then went back through the classroom to his office. Pfc Burns, the clerk, was there now; Tolleson was helping him with the morning report.

"I'm going to see the Captain," Dan said, "and tell him about Freeman."

"Aye sir. Did the Lieutenant have a good time on the beach?"

"Fair."

Tolleson grinned.

"I believe I saw the Lieutenant walking down Thieves Alley with what appeared to be one of them little Jo-sans. Maybe a week ago, sir."

"Me?"

Dan blushed and Burns grinned at him, then went back to his typing.

"Yes, sir. I believe she's employed at the Bar Montana."

"Oh: *that* girl. She was helping me buy a kimono. For my Stateside girl, First Sergeant."

"I see, sir." He grinned and sipped his coffee. "I'm glad to see the Lieutenant buying presents for the ladies back home."

"You should try it, First Sergeant. It's good for the soul."

"Yessir, I guess it is. My old lady thinks so anyway."

Dan was still smiling as he climbed the ladder. Tolleson was the only Staff NCO he had ever been successfully friendly with. As a platoon commander at Camp Pendleton he had, on long field problems or landing exercises, given in to the need for companionship. He had done this with two different platoon sergeants and each time he had regretted it. For he found that when he lowered the barriers of rank, he let in subtle but definite problems: it became harder for him to give orders—especially the distasteful ones, the ones which came from his superiors and which he had to relay as his own—and his orders were sometimes questioned. Then he would become uncertain and on some days he would feel that everything he did was wrong, that he was a totally incompetent misfit. By nature he was not a man who exuded strength and dignity (as Captain Schneider was, drunk or sober, laughing or angry) and he knew that. He often cursed himself, told himself that he was nothing but a frisky puppy in a world of serious men and he would never be a general or a colonel if he didn't learn to maintain the position of his rank and exercise his authority from that fragile height. He supposed many officers were like that, and it was one of the reasons they said a commander was the loneliest man in the world. He was prepared to believe that.

But First Sergeant Tolleson was different. Dan was able to talk with him, had even drunk with him a few times, and their professional relationship remained unharmed. It was not Dan, though, but Tolleson who protected that relationship. On the nights when they got tight in Japanese bars, Tolleson always managed to make Dan feel that he was an intelligent and respected officer. Dan remembered one night when they had sat in a bar for hours, drinking Japanese beer and talking about the Detachment; when they left they were drunk, walking stiffly down the sidewalk, Tolleson on Dan's left. They got a taxi to the *Vanguard* and Tolleson still addressed him in the third person and saluted him good night as Dan turned to the officers' brow and Tolleson went aft to board the ship at the enlisted brow.

Now, swagger stick in hand, he climbed the Captain's ladder; the Marine Detachment waxed its green decks and polished its brass handrails daily: that was supposed to be an honorable duty, but Dan resented using Marines to please a Navy captain's eye. At the Captain's cabin the Marine orderly saluted Dan, then announced him and held the door open as he went in. Captain Howard sat behind a large polished wooden desk; he had a pen in his hand and there was a stack of papers before him. He told Dan to have a seat and Dan sat in a leather armchair.

"Sir, I came to tell you why Freeman's not on duty today."

"I was wondering about that."

Captain Howard was a tall man with a lean face which perhaps several times had been deeply tanned; now, after nearly a year aboard the *Vanguard*, whose crew rarely went above decks, he still wasn't pale. His face appeared rather young, but not as young as the eight-by-ten photograph of him: it had been taken by the ship's Photo Officer, then touched up to remove the wrinkles, making him look thirty years old, and distributed about the ship to be hung on bulkheads.

"I locked him up this morning," Dan said.

Captain Howard screwed the pen into its desk stand. "What for?"

He seemed to frown as he screwed in the pen, but Dan couldn't be sure; like the silver eagles on the khaki lapels beneath it, his face usually showed inscrutable authority, and nothing more.

"He talked back to a corporal during morning clean-up."

"So you locked him up."

"Yes, sir. Three days bread and water."

Captain Howard slowly turned his swivel chair until he was profiled to Dan and staring at the bulkhead. Then he said quietly:

"Don't you think that's a stiff punishment for talking back to a petty officer?"

"An NCO, sir."

Captain Howard did not seem to hear the correction.

"I have never put a man on bread and water," he said. "The book gives us other ways to deal with our men. An effective commander can do much with calm admonishment."

The Captain was still turned away from him and Dan was looking at his parted dark brown hair, his left ear, his face with its tan left over from earlier days.

"Well, sir, we've found that bread-and-water squares a man away."

Again the Captain did not seem to hear.

"It took me a long time to learn judgment," he said. "Because, as you know, most junior officers in the Navy are not given the responsibility of handing out official punishment. Maybe as a young officer I might have let my emotions override my judgment and I might have gone around putting men on bread and water for minor offenses."

"Sir," Dan said too loudly, and the Captain looked at him, so he lowered his voice before going on: "I don't consider Freeman's offense minor. I don't think any Marine officer does. I'll give a man a second chance on almost any other offense—but not insubordination or disobedience. The corporal that Freeman sounded off to would lead a fire team or even a squad in combat and *all* those troops have to learn to respect chevrons."

The Captain was watching him calmly, even a little distracted. Now he looked at the bulkhead again.

"Mister Tierney, I'm aware of all that; I've served with Marines before. But you don't seem to be reading my message. So far, I've allowed the Marine Detachment on this ship to handle its own disciplinary cases. That is a privilege which I don't have to grant, and I can take it away at any time. Now, if you don't want your Marines to come to me for punishment, I suggest you exercise more mature judgment and make your punishments more in accordance with my own feelings."

"Aye aye, sir."

Dan stood up, and Captain Howard swung the chair around and looked at him.

"And next time you want to lock up one of my orderlies, I would appreciate being informed beforehand. I might just know more about my orderlies than you do. Freeman, for instance, is a fine boy and I should think a pat on the wrist would have been sufficient."

"I'm sorry, sir, but not for that offense."

"Mister Tierney, that will be all."

Dan came to attention, clicking his heels, said "Aye aye, sir," and about-faced and strode out.

He went quickly down the Captain's ladder, slapping his thigh with his swagger stick, remembering affronts and conflicts from the past three and a half months: there was the time Commander Craig, the Gunnery officer, had decided to assign Captain Schneider and Dan as boat officers: the officer in charge of a liberty launch which took the crew to and from the beach when the *Vanguard* was anchored in port. It was a duty which usually fell to junior pilots, because pilots did not stand bridge watches at sea and this in-port duty was a settling of accounts. And it was bad duty: responsibility during a half-hour boat trip for eighty or so sailors, drunk, sleeping, or fighting, as they returned from liberty. So Captain Schneider had gone to see Commander Craig and had read him the passage in Navy Regulations which states that no Marine officer shall have command of a vessel at sea. *If that liberty boat sinks*, Captain Schneider had said, *and I'm in charge of it, I wonder who an investigation would find responsible.* Commander Craig had scowled, then grinned, and said: *All right, Marine, no boat duty.*

There were other incidents like that, but the one Dan thought of now as he descended the ladder was the honors ceremony of only three days ago, the last day the *Vanguard* was moored at Yokosuka. Captain Schneider had already gone to the hospital, so Dan had been in charge of the Marine honor guard: the troops dressed in blues, chrome-plated bayonets fixed to their rifles; Dan wore his sword. The Admiral's Band was to the right of the Marines. The *Vanguard* was a flagship and had an admiral aboard, but he did not concern himself with the affairs of the ship, and Dan rarely saw him.

At nine o'clock in the morning the Japanese government officials had arrived and Captain Howard had led one of them to the Marines on the hangar deck; Dan presented the guard, then led the Japanese official and the Captain through the ranks while the band played the "Marines' Hymn." Then Captain Howard took all the Japanese up to his cabin. That afternoon Dan had coffee in the wardroom with Alex Price, who had smiled and asked him how his Fascists had performed at the honors ceremony.

"With their usual beauty and precision," Dan had said.

Alex was a lieutenant junior grade, one of those rare young officers who, having no commitment to the service—in fact detesting much of it—peform as conscientiously as the most fervent career officer. His face was nearly always calm, as were his voice and manner (Dan once accused him of a total lack of passion); he had a crew cut which showed the top of his scalp and he had recently grown a wide moustache which had a reddish hue, though his hair was brown.

"Question is," Alex said, "can there be any beauty—"

The bosun's pipe sounded over the loudspeaker system and Dan turned to the speaker on the bulkhead; the piping ended, there was a pause which seemed to Dan somehow dramatic, as if with over three thousand men staring at speakers all over the ship, a voice was about to announce: "At fifteen hundred today Russian bombers—" but instead came the quiet voice of Captain Howard which had disappointed Dan when he first joined the *Vanguard* and, by now, annoyed him; for he thought a ship s captain should growl, or at least be hoarse from dissipation ashore and bellowing commands at sea:

"This is the Captain. As you know, our chief concern today has been with the visit by Japanese dignitaries. That visit was a success, and I want to personally express my gratitude to all the officers and men of *Vanguard* for their outstanding cooperation and performance throughout the day. And for the honors ceremony, I want to particularly give my personal thanks to the Gunnery Department and the men of the Admiral's Band."

Then he said that tomorrow *Vanguard* would go to sea for day and night air operations and, after two weeks, they would go to Iwakuni. Dan struck the table with his palm.

"Goddammit, I'm going to see him," he said.

"What for?"

Ask him if it d break his jaw to compliment my troops sometime."

"Maybe he thinks you should feel included when he says Gunnery Department."

"I don't care *what* he thinks. If he's that stupid, why doesn't he at least say the Mar*ines* of Gunnery Department. When he knows Goddamn well there wasn't one Gunnery sailor on that hangar deck—Hell with it: I'm going to see him."

He stood up.

"You can't," Alex said.

"Why not? I've got legs, don't I? I've got a tongue, don't I? So I'll go ask him what's wrong with *his* tongue."

"Did you ever walk in on a Marine colonel and chew him out?"

Dan hesitated. He noticed three lieutenants looking at him from across the wardroom. Then he sat down.

"Maybe I should write him a letter."

"Make it original and three. Via the Gunnery Officer, via the XO—copy to each of them. Original to the Captain, and the other copy for you."

"So I'll remember what I said."

"Now you're learning."

That had been three days ago. Now, leaving the Captain's ladder, he crossed the hangar deck: a large space directly below the flight deck, crowded with jet bombers and fighters and the smaller propeller-driven A4D's which, in Korea, the Marine infantry had loved; for it was said that they came slow and close over those ridges and could drop a bomb on a poncho. The wings of all the planes were folded upward and they sat quiet and unmoving, ominous as perched death.

Across the hangar deck he went down another ladder and turned aft, heading toward the barracks. In the passageway Hahn and Jensen were coming toward him. He stood waiting. They stopped talking when they saw him and he watched them coming, Hahn over six feet tall, the biggest man in the Detachment, and he used his size there as he must have used it all his life: the corporals were afraid to give him an order and he was never seen with a mop or rag in his hands unless Tolleson went and found him and gave the order himself. Jensen was shorter, but he fought often, anywhere, with anyone, and the troops— except Hahn—were afraid of him too. Or they would be, if Jensen had wanted that. But as far as Dan knew, Jensen wasn't the bully that Hahn was, and Dan felt if it weren't for Hahn, he might be a good Marine.

Now they reached him and saluted and, since Dan stood in their way, they stopped. He returned their salute, then spread his legs and folded his arms on his chest, looking at their faces which showed not guilt but concealment.

"Where are you two going?" he said, sending out his voice the way he used to make the throw from deep in the hole at shortstop: as the ball left his hand he would watch it with anticipation, hoping he had put enough behind it to get there chest-high and straight. Now his voice failed him; it wasn't harshly ironic like Tolleson's or paternally angry like Captain Schneider's: it was soft, almost querulous, and he thought he sounded like a timid high school teacher trying to scold a sullen football player.

"To chow, sir," Hahn said. He stood loosely, comfortably, at attention, and looked calmly down at Dan whose eyes shifted to Jensen, then back to Hahn—or to the mole on his cheek—and said:

You're in the off-duty section, aren't you?"

Yes, sir.

"And there's a class going on for that section, isn't there?"

"Yes, sir." Hahn said, with that secrecy in his eyes again.

"Then I suggest you two go back to class."

"Aye aye, sir," Hahn said.

His voice and face were calm and courteous and false, showing no more concern than if Dan had merely stopped him to ask how he liked the chow aboard ship; and Dan knew that only the certainty of a court-martial kept Hahn from pushing him aside and going on to eat a late breakfast. He also suspected that Hahn and Jensen had missed the regular breakfast because they had stayed in their bunks while the other troops got up and cleaned the barracks and went to chow. He was thinking all this and hoping his face did not show it, when they saluted. He returned the salutes and they about-faced and walked back down the passageway, talking.

He would tell Tolleson he had caught them going to chow during the map-reading class, and Tolleson would probably give them some extra work to do, but that wouldn't bother them. Maybe he should have done something, reprimanded them loudly and profanely on the spot, though he knew that was useless, for they didn't care whether or not he admired them, and they were not concerned with promotions. He could have charged them with being absent from their place of duty and locked them up; but last summer, for beating up two sailors, they had gone to the brig for thirty days and it hadn't changed them. Hahn had probably done well in the brig: assigned to the lightest work details, given cigarettes by the Marine turnkeys who would be afraid to enforce the regulation allowing only one cigarette after each meal—or, worse, who would not enforce it because they wanted Hahn to like or tolerate them. They were all too young for the job, especially the corporals, who did most of the direct troop handling. They had been promoted quickly and, because they had been in high school only two years ago, too many of them still believed that big men rule.

He walked aft, through the mess deck and up a ladder, then another, and out a hatch onto the sponson deck. He blinked at the sunlight. The ocean was calm and dark blue, the sky lighter, a destroyer tiny and grey against it on the horizon. He went to the guardrail and looked down at the ocean, holding his swagger stick before him in both hands.

The ship began a slow turn to starboard, into the wind. The sponson deck where he was standing jutted out from the side of the ship and, looking up, Dan could see part of the flight deck. Sailors in yellow sweatshirts and pilots in orange flight suits were moving around, then he saw the nose of a jet fighter coming slowly toward the edge of the deck above him; it turned and he saw the cockpit and silver wing and fuselage as it moved onto the catapult. He looked away, at the destroyer on the horizon.

If he were an enlisted man, he thought, it would be different. The first time Hahn pushed him, he'd go after him with a nightstick. And that was it: nonphysical as it was, their relationship still had the elements of a fight or a Western movie showdown. Someday he and Hahn would probably have to face each other in his office and one man was supposed to emerge the winner. The silver bars on his collars wouldn't do it for him, and words wouldn't either: Hahn seemed invulnerable to both.

The jet engine started above him, roaring, and he turned quickly and left the sponson deck, pausing at the hatch for a last look at the sea and sky, but they were altered by that incredible roaring; he went inside and down the ladder. He was going to the brig to see Freeman.

It was his duty to inspect the brig daily and check the prisoners, and that was one reason for his going now. But he had two other motives and he wished he were not aware of them: he had never confined a man before and he wanted to look at Freeman, with that possessive curiosity of a hunter picking up a fallen bird; he also wanted to reassert himself, to regain his dignity. With Freeman he could do that.

Chapter Two

LIKE ALL MARINE officers, Dan Tierney had spent his first eight months of duty as a second lieutenant at the Basic School in Quantico, Virginia. Toward the end of that eight months there was a mess night, a formal stag dinner, the second lieutenants wearing blues and senior officers wearing evening dress: short jackets and cummerbunds and boat cloaks. The evening had begun with martinis and manhattans, then during the meal there was wine with each course, and by the time the guest speaker—a lieutenant-general from Headquarters Marine Corps—made his speech, Dan was drunk. He sat stiffly, his tight blouse and high collar adding to his nausea, and stared at the general. He heard only one line of the speech, and he remembered it: during the rest of the night while they drank beer from silver mugs, and while he leaned over a toilet and vomited without unclasping his collar or soiling his uniform, and he still remembered it when he got to his room at five in the morning. *You hear what that general said?* he told his roommate. *He said—he said: The career of a Marine officer is living the lie and making the lie come true.*

He never forgot that.

He remembered it when he left the sponson deck and went to see Freeman in the brig, and he recognized the lie in his own manner: stern yet paternal, when he felt neither. He also recognized the lie of Freeman's punishment: knew that Freeman did not deserve bread-and-water and no cigarettes and isolation in a cell for three days. But he knew Freeman had expected it; because on the *Vanguard*, sailors were never put on bread and water, while Marines often were. And the Detachment as a whole—if not the particular Marine who was locked up—prided itself on this severe discipline. Beyond this, Dan recognized the essential lie: as he and Freeman faced each other in the cell, Dan saying that as far as he was concerned Freeman would start over with a clean slate and Freeman assuring him that he would be a squared-away Marine in the future, each of them believed they were somehow better men than any sailor or Naval officer on the ship. They both felt that moments like these, spent in a cell below decks, prepared them for that time when they might be called upon to continue the brave traditions of the Chosin Reservoir, of Tarawa, of Belleau Wood.

On his way to the barracks he stopped at the dispensary to see Doc Butler, who was a lieutenant-commander and the senior medical officer on the *Vanguard*. Since early in the cruise, Dan had called him *Major* because he looked like one: he was in his mid-thirties, rather well-built though inactive, and he kept his hair as short as Dan's. When he was a lieutenant, he had served as a regimental surgeon with Marine infantry, and he liked to talk with Dan and Captain Schneider about those days. Doc Butler would know about Freeman, because all prisoners went to the dispensary for pre-confinement physicals.

In the passageway outside the dispensary there was a long line of sailors dressed in dungarees. On the first couple of days after an in-port period there was always a crowd: men who woke in the morning and noticed an ailment they had had for days. Dan opened the Medical Officer's door and looked in at Doc Butler sitting at his desk.

"Morning, Major. You've got all the sick bay commandos here, so who's making the ship go?"

"Just you and me, Dan. I see you've already locked one up."

"Right, Major. Iron hand."

"Good: they know you're the Skipper now."

"Captain Howard recommended a pat on the wrist." Doc Butler smiled.

"A pilot, Dan. They don't worry about discipline and such."

He nodded toward the percolator.

"It's fresh," he said.

"No thanks, Major. I just dropped in to make sure you didn't stay on the beach."

"They wouldn't leave without me, Skipper."

"Semper Fi," Dan said, and left. He walked briskly now,

and when he reached the barracks he was whistling "Scotland the Brave."

That night after dinner he was in Alex Price's room when the bosun's pipe sounded over the loudspeaker and the bosun's mate announced mail call; Dan got up and said "About time" and hurried from the room, leaving Alex grinning and stroking his moustache.

It had been ten days since he had heard from Khristy and he went quickly down the passageway, trying to recall if he had ever gone longer without a letter and it seemed that he had but he couldn't be sure and he wanted to believe he hadn't, that somehow numbers were important and if there had never been ten days without a letter, then surely there would never be eleven. He wrote to her every night at sea because he was lonely and there was nothing to do at night except watch a movie in the wardroom or write to Khristy. His letters were usually four or five pages long. Sometimes he wrote about marriage, although when they had made love for the first and last time, he had immediately asked her to marry him and she had said with a rational voice that—coming from her naked body next to his—had chilled him: *Let's don't even talk about it till you get back from sea duty. I want time to check out my psyche.*

The word *psyche* had also disturbed him.

When the *Vanguard* was in port he wrote to her every third day, on his duty day when he had to stay aboard ship. On the other two days liberty call was at noon and he left the ship then, often choosing as his companions married men who wanted to remain faithful to their wives. They went to bars where the Japanese hostesses did not sit with customers until they were asked, and Dan and his friends rarely asked; when they did, it was because they wanted something soft and responsive and perfume-scented in their booth. They would buy her drinks and tell her in pidgin English that her kimono was very pretty, her face beautiful. By late evening they would have eaten sukiyaki or teriyaki steak or fried rice or sopa, they would be happily drunk, and they would sing; the young officers from eastern schools led them in ribald limericks or sentimental college songs; Dan taught them "Waltzing Mathilda" and usually sang solos of "Danny Boy" and "Irish Soldier Boy." They would return late to the *Vanguard*, oblivious long before they slept.

When Dan wrote to Khristy on those hungover in-port days, he told where he had gone the past two nights and always ended by assuring her that he had only been out with the boys and had slept aboard ship. Khristy had never—either in California or her letters—asked him to be faithful; he respected her strength, and gave her the continual assurance she had not asked for but certainly needed.

Khristy wrote only once a week, but Dan knew the reason: as a senior at UCLA she had little time. But that wasn't exactly right. She had time, but didn't know it, because she was one of those women who have no concept of time, who apparently believe it is to be recorded by facial wrinkles and increasing dress sizes but not by a clock, so she was harassed by its sudden passing in the course of a mere day. Her letters were written on that day which gratuitously stopped and gave her several hours of what she often called *another vacuous Sunday afternoon.* In her letters (which spoke of love but never marriage) she wondered where her time had gone, then she answered her question by telling him of classes and nights of studying during the week and dates on Friday and Saturday. Before leaving Camp Pendleton to report to the *Vanguard,* Dan had said he expected her to date. He had assumed that checking out her psyche involved being with other men. He was rarely jealous. She wrote of several different escorts (naming them, saying briefly where they had taken her) and Dan considered them all boys who lacked the maturity he had earned by being a man among men, boys who bought her drinks and took her to football games and parties but who shared neither her background nor her body.

Her background was the Marine Corps. Her father was a colonel at Camp Pendleton. When Dan first met Colonel VandeBerg, the Colonel had said: *How old are you, Lieutenant?* Dan had told him he was twenty-four and the Colonel had chuckled and said: *I've been in the Marine Corps all your life.* Dan had smiled, blushing; but he was realizing that Khristy had been in the Marine Corps all her life too: she had already—though secondhand—experienced most of his future. If she married him, she would leave a colonel's house to live in a lieutenant's.

He felt that her father's profession and her mother's commitment to it were the causes of Khristy's subtle abeyance, her resistance which was more than physical, and their differences which they rarely quarreled about but usually touched on, even on their last night together

before Dan drove north to join the *Vanguard*. They had begun that evening at a restaurant in Oceanside (she did not like the officers' clubs on the base); Khristy was drinking martinis, saying she was determined to get happy and fuzzy like a child falling asleep. He drank them too. After his second, he was telling her of almost getting lost in the field with his entire platoon because he had been in new terrain and for some reason he could find none of its contours on the map. So he had marched the platoon up a hill and given an impromptu lecture, showing them how you could find your position by doing a two-point resection with a map and compass, and they sat on the ground watching him, the platoon sergeant standing behind them looking interested too, and then Dan had known the sergeant was also lost. He had squatted on the ground and done the resection and it had worked: he had been able to stand up and say: *So you see we're on this hill, right here—*
Then Khristy had said:

"You should get out of the Marine Corps."

His first thought was that she was disgusted by his incompetence, and looking at her with his mouth open but quiet, he thought her father—whom he only saw at his quarters—had somehow judged him and told Khristy he didn't pack the gear. She reached a hand across the table and laid it on his.

"I hate to see you get old," she said. "They get so old. They go to a couple of wars and after twenty, twenty-five years, they retire and they're lost. Did you ever notice how many of them simply fall apart when they retire? Old wounds start bothering them and they look restless or confused or even scared, some of them. My God, how many times have I heard my father say: 'When I go I want to catch one right between the horns—'"

She withdrew her hand and touched her forehead.

"And you," she said. "You're on fire with it: you'll be yelling gung-ho on beaches and someday if you're still around you'll retire and they'll give you a regimental parade and you'll cry when they march past playing the Hymn—unless you've changed a lot."

Then she looked away from him, toward the piano bar, and said:

"And for what."

He started to reach for her hand again but, pretending not to notice, she moved the hand away, to her cigarettes. When he gave her a light she settled back in her chair, out of his reach, and said:

"I'm fuzzy but that's all. Let's have another."

Her voice then had been sad, resigned, and her letters which began the following week, shortly after he had reported to the *Vanguard*, had the same tone. That tone had never changed. He grew accustomed to it and the weekly letter, accepting his allotted time in the flow of her life. Still, every day when mail call was announced, he faced the distribution of letters with the anxiety of a waiting lover.

When he reached the barracks, mail had been passed out; there were six letters stacked on his desk. He spread them out like a hand of cards and in one glance saw that each was addressed by a feminine hand and each was for a prisoner in the brig. There was no letter for him.

Though he was alone in the office, he assumed a calm expression, then sat at his desk and slowly looked at each letter. One of his functions as the man in charge of the ship's brig was to read all outgoing and incoming mail. At times it was boring, but often he enjoyed it. In September there had been witty letters from a girl in Alameda and, for her sailor's two weeks of confinement, Dan had looked forward to reading them. Last month a Negro sailor had served thirty days in the brig and his mistress in Oakland had written him daily: her love passages sounded like a combination of popular songs and romance magazines, but Dan believed her anyway; what he liked most was her anecdotes of Oakland night life which, she wrote, she enjoyed with a girl friend. She told him of a world of music and gin and violence which he had never known.

Tonight there was a letter from Freeman's girl and Dan saved it for last.

When he pulled out the four sheets of thin folded stationery, a small colored photograph fell on his desk: the girl, standing on a blanket in a small lawn with a low green fence behind her and, beyond that, tall apartment buildings. She wore a two-piece aqua bathing suit and stood profiled to the camera, and her hair was indeed bright red, as Tolleson had told him. Her belly was flat and white and her face, turned to the camera, was smiling. She held a can of beer. On the back of the photograph was written:

All my love,

Jan

(I don't remember the date.

Do you?)

Then he studied her face, as if to intercept that look in her eyes before Freeman saw it. And he was thinking they were not at a beach and apparently there was no one else there, they were sunbathing together on a bright California day and they would leave the blanket and go into her apartment—wherever that was, probably behind the camera—and they would make love and lie in bed drinking beer, maybe three dollars worth of beer, three dollars and a sunny afternoon and a young red-haired girl, and then they would—*oh Khristy oh Goddammit—*

Then he read the letter.

Ted Baby,

I finally used up the rest of that roll. The others didn't come out so good but I'm glad this one did. I wanted you to have it so you could remember what I looked like. Believe me, next time you see me you'll notice the difference! But don't worry, next summer I'll get in that same bathing suit. I wonder if that was the day it happened. I hope it was, because it was such a good day.

Dan read faster, sensing—as if she sat talking in his office—her voice changing from nostalgia and love to desperate practicality:

—have to go by the regulations but Baby I'm going on four months and I can't cover it up much longer. If we wait til the ship comes home in March I'll be seven months! Please Baby can't you talk to your Captain, you told me he was a good man—

Dan got up and opened the door. Across the room, the Corporal of the Guard was sitting at his desk, reading a letter. Dan told him to have Freeman sent up from the brig and he waited at the door until the corporal was dialing the number. Then he finished reading the letter.

While he waited for Freeman he looked up the order that had been issued by the Commander of the Seventh Fleet before the *Vanguard* had left the States. He did not really have to see it again, for he knew what it said: that during the Western Pacific deployment, members of the Seventh Fleet would be granted emergency leave only under the following circumstances: father or mother dying, wife dead or dying, child dead or dying, or father or mother dead provided the serviceman was necessary for settling the estate.

Then he left his office and knocked on the door of Tolleson's stateroom and went in. Tolleson rose from the leather chair where he had been reading a letter. He wore khaki tropical trousers, a T-shirt, and shower shoes. On his left bicep, above the dark hair, was a tattoo of a Marine emblem. Dan sat down, then Tolleson did.

"Freeman's girl is knocked up."

"Well, sir," Tolleson said after a moment, "it's kinda tough when these little girls take serious what you poke at 'em in fun."

"She'll be seven months when we get back to the States."

"Goddamn, sir, you know what I think? The Commandant of this man's Marine Corps ought to issue a general order that *all* Marines will be schooled in the function of the birds and the bees. I swear to God, sir, half of 'em don't know how they got here."

Dan was looking at the bulkhead and scratching his jaw, waiting for Tolleson to subside, and he was thinking that for four or five years now he had needed to shave again in the evening, with a blade, if he were going out; Freeman would be married soon and his electric razor would disturb the apartment's morning quiet only three or four times a week.

"How well do you know that chief in charge of passenger lists?"

"Sir, I hope the Lieutenant's not thinking about sending Freeman home, because if I remember correctly—"

"I know. I just read the order again."

"From ComSeventhFleet, I believe, sir."

"It is. But it occurs to me that this is an aircraft carrier and it has a mail plane that takes people to Japan and if Freeman can get to Japan he can catch a hop to California."

"Yes, sir. However—"

"And I know this, First Sergeant, and you know it too: a lot of things get done, whether admirals authorize them or not."

"Yessir, that's true."

"So why don't you give that chief a call. We'll just look into it and see what it'd take to get Freeman home."

"Aye sir, I'll give it a try."

Dan went back to his office where Freeman was waiting, just outside the door, standing at parade rest with a prisoner chaser behind him. Dan told him to come in and shut the door and stand at ease.

"Why didn't you tell me your girl was pregnant?"

"Sir, Prisoner Freeman didn't think it'd do any good, sir."

This time Freeman was not afraid; he stood at rigid parade rest and stared with pain and defiance at the bulkhead behind Dan, who felt that defiance, retreated from it and all it represented—his past and future days of working with men whose enslavement to his rank enslaved them even further, so they were not free to look at him as a man, stripped of his uniform and its accouterments of rank which were, to them, his name: The Lieutenant. As gently as he could, he said:

"Look—we've got a lot of talking to do, and it'll save time if you knock off that prisoner talk."

Freeman's face did not change.

"Aye aye, sir," he said.

"Now: maybe there *is* something we can do. You can't tell until you ask."

Looking at Freeman's face, he was imagining it suddenly changing: saw the jaws and lips softening, the eyes focusing gratefully downward toward his own. He saw Jan in the apartment doorway, her hair somehow brilliant even without sunlight, and Freeman, uniformed, dropping his seabag to the corridor floor: *Lieutenant Tierney sent me home!*—clasping her—*he took care of EVERYthing.*

"Do you love this girl. Freeman?"

"Yes, sir."

"Did you plan to marry her?"

"Yes, sir."

"Pregnant or not? You're sure?"

"Yes, sir: we were gettng married after the cruise."

"Where do her parents live?"

"In Stockton, sir."

"Do they know she's pregnant?"

"No, sir."

"But they see her often enough so they'll find out?"

"Yes, sir. I suppose they will."

"What about your folks? Do they know?"

"No, sir."

"They're in California too, aren't they?"

"No, sir. Bellingham, Washington, sir."

Know your men, he had been told at Basic School, *keep a platoon commander's notebook*; and he faithfully had: a small pocket notebook with a red leather cover that bore the Marine emblem. Inside, there was a page for each man with blanks for essential information; the process of knowing a man began with your filling these blanks. As you copied the information from his service record book, you felt that you were taking possession of a part of him: as if you were watching him sleep, and sharing the privacy of his slack jaws, his snores, his mutterings. Then you memorized the information and the process was complete. If your commanding officer asked, you could tell him where a man was from, his age, his approximate height and weight, whether he was married or single, and whether he was a marksman, sharpshooter, or expert with the rifle. And now Dan had blundered: had forgotten and then let Freeman know it. He would study his notebook before going to bed tonight.

"Well, Freeman, there's a chance—just a chance, understand—that we can get you off this bird farm and fly you back to the States. If the First Sergeant can—" he paused "—swing something."

Now Freeman was looking down at him, not grateful yet but anxious, dependent—and surprised.

"Tell me, Freeman: what made you say that to Corporal McKittrick this morning?"

"Personal reasons, sir."

It was what they always said when they wanted to see the chaplain or the company commander or battalion commander or the inspector general, and you were not supposed to pry; you had to let them go, and you did—with the sense of alienation of a man watching his wife enter a confessional.

"I'm sure that's true, because I don't think you'd be insubordinate without some reason. Now I don't mean to pry, but maybe if you could tell me it would help you with this other thing."

He held up the letter from Jan. Freeman looked at it, then looked at the bulkhead and said:

"He was harassing me, sir. About my girl being pregnant."

"What did he say?"

"Sir, he said the Detachment was going to have another Teddy-Baby."

"He said that in front of other troops? While he was supervising clean-up?"

"Yes, sir."

"Did he say anything else?"

"Yes, sir, but I'd rather not repeat it, sir."

"All right," Dan said.

He stood up.

"Tell you what: you stay here and read your letter and I'll step out for a while."

Freeman came to attention, clicking his heels.

"Aye aye, sir. Thank you, sir."

Dan went out and shut the door, then knocked on Tolleson's door.

"Sir," the Corporal of the Guard said, "First Sergeant said to tell the lieutenant he's gone to the chief's mess."

"All right. How 'bout getting hold of Burns for me."

Dan waited in Tolleson's stateroom for Burns, a tall lean boy with dark hair whose cutting at Boot Camp he probably still regretted; he was a saxophone player. Or he had been before joining the Marine Corps, and he meant to play again, professionally, when he got out. He had the qualities of a good clerk: he was smart enough to work in the small office with Dan and Tolleson every day, to join their small talk when he was invited or allowed, while never making Dan or Tolleson feel that he was trying to have anything more than a professional relationship with them. When he came to Tolleson's door, Dan told him to prepare a release order for Freeman.

"And Burns—"

"Yes, sir?"

"When you go in there to type it, don't tell Freeman what it is."

Burns smiled, like a friend planning a surprise party.

"Aye aye, sir," he said.

Then Dan was alone. He closed the door and sat smoking because things were happening fast now and he had to think. First he would release Freeman, telling him that he could understand the causes of insubordination (he would not say that Corporal McKittrick had been wrong, had used his rank for bullying, because he did not want to undermine that rank); he would say that, considering the circumstances, he felt one day in the brig was sufficient punishment, and that he expected Freeman to control himself in the future and to come see him or the First Sergeant if he had any more personal conflicts with NCO's. Then, with Tolleson, he would arrange to fly Freeman home. And last, before leaving the barracks that night, he would reprimand Corporal McKittrick. Then he would go to his stateroom and study his platoon commander's notebook, and write to Khristy.

He would reprimand her too.

He went into his office and told Burns to step outside. He signed the release order, leaning over the desk, then slowly straightened and turned to Freeman who stood at parade rest. He told Freeman he was released from confinement, and he told him why, watching the fading defiance in his face. Then he told him to stand by for word on a flight off the ship.

"I don't know if it can be done," he said. Then he smiled. "But after all, Freeman, it occurs to me that this is an aircraft carrier and there's a mail plane that takes people to Japan."

Freeman smiled and said: "Yes, sir." Dan told him he could go and, still grinning, Freeman clicked his heels, smartly about-faced, and walked out.

Dan sat in the office waiting for Tolleson, sipping a cup of coffee which he got from the percolator near the Corporal of the Guard's desk, having crossed the classroom where several troops were shining shoes, having felt so completely in control of the Detachment and himself that he had been unaware of those troops and—for once—had not bothered to fix on his face the public expression of an officer: a look of serene confidence, as if he had transcended all the problems of the enlisted world and was now preoccupied with the logistics of an amphibious landing on the shores of China. He had merely crossed the room, watched by the troops, thinking of Freeman and Jan starting a baby on a sunny afternoon in Oakland, and as he recrossed the classroom to enter his office, he was smiling warmly to himself.

He leaned back in the swivel chair, looking at the overhead and thinking of Khristy, having forgotten the time difference and wondering what day and what hour of that day it was in California: perhaps morning and she was walking to some place on the campus for breakfast, her long brown hair curling upward at her shoulders, her lips freshly and lightly reddened, the scent of toothpaste still on her breath, and her greyish-blue eyes as calm and alert as her father's might be while he read an operations order from higher command. Her eyes were not always that way. When she and Dan laughed together they would brighten, looking at him with a sudden intimacy that made him feel he had known her all his life.

On that last night with Khristy, after she had told him he should get out of the Marine Corps, they had with their usual facility changed their conversation and their moods. They had been in one of the two restaurants in Oceanside which provided left-over atmosphere: a dark place, behind whose bar was a large stuffed marlin flanked by sections of a fishnet arranged as neatly as bunting; on another wall a black low-crowned flat-brimmed hat was suspended as if a Flamenco dancer had come through head first and lodged there, his bent-over body trapped outside in the moving fog—and Dan thought of Winnie-the-Pooh caught in Rabbit's hole, and told Khristy; and squeezing his hands on the table she laughed until tears sparkled her eyes. Beneath the hat was a red poncho. Farther left there was a sombrero, a white one, with a green serape below it; directly between the two hats a coiled bullwhip hung over two crossed banderillas.

"That's the wetback wall," Dan said over the organ music, loudly enough so that he quickly looked around to be sure his next statement was true: "Only thing is, they can't afford to come see it."

"*Si*" Khristy said, and lifted her martini in a toast, whether to his sense of justice or to the huts and dirt floors of fruit pickers, he didn't know.

The organ music came from what the management called a piano bar. On the wall above the organist's head was a photograph of the restaurant-owner shaking hands with a steady-working mediocre Hollywood actor who, Dan recalled aloud, had been twice nominated for Oscars but had not won.

"So they'll give him one someday," he said. "They'll say he's been a fixture in the industry."

Then he picked up the menu and asked if she would like to start with a shrimp cocktail, for he was sorry he had mentioned movies. Some time ago she had accused him of having seen more movies than any person his age in the United States. They're not *real*, she had told him and he replied that he was well aware of that but he didn't care; besides, he had said, sometimes they're more real than they seem to be. Once he had told her that Gary Cooper had been his hero since he was a boy, that he had seen *The Pride of the Yankees* and *For Whom the Bell Tolls* several times when he was very young and he had cried each time. So she had given him a large paperback edition of *For Whom the Bell Tolls*, inscribing it: *To a good trooper from a rather uncertain Maria*. Taking the book from her he remembered Gary Cooper lying on his belly, aiming what Dan believed was a Lewis gun at the audience, firing, as two guerrillas rode away holding Ingrid Bergman on a horse between them.

He had felt like crying at the end of the book too, then told her that Hemingway should have known better, that when you cross a road or trail in daylight you make everyone cross at once before they can zero in on you, because if you cross one at a time it'll be just like the book, they'll get the gun around and the people at the end of your column will have had the course. Just as she was beginning to scowl he said: *Wait*, and told her he was glad it worked out that way because otherwise Robert Jordan wouldn't have had to stay behind, which was the best by God thing he could have done.

I thought you'd like that, she had said.

So in the restaurant he ordered two shrimp cocktails and lobster and more martinis, having a quick fantasy of being unable to buy gasoline for his trip north tomorrow, and Khristy said with more irritation than music alone could have caused:

"Why should a town in Southern California, of all places, have nothing but organ music?"

She was looking at the piano bar whose stools were all occupied by middle-aged couples; even as she looked they began to sing "Heart of My Heart." The organist was about fifty, a lean almost bony man, having slicked long hair without a visible touch of grey. He was smiling, with lips closed, at the singers. Khristy said he looked like he had slept with every peroxided girl and woman from San Diego to Santa Barbara and was playing his own funeral music while he waited to die.

After the martinis and shrimp cocktails and lobster, the sweetness of chocolate-covered mint patties—one apiece—which Dan bought at the candy counter in front of the cashier, the hot bitterness of coffee that sweetened their cigarettes, they sat quietly, full and rather tight, smiling oddly at each other, and Khristy said:

"Well, we might as well."

"Might as well what?"

"Dance to this stuff. Come on."

They danced among couples who were, in a last-lap sort of way, attractive: women whose lined tan faces suggested boats and beaches rather than age, and whose hair refused to be grey; men whose hair either silvered or did not change at all, though some had owned faithless hair which had left them to live the rest of their lives under a series of seasonal hats. Dan assumed these people inhabited the town of Oceanside, a town he referred to as a service town: a main street of barbers, tailors, dry cleaners, laundromats, and bars without even facades: mere four-walled structures where young enlisted Marines could continue their baptism into the world of men by drinking and talking as they pleased. He did not know what these dancing men did for a living. He had never been in the pastel residential section on the hill overlooking the main street. He figured of course that Oceanside had its mayor, its judge and lawyers and doctors; there must be teachers and men who erected buildings and houses; certainly there were managers of supermarkets, owners of service stations, pharmacists; there would be the ubiquitous insurance men, and someone owned the women's clothing store which seemed to display always a brightly colored bathing suit in its window. But he could account for no one else. Then Khristy said:

"My *God*—let's get out of here."

He left a good tip, his fantasy of being utterly broke by morning now washed away by gin, and its vestiges tamped firmly beneath consciousness by lobster and potatoes; he paid the bill with the same insouciant grace; and with his arm lightly encircling her ribs, they stepped into the fog. She took his hand and led him away from the parking lot, toward the beach: she descended steep wooden steps to a pier and he thought she was going to the end of it where they would kiss swaying over the dark white-capped tide smacking against the pilings. But a third of the way down the pier, as he was reaching for her waist again, she turned in front of him and stepped rather than jumped to the sand three feet below. So he jumped after her.

"Let's go to that place at the south end of the beach," she said.

He had just straightened from his jump, standing close to her, her grey-blue eyes looking dark now just below his, and he was about to tell her the bar at the south end was off-limits, but instead he kissed her; taking her by surprise so that her teeth clicked against his for an instant, then she was returning the kiss and he was seeing her prone on the sand, wondering if she would ever be prone for him— although he wasn't sure that he would, on the sand; for just as he could not look at any landscape without a tactical eye which sought out critical high ground and draws and treelines that would serve as avenues of approach, he could not see or feel sand under his feet without being reminded of amphibious landings and the difficulty of running on it wearing boots and a haversack and, once off the beach and your uniform dry, your clothes and flesh and weapons carried sand that you could not entirely brush away. But with Khristy he guessed he would, sand or not, though he imagined that somehow sand would cling to their bodies, even at their point of fusion.

Then she pulled away and he said he loved her and she cried out louder than the surf that she bet no one in the world could kiss like he could, and taking his hand she led him down the beach, past the backs of restaurants and bars and darkened stores above them, crunching through burnt wood from beach fires, stepping over dried pale driftwood, saying *ooh* when a sand crab fled across her path. To their right the tide rushed in with dark power, emanating some preternatural sense of omnipotence and threat, and it occurred to Dan that if you really wanted to be alone you merely had to stand on an empty beach at night. Khristy was breathing hard now and he thought of her high heels driving into the sand, and of his cordovans losing their layers of spit-shine so he would have to spend an evening in Alameda working on them before he reported aboard.

Sitting in his office on the *Vanguard*, thousands of miles and nearly seven months from that evening, he could still see her walking on that beach. Then he thought of her at UCLA now, walking across the campus, and he hoped no hand was in hers, that no one walked beside her; that, lost and without purpose, she moved through smog with books pressed against her sweatered breasts.

Then Tolleson came into the office, his eyes for an instant puzzled by Dan's face. Tolleson had brown eyes which were hard only when he was angry; at other times, when he was serious, they had a soft shine of disillusion, as if he had refused to cry ten years ago but the tears were still waiting there, ready; when he was joking his eyes were bright as a child's. Looking at Tolleson's firm jaw and erect back, Dan was suddenly convinced that he should not have released Freeman and, above all, he should not have considered sending him home.

From his own desk, Tolleson got his coffee cup, a large white mug with First Sergeant's chevrons painted on one side and the Marine emblem on the other, and went for coffee; as he crossed the classroom he said loudly, hoarsely: "Corporal, you keep your ass glued to that desk."

"I had to make a head call, First Sergeant."

"Goddammit, if it takes you that long I'll get a God-damn piss tube installed under the desk—you're back there paying a social call on your Goddamn buddies." Then his voice softened, became sarcastic: "Well, I'll tell you a little secret. Corporal. A corporal doesn't *have* buddies: he's got military acquaintances."

When Tolleson returned to the office, shutting the door behind him, Dan's feet were off the desk—though he still leaned back in the chair—and he was thinking of nothing at all, but he knew that his face made him appear to be thinking six steps ahead of Tolleson.

"What did the chief say?"

"Well, sir, he said there's a plane leaving tomorrow morning and all Freeman needs is emergency leave papers." He paused. "Signed by the Lieutenant, sir."

"That's all?"

"Right, sir. He says as long as the Lieutenant is authorized to grant leave, it ain't his business to ask questions."

"Well—"

"Also, sir, he says this conversation between me and him never took place."

"Good. Let's do it then."

Dan waited as Tolleson bent over and took his cigarettes from his sock.

"With all due respect, sir, I ought to tell the Lieutenant that it's a big risk."

"You don't have to worry, First Sergeant. The responsiblity is mine."

"Goddamn, sir, I've got nineteen and a half years in this man's Marine Corps and I've gone as far as I can go. They can't hurt me. Sir—if Freeman gets on that plane and it goes down in that ocean, there'll be an investigation—right, sir?"

"I suppose so."

"And they'll want to know how come one young Pfc Freeman was on that plane—right, sir?"

Dan looked away and sipped his coffee.

"Sir," Tolleson said, his voice soft, near pleading, "I hate to see the Lieutenant stick his neck out. Lieutenant's got a long career ahead of him."

"I've also got a promise to Freeman."

"A promise, sir?"

"Well, not exactly: I told him I'd do what I could."

"Well, sir, the Lieutenant can go down to the brig and tell that young Christian there ain't nothing to be done."

"He's not in the brig. I let him out."

"Goddammit, sir, why? He committed an offense, he was brought in to office hours—"

"Because Corporal McKittrick was harassing him."

"Sir, I've been harassed for nineteen and a half years."

"Maybe you shouldn't have been."

"Well sir, my Drill Instructor got my cherry and after that I sort of expected it."

Dan looked away. The mention of Drill Instructors or Boot Camp always made him feel that, in some irrevocable way, he was a coward: no matter how often he convinced himself that officer candidate training had been harder, both physically and mentally; no matter how often he told himself that candidates were not harassed as steadily and harshly as recruits were, because candidates were supposed to become leaders, were expected to get through their training on their own initiative, or give up and go home—he still believed he had basely avoided that common experience of humiliation and final reward which all enlisted Marines shared. So whenever Staff NCO's told stories of Boot Camp, he listened in embarrassed silence; even if he could recall similar incidents from his officer candidate training, he never told them, because he knew they would listen with condescension, with impatience, if they listened at all: for they prided themselves on having suffered most, on having borne it best—

"Sir, we got problems," Tolleson was saying. "What's going to stop every man in this Detachment from telling these corporals to go fuck themselves—which, sir, is what Freeman did this morning."

"You will, First Sergeant; and I will."

"One moment, sir: *also*, if the Lieutenant sends Freeman home, then what happens when the next man comes in with a letter from *his* girl? Sir, if Freeman goes home, we'll have fifty Goddamn emergencies before this ship gets to Iwakuni and Captain Schneider comes aboard."

"You have a point there," Dan said, and his cheeks were warm and flushed.

"Yes, sir. Also, there's the Lieutenant's career to think about."

"That's not important."

"Sir, the Lieutenant's a good officer and it *is* important."

"Well—not in this decision." Dan stood up. "But I'll take your advice on that other point. You can send Freeman in now."

"Aye aye, sir," Tolleson said, grinning, turning and going rapidly out the door, like a man with good news.

THE NEXT DAY Freeman was Captain Howard's orderly again. The Captain was surprised to see him, and said, "I thought you were in the brig," and Freeman told him the Lieutenant had released him the night before. The Captain seemed to think about that for a moment, then he said: "Good." All day Freeman stood on the bridge with Captain Howard, watching planes landing and taking off, or followed him about the ship, with that protective attitude he had acquired from carrying a loaded .45 while Captain Howard—who could probably not fire one anyway—was unarmed. After the evening meal he polished his shoes and brass and wrote a letter to Jan, telling her there was nothing to do now but wait. Then he undressed and lay in his bunk.

In the light of the small reading lamp above his head he stared at Jan's picture near his feet. He was not as disappointed as he had thought he would be, because he had never really hoped: since Jan had first written that she was pregnant he had been certain that he could not return to the States and marry her, so his energy and preoccupations were directed toward waiting. He became a habitual watcher of time: every other day, on his duty day, as he

stood on the bridge with Captain Howard, he glanced ha-
bitually at his watch, only occasionally aware of the time
on its face or even aware that he had looked at it.

On the days when he was off duty, he sat through lec-
tures on military subjects and, at three o'clock, he would
go with his section to a sponson deck where the Lieutenant would lead them through calisthenics for an hour.
That was one of the peaks of his waiting: in stationary
double-time, lifting his knees high and pounding his
booted feet on the steel deck, he would look at the horizon—on most days a fusing of shades of blue, on others
the living grey of choppy sea and the dead paler grey of
the sky—and he would feel that he had almost made
another day.

His second peak would come that night, after shining his leather and brass and watching a movie on the
ship's television in the classroom or on the screen set up
on the enlisted mess deck, then writing a letter to Jan and,
on some nights, working on a correspondence course in
squad tactics—then he would climb into his bunk and
look at his watch and take the calendar from the small
locker near his pillow where he kept toilet articles and
cigarettes and stationery, and with his ballpoint pen he
would block out that day. Then he would turn out the
reading lamp and stretch his legs under the taut blanket,
lying on his back, not sleepy for he was nineteen years old
and a day on the *Vanguard* rarely tired him. He would try
very hard to avoid thinking of the number of days left, for
a three-digit number was unbearable: he would lie there,
thinking he had made one more day.

So last night when the Lieutenant had released him from the brig and told him to wait for further word, he had climbed onto his bunk and sat with his feet hanging over its side and told himself there was no hope of his going home—no matter what the Lieutenant said. An airplane seemed to involve so much more than Lieutenant Tierney and the Detachment; it involved the ship itself, anonymous Naval officers behind grey hatches; it involved the Seventh Fleet and, by boarding a plane and rising above the *Vanguard*, it seemed that somehow you were involved with the command and staff of the entire Western Pacific. He was certain of that. He remembered the order about emergency leave which Captain Schneider had read to the Detachment before the ship left the States. When the First Sergeant had hollered at him from the classroom he had jumped to the deck and gone through the curtains between the berthing area and classroom, trying—as fervently as he avoided thinking of three-digit numbers, of Jan's expanding belly—not to hope. The First Sergeant had told him to report to the Lieutenant and he had; and when he saw the Lieutenant's face—that solemn look they always gave you just before they crapped on you—he knew he had been right.

But Lieutenant Tierney had told him something totally different from what he had expected. The Lieutenant had not said that it was impossible to send him home; he had said that it was possible, but he couldn't do it because if he broke regulations for one man he would have to break them for everyone. Then he had said: "I know how tough it is, Freeman."

"Thank you, sir."

"If there's anything else I can do, let me know."

"Yes, sir. Thank you, sir."

And the Lieutenant had said: "That's all, Freeman."

Now, twenty-four hours later, he looked at his watch, even read the actual time: eleven thirty-two. Later he would remember that: would vividly recall that, at eleven thirty-two, he had been lying on his bunk and it had just occurred to him that he had to piss.

But he did not go to the head: he lay there silently cursing Lieutenant Tierney and looking at the eight-by-ten picture of Jan's face and thinking of one hundred and fifteen days until the ship got home, then he thought of his father in Bellingham: a barber whose own hair had long since fallen out, the top of his head smooth, and only short grey hairs at the sides and back now; a short man with narrow shoulders and a pot belly and a high laugh tha ended in wheezing; he was grouchy in the morning, tired and quiet at night. If his father were dying, he could go home.

He was sitting up to go to the head when he heard footsteps on the rubber tile deck, stopping at his bunk; he turned and saw at eye-level Corporal McKittrick's spit-shined cap brim, the black Marine emblem above it. Then he looked at McKittrick's eyes and, farther down, at his white pistol belt and holstered .45; McKittrick was the Corporal of the Guard.

"What did the Lieutenant tell you last night?"

"He let me out of the brig."

"No shit, Freeman: I ain't blind. He said you can't take leave, didn't he?"

"That's right."

"You went crying to that sonofabitch and he chewed me out."

"You want me to tell the Lieutenant that?"

"You better square away, Freeman, that's what I'm telling you," McKittrick said; but he turned and walked away, retaining a swagger: his holstered .45 at his hip, his right arm out from his side, swinging. Then Freeman dropped to the deck and went toward the head.

He did not want to, for he knew that Hahn was in there, and Jensen too, shining their shoes and talking with that group which gathered in the head at night. When he pushed through the swinging wooden hatch, Hahn was standing profiled to him, talking loudly and grinning at the others who sat on the deck near the lavatories, shining shoes, grinning and nodding at Hahn who was gesturing with his left arm (he wore utility trousers and a T-shirt); beneath his vaccination scar, on the broad surface of his left bicep, was a tattooed Marine emblem. Then Hahn saw Freeman.

"Jesus! It's the brig rat."

Freeman turned to his right and went to the urinal.

"Hey, Teddy-Baby," Hahn said. "How come Dangerous Dan let you out? You do something for him?"

"No," he said, shaking his head, unbuttoning his fly and wishing he had not answered, now pulling out his penis that shamed him so, and it seemed even smaller than usual, as if it too shrank before their derision.

"Let's see it," Jensen said. "Maybe there's toothmarks on it."

Laughter bounced off the bulkhead in front of him as, shivering. Freeman pissed. He left the head without looking back, stepping hot-faced into the dark of the berthing area, moving between the bulkhead on his left and the cubicles of metal bunks on his right, turning into his own cubicle and climbing onto his bunk. In the upper bunk opposite Freeman's, Jack Burns sat up and said:

"They giving you a hard time?"

"Bastards."

"Somebody ought to tell the Lieutenant what goes on around here," Burns said, then lay down again and, pulling his blanket to his shoulders, rolled on his side, his back to Freeman, who was about to unlace his boots but stopped. The swinging hatch of the head had just slammed shut and he heard them coming, knew they were coming for him, and he straightened from his boot and sat holding the edge of the bunk as Hahn and Jensen stepped into the cubicle—then Hahn grabbed one of his dangling legs, just below the knee, in a grip that Freeman knew he could never break. Gradually Hahn pulled the leg downward, and Freeman held the bunk with both hands as he slid forward, closer to Hahn's face which was level with his chest: Hahn grinning and his eyes brutal and unyielding; now he said:

"Let's see the toothmarks, Teddy-Baby."

Freeman looked down at Jensen, shorter than Hahn, grinning too; his left arm was bent upward, so the sleeve of his T-shirt stretched around his bicep, and Freeman saw the can of shaving cream in his hand.

"Aw, come on," he said, hating the whine in his voice. "Come on now."

He looked at Burns, who was still on his side, the blanket over his shoulders, his back turned. Then Hahn pulled again and Freeman tried to stop himself but couldn't and he knew he would scrape his back and hit his head on the bunk's edge as he fell—but then from the classroom beyond the curtain he heard the slide of a .45 slamming forward and the click of the hammer and Hahn wasn't pulling on his leg anymore, though gripping it still as he stood with his head cocked toward the curtain, listening to the sounds of the changing of the guard: the sentries clearing their .45's.

"Mac's getting relieved," Hahn said. "Let's get him."

"All right," Jensen said, and he moved farther into the cubicle and stood with his back against Burns' bunk.

"Come on, Teddy-Baby," Hahn said. "We'll get old Mac."

"Okay"—nodding his head—"okay: good."

He slid down from the bunk and stood with them and listened as the new corporal of the guard took his sentries up the ladder. He heard McKittrick coming through the curtains, into the dark, approaching the cubicle, his heels clicking. Then he saw him. Jensen and Hahn sprang from the cubicle and he followed them, saw McKittrick going to the deck on his back and Jensen pinning his arms; Freeman kneeled on McKittrick's shins and with each hand pushed down hard on a knee, watching as Hahn unbuckled McKittrick's belt. He looked away, down at McKittrick's struggling legs, heard McKittrick's voice murmuring curses without malice, curses that became strange laughter from his throat; then cursing and laughter both stopped and Freeman heard what he thought was a groan and McKittrick's legs stopped struggling though their muscles were still tight, and Freeman looked up from the legs and saw what Hahn was doing and for an instant he could not move, as if an intense nausea had suddenly rushed up from his knees to his throat—then he moved: he rose quickly, turning, his left ankle tripping on McKittrick's outstretched legs and he stumbled but did not fall. He ran out of the berthing area, through the curtains, into the lighted classroom.

Chapter Three

AN HOUR LATER, trying to sleep, he heard Burns shifting in his bunk, pushing away a blanket and sitting up.

"Jesus," Burns said. "I saw it all."

"You did?"

"Jesus Christ, I don't care what they do to me, I'm telling the First Sergeant tomorrow morning. I had to go to the head and *puke*, for Christ's sake."

So now, though Freeman had always been their victim, it was Burns who would tell. Lying there in his bunk, Freeman thought that for years he had been wandering around, trying to decide what to do, while someone else was already doing it.

In high school, surrounded and defined by blackboards and the semi-enclosing blond wood of his several desks, by teachers who seemed old and certain, by young boys whose dress and manner he imitated, and girls whom he at once desired and shied from, Freeman had never paused to consider what he was. He thought he knew, and had he ever articulated this knowledge, he would not even have said *student:* he would have said *high school boy.* Then he was graduated.

During the first weeks of that summer, as a bag and carry-out boy at a supermarket, he was all right. But after a month had passed he was restless. At the check-out counter he tried to pack each bag as quickly as he could, was conscious only of the damp cold of milk cartons, the hard cylinders of soup and vegetables, the crisp lettuce that yielded to his squeezing fingers, and time that was measured by empty bags becoming filled. When there were few customers, he swept the floor and arranged canned goods on the shelves and measured time by the hands of his watch. At night he would walk home, feeling somehow severed from the world as he had known it.

He had assumed that he would go to college at the end of the summer. But now this troubled him. At college he would have to tell people what he wanted to study, what he wanted to become. He began to think of joining the service.

So on a Saturday afternoon in midsummer he stood ouside the courthouse, confronted by a large recruiting poster luring him to the service which, after many walks from the supermarket to his home and many wakeful hours in bed, he had decided would do for him what he had not been able to do for himself. The poster showed a rifle inspection at Boot Camp, focusing on a tall young recruit in the front rank and the corporal who was inspecting him. The recruit wore utilities and a cartridge belt and stood stiffly at attention. The corporal wore tropical khaki, and a campaign hat cocked over his eyes; his fists were on his hips, his face—suntanned as only technicolored movie actors are—was leaned toward the recruit, and he looked like a very young man who could do anything he chose. The large caption of the poster was THE MARINE CORPS BUILDS MEN. Freeman thought of himself as the recruit on the poster, afraid but efficient (you could see that) in a strange, harsh world. Then he looked at the corporal and thought of himself too: standing before a group of men with his fists on his hips, or home on leave and people turning to look as he sauntered in uniform down these same streets. *Oh*, he would say at a bar, *it's not bad: you just do what you have to.*

After what seemed a long time he walked up the sidewalk and the steps and into the courthouse, past the blind man who worked behind the candy and cigarette counter, and down the stairs into stale subterranean coolness and the smell of a spittoon at the bottom of the stairs, and into the office where a sly lean staff sergeant in blue trousers and a tropical khaki shirt with campaign ribbons looked up from his desk, rose, and extended hand as he smiled and said: *Come on in.* Months later Ted felt the same fear and discomfort when, in Tijuana, he entered a whorehouse. In the whorehouse he quickly said no, and left; but that day in the recruiting office he said yes, although nothing the sergeant talked about appealed to him: in fact, the entire interview increased his fear—and his final yes was really spoken to himself, an affirmation of his need to endure Boot Camp and infantry training, to be somehow transformed.

Boot Camp did change him, but not enough. By the end of it he could run two miles with a haversack on his back, though he still could not approach that run with confidence and he felt that he was able to keep up with the platoon only because he was afraid of his Drill Instructor. Freeman would always remember him: leaning forward, his eyes wrathful under the brim of his campaign hat, his harsh Boston voice taunting and cursing until tears came to Freeman's eyes, and two fists struck his chest, grabbing his shirt before he fell: breathless and stiff and open-mouthed, he felt his face paling and his knees going weak as rope, just before he was shoved backward against the bruising corner of a foot locker, going over it, legless now, his back and head hitting the deck, and above his sudden pain, the voice:

"Goddamn you Freeman you skinny little shit you can't even *fall* like a Marine. Get up get *up*. Freeman did you ever just once—just one tiny little fucking time in your whole life play football?"

"Sir no sir."

"Well what the fuck *did* you do? Did you ever get a piece of ass?"

"Sir no sir."

"Freeman you are an asshole. Now I'm going to ask you one more time, Freeman, just one more fucking time: describe the M-1 rifle. *Describe* it, I said."

"Sir the M-1 rifle is a gas-operated semi-automatic—"

"What does gas-operated mean, asshole?"

The sergeant spun away, out of his vision which was not really vision, for he did not see the recruits standing at attention on the opposite side of the squad bay, nor did he see the bulkhead: he saw, through a mist, only himself. Then a rifle muzzle was inches from his face, at eye level, and the sergeant's long forefinger was touching it.

"See that Freeman. That is the gas cylinder. Now, Freeman, what does it *do*?"

"Sir—"

Then the rifle was smacked against his chest before he could raise his hands to grab it, then he had it, not knowing what to do with it next, and he was about to hold it at port when the sergeant said:

"Now you hold that piece out in front of you. *Straight* out, Freeman: horizontal. Freeman if you drop that weapon I'll break your skinny fucking arms. Now you hold it. How much does it weigh, Freeman?"

"Sir the M-1 rifle weighs nine point five pounds sir."

"That's not very much, is it. Freeman?"

"Sir no sir."

"Then why the fuck is your whole Goddamn body shaking? Freeman you are an asshole. Do you know why you never got a piece of ass? I know why. Because, Freeman, you are nothing but a skinny turd and you would fuck up a wet dream."

He did not, at Boot Camp, have wet dreams. But often he dreamed of his Drill Instructor and one night the recruit who had fire watch duty found him crouched in front of his steel wall locker, still asleep, murmuring in a forlorn and desperate voice: "I can't find it; I can't find it." Then he gripped the bottom of the wall locker and with his arms that had so much trouble with chin-ups and push-ups and the obstacle course, he lifted the wall locker and stood, holding it tottering above their heads until the firewatch said: "Goddamn, what are you doing, Freeman?" And he said: "I lost my blanket roll strap." The firewatch helped him lower the wall locker, and led him to his bunk, assuring him that his blanket roll straps were on his pack and he could see them in the morning. Next day they told him about it and he was surprised. He had never walked in his sleep before, he said. Later, when no one was watching, he tried to lift the wall locker. He could not.

The trip to Tijuana was after Boot Camp, on a bus. When Ted and the four others were high on beer (which they drank boisterously, watching strippers, their language tougher now, less awed than it might have been before their enlistments) they took a taxi to a whorehouse. Passionless, Ted followed a girl as far as her room; then he looked down the corridor and saw that all his friends were in rooms now, and he told the girl he was sick, he had drunk too much, and he had to go outside and throw up. She started cursing him, so he paid her, then went out and waited. On the ride back he told them it was a good piece but he had come too fast. "That's 'cause it was your first time," one of them said.

From Boot Camp he was sent to the Infantry Training Regiment at Camp Pendleton. He had thought his legs and lungs were in good condition, but at Camp Pendleton there were hills. The steepest of them was Old Smoky, which seemed to rise straight into the sky above Southern

California. Ted's platoon sergeant prepared them for it with the usual Marine Corps warning: "You people maybe think you're in good shape, well we're going to climb Old Smoky tomorrow"—turning to point at its brown peak, the wavering fire trail up its slope; Ted looked away from it, at the sergeant who was still pointing, looked at his green starched utilities faded near white, at his profiled red-brown face, and beyond him, at the other brown and treeless hills; and he thought that for the past three months, which now seemed his entire life, men had been telling him that tomorrow or next week he was going to have to do something that he could not do—the sergeant turned, faced them again—"and you people are going to wanta crap out, but you better forget it 'cause I'll be kickin' asses all the way." He did. On the march he used a walking stick, a long shaved branch, and after a third of the climb he jabbed Ted's back: "Close it up, Freeman, or you'll be running all the way."

The platoon was formed in two columns, the tallest men in front setting the pace, the shortest in the rear, and Ted was at the end of one column. So to keep up he had to walk faster—or take more steps—than the pacesetters; and when someone at the head of the column momentarily lagged, then increased his pace to catch up, the whole column felt it: each man in turn stretching his legs farther and faster to regain those two yards, the yards increasing toward the rear of the column so that when it was Ted's turn to catch up he had to cover five or six yards and he could only do it by running. He began to hate marchers with long legs.

Halfway up the hill he thought he would not finish. The muscles in his calves were burning; and each time his weight shifted to his forward leg, he felt that its horizontal thigh would stiffen, that he would not be able to straighten that leg or thrust his rear leg forward and up the slope. And he was winded, his lungs demanding oxygen again even before he finished exhaling, his mouth and throat dried by his rapid open-mouthed breathing so that he at once cursed and longed for the two canteens on his hips. In the squad bay before the march the canteens had seemed weightless but now they rubbed his flesh and pulled at his cartridge belt like the hands of a boy, tugging him backward. The haversack had been an alien weight—but not heavy—even in the squad bay, and its shoulder straps were tightened so that it rode high on his back. Now it was heavy too. He bent under it, leaning into the angle of the slope, and its sliding pressure and his soaked utility shirt chafed his back. He hooked his thumbs under the shoulder straps to keep them—he felt—from cutting through his flesh. But when he did that with his right hand he released his rifle sling and the stock bumped his leg, so he grabbed the sling and pulled the rifle tight against the back of his shoulder, then stretched out his thumb and hooked it under the shoulder strap again. He looked fearfully at a man ahead of him carrying a BAR. His rifle was only half as heavy as that and already it seemed too heavy for any sensible man to consider it a good weapon, to consider it a good thing at all—

And that was it: his personal equipment—the steel helmet squeezing and pressing his head, the rifle, the haversack which contained his food and mess gear and socks and underwear and poncho, the canteens with two quarts of water that he so badly needed—all these things were suddenly impersonal, or worse: they were devised by someone who wanted to show him another thing he could not do. And they had won. He could not: not another stride up that slope—

This time, if he could have heard anything but his own breathing, he would have heard the platoon sergeant's stick swinging toward him. The sergeant had swung like a baseball player, striking Ted's pack, jarring him so he stumbled, then straightened himself and found that his legs had taken him ten yards farther up the hill before he felt their pain and heard his breath again in the silence after the sergeant's hoarse and angry and also tired cry: "Goddamn I said *close it up*"—

The sergeant did not have to hit him again. He would not, Goddammit, drop out; would not be the only one who didn't make it or didn't keep up, because if he couldn't get up this hill, then people at home, the people from high school who were probably thinking he could never get through Marine training, would be right: and he would be a phony. So he went up, not daring to look at the peak for he did not want to see how much farther he had to go, his eyes on the pack and helmet in front of him, and when someone in the column dropped back then caught up, forcing him to run, he yelled, expending the little oxygen he had, his voice breaking shrill and petulant through the sound of the march—stocks bumping against legs and canteens, and booted feet climbing slowly but still too fast, and small rocks kicked loose and rolling downhill—"Goddammit keep it closed up!" After yelling and running those few paces to gain on the forward-tilted haversack and helmet ahead of him, he knew that his lungs would lose: they would never get the oxygen they wanted, not until he reached the peak; and now with tears as well as sweat dripping from his cheeks, he climbed, his eyes on the hard dirt of the fire trail, the muscles of his legs burning and swelling as if they meant to burst through his taut flesh—

He made it. At the top he stood on quivering legs and drank while, as if in shock, his body cooled rapidly, his sweat drying in the breeze which passed them on its way to the bright ocean. Out there he saw grey ships and, around his uptilted canteen, he stared at them.

After four weeks of combat training, when he was ordered to Sea School at San Diego, he was happy—although he recognized a certain cowardice in his reaction to the orders, and that shamed him. But he got over it. He did well at Sea School where tailored uniforms, shined brass, polished leather, and learning shipboard duties were all that counted. At night, on liberty in San Diego, he wore his uniform, and after a couple of beers he felt tough, competent with his hands and knees and feet, remembering the hand-to-hand combat classes in Boot Camp. In those classes he had learned—or had been introduced to—several judo throws; more important, he had been taught the vulnerable parts of a man's body, and he now believed that lacking the strength and speed of a boxer he could still disable another man with his knee or one chop from his open, stiff-fingered hand. He had not thought it odd when the hand-to-hand combat instructor had so often referred to barroom fighting, as if that were the course's reason or goal (*You're out with your girl, and this swabbie's giving you a hard time and he shoves you like this*—). In fact, because of those references, he was more interested in hand-to-hand classes than in bayonet training. So drinking in San Diego bars, the hills and marches and Camp Pendleton well behind him now and knowing the next day at Sea School would be neither difficult nor especially challenging, he imagined himself disarming a knife-threatening Mexican or kicking a large sailor in the groin. Then Sea School was over and he was sent to the *Vanguard*, home-ported at Alameda, across the bay from San Francisco.

Shortly after he came aboard, the *Vanguard* went to sea for five days. On the third night, while he was lying in his bunk and waiting for sleep, they came for him: Hahn and Jensen and McKittrick, who was still a Pfc. They lifted him from the bunk and, holding his feet and arms, carried him toward the head. He was conscious of grinning faces watching as he passed. Inside the head, when they lowered him to the deck, he was smiling too and only half-struggling. But he was afraid he would cry. He had not expected this, had even—during his months of training—forgotten that it existed, forgotten that during his twelve years of school he had always been a victim of bullying, even in high school where it took subtler forms, questions like: *You coming out for football? You got a hot date for the prom?* Now here it was again.

Then someone—Jensen—pulled his T-shirt up to his armpits, pressed his arms to the deck and, behind his head kneeled on Ted's biceps.

"Come on, get off now Goddammit—"

But Hahn was pulling his shorts down, over his thighs, past his knees; and McKittrick was laughing now, falling backward against a shower stall, holding his belly and pointing. Hahn was looking at Ted with a bemused smile; but his eyes were more savage than any Ted had ever seen, and he looked away, struggling now, arching his back and trying to move his legs under Hahn's weight.

"Hey, I think it's a cunt," Hahn said.

Then Ted screamed, cursing them all: Hahn and Jensen and McKittrick and the ones who stood watching and laughing. His eyes were shut on tears and all that he felt or heard was his own screaming and once, at the height of a cried-out curse, he saw as in a dream Captain Howard, on the bridge, hearing that final curse shouted far below him. Then Jensen's hand was on his mouth. Another voice had replaced his own but he could not distinguish it, understand it, and he opened his eyes. Through his tears he saw Hahn's face, the mouth savage now too:

"You wake up the First Sergeant and your ass is mine, Teddy-Baby."

He stopped struggling. He smiled. People made jokes and he responded with good-natured grunts as Hahn spread shaving cream on his groin, shaved the hair, and painted his flesh with Mercurochrome. Then on his chest and belly, which were already hairless, Hahn carefully painted something. When he was finished they were all laughing and Ted smiled up at them, then felt the weight going off his arms and thighs and now he had to get up. He pulled up his shorts, pulled down his T-shirt, and quickly left the head.

In his bunk he waited until the berthing area was quiet, until the last flap-flap of shower shoes had gone from the head to a bunk, then he got up and, barefooted, went to the head. The lights were on. At the mirror he pulled up his T-shirt. The words were reversed and it took him several moments to read them:

I

LOST

MY

PRICK

LATER, AFTER HE met Jan, he would think: *Jack Burns is my best friend.* For it was Burns who, from the opposite bunk, began talking to him the night after he had been shaved and painted. After another day at sea, when the *Vanguard* returned to Alameda, it was Burns who asked him to go on liberty. And it was Burns who, two weeks later, brought him to the party where he met Jan and where, because he and Burns were the only Marines and even the boys at the party were impressed, and because he was a bit drunk as well, he was able to talk to her without timidity, to laugh naturally and joke and tease. By the time she went home with her date—a young sullen civilian with long hair— Ted had arranged to take her out later in the week. That first date was easier, less discomforting, than one had ever been; because he already knew she liked him.

On their third date, three months before *Vanguard*'s deployment to the Western Pacific, he arrived to find her in bed, watching television, and she told him she had the flu or something and she had tried to call the ship but it was too confusing, all those different extensions, and finally she had given up. So he went out and bought two six-packs of beer, having carried only one to the cash register before—on impulse—he went back for another. Even walking back to her apartment with twelve cans of beer cradled in one arm and an overnight liberty card in his billfold he did not allow himself to think of seduction. For if he considered that, he would have to consider the rest: his total lack of experience and therefore confidence, and the jokes he had heard, jokes which convinced him that female pleasure was all a matter of a man's size. He reentered her apartment, where both of them knew—and had known since he first appeared that night—they would make love.

She sat with two pillows behind her back, the sheet and pale green spread covering her bent-kneed legs, making a tent containing that sweetness he had never touched in his nineteen years—and though he averted his eyes he was aware of nothing else in the room, in his life. The sheet and spread were pulled up to her waist; above that, her breasts and shoulders and arms to the wrists were covered by a light blue nightgown: her body not hidden but assuming a subtle form of exposure because all its coverings were those of bed and night, the trappings of his fantasies. After her fourth beer she was grinning and patting the small available portion of mattress beside her; he left his chair, moving dry-throated to the bed, and he sat there and with his palm touched her cheek, hot with fever, and she stopped smiling.

Then he kissed her: what seemed one long deliciously maddening unbroken kiss, his hands going downward from her shoulders, pausing unchecked at her breasts where he did what he had been told by other boys he would like to do, his hands actually stopping at her breasts only because he had been told that—and down again, one hand now sliding over the nylon nightgown and the loose yielding flesh of her belly. Then her hand was on his, pressing, stopping him. He pushed hard and her hand was gone, somewhere on his back now, but her legs were together: in turn squeezing and relaxing until finally his hand was there, pulling the nylon away and still he would not allow the final image of lovemaking to form in his mind, not even when her legs spread and she. moved against his hand and whispered or exhaled: "The light," and as he turned to reach the lamp on the bedside table he felt her moving, shifting, and when he turned to her in the dark she was sitting up, the nightgown rising from her raised arms, then dropping to the floor. He was suddenly out of his clothes. Still he would not think: *I'm going to—* He was on top of her, starting to kiss her, when she whispered again or made that sound of urgent breath which alone was more than he had ever heard, ever experienced: "Do you have something?" At first he did not understand, for by refusing to think of lovemaking he had fled from any thought of its consequences too. Then he shook his head and was rising on his elbows when her arm slid under his ribs and belly and her hand nested beneath what had shamed him, guiding it forward: and without shame or fear he entered—poised then for a motionless and startled instant. It was scalding hot, beyond prediction and belief, and still in that instant of nonmovement, he remembered a high school boy who had gone to a whorehouse and had this for the first time and had told him it was like sponge rubber and Ted almost told Jan now, almost sang out how wrong that boy was— But instead he began to move, opened his mouth to speak but there was no time: and with a soft boyish cry that he did not even hear, he spent himself, collapsed, seemed to melt and spread over the length of her body, which settled under him, warm and reposeful, and he was aware of sounds again, of her breath and heart. . . .

Wrapped in manhood as tangible as the heat from her naked feverish body, he slept with her that night. After a couple of hours he woke, confused until he felt her body against his; then he made love to her again, taking longer this time, knowing he pleased her.

In the weeks after that, when he had to stay aboard ship for guard duty, or when the ship was at sea for five or six days, or sometimes even when he lay in her bed, sapless and sleepy, he thought sorrowfully of all those girls in high school who might have been his if he had only tried hard enough, if he had only been confident of his good looks and personality (he could always make Jan laugh) but he had not been confident, he had not tried, and now they were gone: sweaters and perfume and tossing hair, up in Washington, lost. . . . But he had this.

Hahn and Jensen and McKittrick, though, took it away from him a second time: in July, when the *Vanguard* was conducting air operations off the coast of Southern California, they held him down and shaved his groin again. He could not stop the tears and they trailed down his flushed cheeks as he silently submitted. He had believed the first time would be the last: that he had been initiated as a new man in the Detachment. But, held to the deck for the second time, he saw this happening again and again, as often as they wanted.

He did not tell Jan. In those last weeks before the ship deployed to the Western Pacific, he kept hoping something would happen to them. When the ship was in port and he saw them leaving for liberty, the three of them walking down the long concrete pier, slapping backs, laughing, faking left hooks, he wished he would never see them again: that they would get involved with dope peddlers that night or would roll someone in San Francisco and go to jail, staying there while the *Vanguard* deployed.

But nothing ever happened to them, or nothing really bad. Hahn and Jensen were court-martialed once, but got light sentences. In August, while the ship was on its way to Japan, McKittrick was promoted to corporal. Ted stood in the formation on the mess deck and watched him going front and center and saluting and taking his warrant from Captain Schneider, and Ted thought even the First Sergeant and a mustang like Captain Schneider were snowed and if they really wanted to know who rated promotions they ought to ask the troops.

A week later, the night after Ted was promoted to Pfc, Hahn and Jensen dragged him to the head again. But as they started to bring him to the deck, he swung once: an impotent blow which he regretted even before it struck Hahn's chin. Hahn slapped him, five or six times, slowly.

McKittrick wasn't with them, because he was a corporal now, and his safest act of collusion was noninterference. But he did not stop harassing Ted. When the word got out that Jan was pregnant—somehow the word always got out and everybody, except the First Sergeant and the officers, knew everything—McKittrick teased him about it so often that it finally became boring. But yesterday morning during clean-up he had said more than: *Looks like the Detachment's goin' to have another Teddy-Baby*. He had said: *She must be fuckin' somebody, Freeman. That little pecker you got couldn't have knocked her up—*

So, twenty-four hours out of the brig, when Hahn utterly surprised him by saying *We'll get old Mac* he had joined them until he saw what Hahn was doing. Then he had run to the classroom and sat there, in the light, reading a month-old copy of *Leatherneck*. An hour later, climbing into his bunk, he was beginning to understand why they had gone for McKittrick. But when he thought about it he felt uneasy and wicked too, the way he had felt in high school when he heard that a cheerleader, an older girl with long dark hair whom he watched through every football game, was putting out.

When Burns sat up in his bunk and told him what he had seen and that he was going to tell the First Sergeant in the morning, Ted could not even think of revenge. He only wished that he had never seen this ship or anyone on it, that somehow he could have met Jan without joining the Marine Corps.

AT EIGHT O'CLOCK next morning Jack Burns was sitting in his chair, at his desk; First Sergeant Tolleson stood to his left, drinking coffee and frowning; and Lieutenant Tierney sat at his desk, his swivel chair turned so that he was lookingat Burns. After a pause, which had not been necessary when he had told the First Sergeant half an hour ago, Burns found a word he could use:

"Then, Sir, Corporal McKittrick ejaculated."

Lieutenant Tierney's eyes, in the sudden pallor of his face, were black.

"Tell the Lieutenant the rest of it," the First Sergeant said.

"Well, sir, then Hahn had shaving cream and that stuff, sir, all over his hands. And he and Jensen rubbed it on Corporal McKittrick's stomach, sir."

"*Goddamn.* Then what?"

"Then, sir, they left and I went to the head and threw up."

"Good for you. What about Freeman?"

"Like I said, sir, he took off as soon as Hahn started fooling around."

"He helped them tackle Corporal McKittrick, though—is that right?"

"Yes, sir. But he took off—"

"You already said that, Burns," the First Sergeant said.

"That's all for now, Burns," the Lieutenant said. "Thank you."

"And you keep your mouth shut," the First Sergeant said.

Dan closed the door when Burns had left.

"Let me see McKittrick first," he said.

Tolleson went out, shutting the door, and Dan snatched his swagger stick from his desk and began pacing the length of the office, only six strides, striking the palm of his left hand with the dark waxed cherry wood stick. His back was to the door when they came in, and he spun around, his arm jabbing straight out at McKittrick, the swagger stick a quivering rapier-like extension of it.

"You're a Pfc now, McKittrick. That promotion of yours is probationary and I just took it away. Administratively. That means you can still come in for official punishment at office hours."

Now he lowered his swagger stick to his side. McKittrick was at attention, his tropical shirt tight around his chest, his shoes reflecting the overhead light; and Dan was proud that even this inefficient corporal stood so tall and straight in an impeccable uniform.

"Since you're looking so hurt and innocent," Tolleson said, "I'll refresh your memory. The Lieutenant's talking about last night. What should I call it—a circle jerk, McKittrick?"

"It's worse than that," Dan said. "You know what it is? Your friends violated that rank you had. Whether you know it or not, those two chevrons mean something—a lot of dead corporals in a lot of wars, for one thing. And leadership, McKittrick. But last night you chose to let people take away the dignity of a noncommissioned officer in the Marine Corps. You could have yelled for the First Sergeant—or even the other corporals—but you didn't because that wouldn't be popular. Well, you can be popular now. You're not an NCO anymore."

He paused, looking at McKittrick's shameful eyes. Then he said quietly: "Get out of here. Go join your buddies."

He sent Tolleson for Freeman, who came in, shined and pressed and tailored, and already afraid, so Dan spoke calmly.

"Freeman," he said, then paused and looked at the silver tip of his swagger stick, tapped his palm with it, and looked at Freeman again. "Freeman, this is getting old. You were in here two days ago for insubordination to Corporal McKittrick. You went to the brig, but you didn't even have to spend the night there. I let you out, Freeman, when I found out that you had been provoked: and since that man isn't a corporal anymore, as of a couple of minutes ago—" Freeman looked surprised, then almost victorious, before his face tightened again "—I can tell you that he was wrong. That's why I let you out. And I told you if you had any more personal problems with NCO's to come see the First Sergeant"—nodding at Tolleson, who was standing with one foot up on a chair and frowning at his shoes—"or me. Then last night, for some reason that I can't understand—unless you were drunk and I don't think you're hiding booze—you jumped Corporal McKittrick. That *might* constitute striking an NCO, Freeman: I haven't decided yet. Maybe it's just disorderly conduct, since from what I hear, that Corporal was grab-assing as much as anybody else. But what's important is this, Freeman: you laid hands on a man wearing corporal's chevrons. And there was a time when you wanted to be a corporal. But if you still want that promotion you'll have to wait a long time for it, because your first six months as a Pfc arc probationary—you know that. And I have just taken away that rank, Freeman. You can still receive disciplinary action for this offense, and you probably will."

He waited a moment, looking at Freeman's eyes, then having to look away, at his lips and jaw, for he knew what Freeman was thinking.

"You haven't helped your girl," he said. "This means less pay and a hell of a long wait for a chance at corporal. Do you have anything to say?"

"Yes, sir. Am I being busted because—"

"You're not getting busted," Tolleson said. "That happens at office hours. You're being administratively reduced."

"Yes, First Sergeant. Sir, am I losing my rank because of what they did to McKittrick? Because I left when I saw what was happening, sir."

"No, I'm not talking about that. I'm talking about your part in it up to that time. You *did* help them, didn't you?"

"Yes, sir."

"That's all, then."

"Aye aye, sir."

Freeman about-faced and left, shutting the door behind him.

"So we've got vacancies for one corporal and one Pfc now," Dan said. "What do you think about making Burns the corporal?"

"Yes, sir: he's a good clerk."

"He also seems to be the only man around here with any guts. Okay: we'll promote him."

"All right. Now, sir: we still haven't figured out what to do, is that right?"

"Office hours. For disorderly conduct."

"But how are we going to write up the specification for the record? Sir, if we put on that unit punishment sheet: *to wit, they jacked off the corporal of the guard*, we got troubles. Someday an inspecting officer's going to come down here and look at the files and he's going to ask questions. What would the Lieutenant give 'em at office hours?"

"Three days' bread-and-water."

"Yes, sir: and that officer from Headquarters Marine Corps will want to know how come they got off so easy."

"I could send them up to Captain Howard and recommend a special court. But I don't want to do that."

"Exactly, sir. If this outfit was a rifle company at Camp Pendleton I'd say run 'em up to the battalion commander and let him handle it. But we ain't: we're fifty-five Marines and two officers—"

"—Fifty-seven Marines, First Sergeant."

Tolleson grinned.

"Right, sir: fifty-seven Marines living with thirty-five hundred swab-jockies and if the word gets out, then we've shot our reputation all to hell."

"I know," Dan said.

He had, in fact, been thinking just that: with the certainty of a father who knows his daughter is pregnant, he saw that his most important function now was to protect the name of the Detachment. He sat down, put one foot on his desk and, looking at his miniature reflection on its shined toe, he tapped its sole with his swagger stick.

"I'm not a Marine just because I like military life," he said. "If there were no Marine Corps, I'd be a civilian—"

"—So would I, sir—"

He did not look at Tolleson: he kept looking at his shoe and the slow-tapping swagger stick.

"What we have is tradition. We live the lie and make the lie come true: we tell these kids they're the best fighting men in the world and they believe it and so does everybody else: these sailors don't like us, because we're so cocky—but they believe we're the best. They won't salute a Naval officer under the rank of commander, but they salute me and Captain Schneider. And I know we *are* the best—"

"—That's right, sir—"

Still he did not look at Tolleson; as if they had emerged from the layers of polish on his shoe leather, he felt the presence of ghosts: *In the Chosin Reservoir I was a corporal*, Captain Schneider had told him. *You know what kept us going? Every morning I'd go around, with the platoon sergeant and a couple of corporals, and we'd kick 'em out of the sleeping bags. Some of those troops would still be zipped in their bags if we hadn't kicked 'em. Then we'd move out and we had to kick their asses all the way. . . .* If Dan had closed his eyes he could have seen them: moving on a road of tire-tracked snow between white ridges, slow columns of boys in heavy parkas, with haversacks and rolled sleeping bags and blanket rolls on their backs, carrying rifles in cold gloved hands, and moving on: thirteen days of fighting to cover thirty-five miles—

"So we've got thirty-five hundred sailors here who believe we're the best. And I'll be Goddamn if I'll give them a chance to change their minds."

Now he looked up at Tolleson.

"We'll cover for those bastards," he said. "We'll hush it up."

He told Tolleson to arrange office hours for one o'clock, then he left the office, stepping into the classroom where guard school had ended and the troops were standing or moving toward the coffee percolator. Someone said: "Gangway, the XO!" and they stepped aside and he walked through the corridor they made, to the ladder, his face pensive and stern. He climbed the ladder quickly, without touching the handrails, as if—clutching his swagger stick—he were charging up a hill.

Then he crossed the mess deck, went through two hatches, and up a ladder to the hangar deck: sailors in yellow sweatshirts were pushing a jet bomber onto an elevator and, through the large rectangular hangar bay door he saw the blue ocean and sky. From the flight deck just above him came the short diminishing roar of a jet being catapulted. Dan climbed to a sponson deck on the starboard side of the ship and watched as the elevator below him rose with a bomber and sailors, passed him and went up to the flight deck, and the sailors started pushing the plane off. Above him, out of his vision, another jet revved its engine and was catapulted; alone in that sound, he turned to the ocean, squinting at its glare from the sun he rarely saw.

On most days his duties confined him to the barracks and the interior of the ship and he did not know what the weather was like until he took the troops to the sponson deck, at three o'clock, for physical conditioning. He was on that sponson deck now. It was one of the few places on the ship where he felt he belonged, for every day at sea he stood here, dressed in a T-shirt and utility trousers and boots, and sang out rapid cadences to a spread-out formation of young crew-cutted Marines, frisky and grinning in the ocean air, sweating in the sun, as for an hour they worked their restless muscles. It was where he kept them in condition so they would not shame the Detachment when they were transferred to the infantry; and it was here he kept his own body hard. So he had come there now.

He had postponed office hours to allow himself time for planning. He leaned on the guardrail, touching it only with his hands, keeping his sleeves clear of its moisture. The wood and silver tips of his swagger stick were shiny in the sunlight. He stayed there for nearly an hour, finally oblivious of the catapulting jets above him, and decided what to say at office hours and what to tell the rest of the Detachment.

He avoided rehearsing what he would tell Hahn, for he could not think of him—strong and certain and staring with implacable and narrowed eyes—without rage: and he did not want to expend that rage here on the sponson deck; he wanted it to remain like a submerged log beneath the nervous beating of his heart, to be ejected within the close bulkheads at office hours. So he thought about Freeman.

Two nights ago he had betrayed Freeman, and it had been entirely his fault. He had allowed Jan's letter to affect him, had started making decisions based on pity, and no leader could afford that. It had been his second day in command of the Detachment and, given another chance, he would have kept Freeman in the brig for three days, right or wrong, and he would have spoken to McKittrick about the relations between NCO's and subordinates. That was all. He would never have considered sending Freeman home to Jan, who—even now, on the sponson deck—was part of him: as if she stood on one of those hills near San Francisco Bay and gazed across the sea.

He had given in to her and Freeman once, and though he was glad Tolleson had saved him, he wished at times he had followed his own course, as wrong as it was. For two nights and a day—in his stateroom, or talking with Alex Price, or checking posts about the ship—he had heard his own voice: *Freeman, if I made an exception for one man I'd have to make it for the whole Detachment,* and he had remembered Freeman's betrayed and bitter face, turning to look at him, breaking the rigidity of parade rest.

During the time since that night he had begun to question his motives. He knew that if Tolleson had not argued with him, he would have sent Freeman home; and at first he had assumed that Tolleson, with his experience, had merely shown him what was right. After a while, though, he thought it was not respect but fear of Tolleson's experience and certainty which had made him change his mind. That had occurred to him when he was in his bunk, about two hours after reneging on Freeman, and he had lain there for some time, feeling as he had when he was a second lieutenant with his first platoon at Camp Pendleton, when every day he faced his platoon sergeant with indecisiveness and uncertainty. He had not felt that way for about two years: by the time he was promoted to first lieutenant he had discovered that he knew as much as his platoon sergeant—and sometimes he knew more. He had gained a professional confidence which was echoed each time he spoke to his platoon sergeant or gave him a command.

But as a platoon commander his decisions and orders had affected only his platoon, and most of those decisions were made by the company commander. Now it was different: he had no Marine captain to stand between him and the ship. Which brought about his final and worst doubt: he had never, in three and a half years of service, had to make a decision that could affect either higher command or his own career. He had never worried about his future: he hated careerists, those officers who talked lustfully of promotion zones, hurried through Marine Corps correspondence courses to get them entered in their record books, and tried to get command billets for the same reason; and, once in the command billets, were concerned primarily with how their companies performed when field grade officers were watching; they were the ones who adapted themselves to each new commanding officer, and they were the first to put away their swagger sticks when the new Commandant had implied that he disliked them.

He tried to remember if Tolleson's warnings about his career had affected him, but he could only recall that as soon as Tolleson had returned from the chief's mess and entered the office, he had begun to feel like a very young and inexperienced lieutenant. He did not know whether he had realized, when he saw Tolleson, that sending Freeman home was wrong; or whether he had simply felt that he could not resist Tolleson's objections; or whether it was Tolleson's mention of his career that had finally worked on his original discomfort until he had weakened and given in entirely to what Tolleson wanted. He could only assume that all these forces had probably influenced him but he still hoped that at least any fears about his future as an officer had been slight, if they existed at all. And slapping his swagger stick on his palm, he wished that he had never got himself into that position. He had taken the wrong hill and, once on top of it, he had given it up to the first probing attack.

He left the sponson deck. During the rest of the morning he inspected posts, spending several minutes with each sentry, asking questions about the special orders for the post, and safety procedures with the .45 pistol. When he inspected the brig, the prisoners were on working parties around the ship; the turnkey, a Pfc, was able to tell him where each prisoner was working and which Marine chaser was supervising. Dan described several imaginary situations, asking the turnkey what he would do if they occurred: an injured prisoner, an attempted escape from the chow line when the mess deck was crowded, a fire on the hangar deck. Without hesitation, the turnkey answered them all. Dan knew he would, just as he had known the sentries would; he had questioned them to show that he knew their jobs as well as they did.

He went to the Captain's ladder. Some time that morning, watched by a Marine chaser, Navy prisoners had swabbed the landings, then waxed and buffed them; they had shined the ladder's brass handrails; and they had left a dark purple rag, smelling of Brasso, lying on the steps. Dan went all the way up the ladder, to the Captain's cabin (there was no orderly outside the cabin: Captain Howard would be on the bridge) but the prisoners and chaser had gone to chow. So, using the orderly's phone on the bulkhead, he called the Detachment office and when Tolleson answered he told him the prisoner detail had left a rag on the Captain's ladder.

"Aye aye, sir. I'll get on that chaser about it."

Then Dan was suddenly chuckling.

"I didn't pick it up," he said. "It's on the o3 level."

Tolleson laughed.

"Chaser'll take care of it, sir," he said.

At lunch in the wardroom, Dan ate soup and a salad and iced tea without sugar. He had been eating carefully since joining the ship, and it had worked: his belly was still flat and easily contained by his trousers and his tailored, close-fitting shirts. Beside him Alex Price was eating curry. Alex was taller and heavier than Dan and, in his loose Navy uniforms, he looked firm enough. He wiped his moustache, then his mouth, and turned to Dan and asked how the Marine Corps was holding up. Dan said that everything was squared away.

"I'll switch jobs with you," Alex said. "I've got three special courts in the next ten days."

He was the *Vanguard*'s Education Officer. A year ago he had attended the Naval Justice school and since then he was continually appointed to serve as trial or defense counsel on special courts-martial. His reputation as a conscientious and smart counsel had spread among the crew; so, besides the courts he was appointed to, he had performed in many others, because sailors requested him. Marines never had to request him; Dan always did it for them.

Last July a squadron commander had accused Hahn and Jensen of beating up two of his sailors. Captain Schneider had told Dan to investigate and, based on the sworn written statements of Hahn and Jensen and the two sailors (who were both skinny, bruised, and visibly afraid of further involvement), he recommended that the case be dropped. The beating had occurred at night and Dan had a reasonable doubt, as the book put it, that the sailors had clearly seen the men who attacked them. Captain Schneider agreed and sent the investigation, with his endorsement, to Captain Howard. But Captain Howard ordered a special court-martial. Even then Dan believed the Marines were innocent (he had been aboard only two months and didn't know them yet), and he thought Captain Howard was either stupid or showing his dislike of Marines, or both.

He had asked Alex to defend Hahn and Jensen. Before the court-martial Alex talked to the sailors, then came to the Detachment office, asked Dan to call in Hahn and Jensen, and told them he was tired of being snowed, they were guilty of assault and battery, of lying under oath, and if they didn't start telling the truth he would refuse to defend them. So they told him that, while drunk, they had beaten up the sailors, but they were sorry, especially after seeing in daylight how small those sailors were. Alex said he didn't believe they had been that drunk and he didn't for one second believe in their remorse, but he would do what he could. At the court-martial he pleaded guilty and got them a light sentence: reductions from private first class to private, and thirty days in the ship's brig. They got out five days early for good conduct.

"I think I can get a suspended sentence for one of these sailors," Alex said now. "He was sleeping on watch."

"Do you *want* to?"

"Sure. He shouldn't have *been* on watch. He had just come off four hours before and they put him on again because they couldn't find the sailor who was assigned the watch in the first place. He also had fever and he told them so."

"But he slept on watch."

"He slept on the short end of the stick."

"Okay: good. Go on in there and expose all these commissioned sailors who don't give a damn about what's happening to their troops."

Then he smiled. Across the table from him, an ensign looked up from his bread pudding and returned the smile.

He was from the Naval Academy, having reported to the *Vanguard* a week before she left the States; when he used terms like *deck* or *bulkhead* or *aft* or *deploy for air ops* he spoke with that rather uneasy pride of young officers who have recently adopted the language of their service as their own; his cheeks flushed brightly when he smiled, which was often, though his mouth did not appear suited for it: it was narrow, and his lips were thin, and usually closed tightly.

"We're not sailors," he said. "We're Naval officers."

"Well, I'm a Marine. And I know what they taught you at Canoe U. They said remember three things: enlisted men don't count and they won't salute you anyway; a commander's wife outranks everybody below the rank of commander; and you can make or break your career in the wardroom. Do you know what the troops are eating on the mess deck while you're having curry and pudding? Beans and franks."

He was still smiling. The ensign's cheeks were flushed, and his lips had narrowed.

"Maybe you should eat with them," he said.

"Oh no: they can't eat with me, so why should I be able to eat with them? But do you know what happens when a Marine battalion goes to the field? The privates eat first and the colonel eats last."

"Oh come on: what if he doesn't get anything?"

"That's the point."

"An army," Alex said, "marches on its stomach. Let's go, Leatherneck. You're disturbing my colleagues."

In the passageway, Dan said:

"Well, I'm going down to my island of military discipline and instill some of it."

"Office hours? What for?"

"I don't know, Alex. But they won't get away with it."

"Keep your powder dry."

When Dan was halfway down the ladder to the barracks the Corporal of the Guard shouted *tenhuhn*; Dan walked quickly through the stiffened troops, not seeing any of their faces, looking directly ahead of him as if he were passing through familiar trees. At the office door he said loudly: "Carry on."

Since his leaving the barracks four hours ago things had happened: the office had been prepared, the green decks shined, the tops of desks cleared and dusted; on the glass cover of his own desk were four typed unit punishment sheets, the *Manual for Courts-Martial*, and the service record books. He knew that word had been passed too, and Freeman and Hahn and Jensen and McKittrick were standing by in the berthing area, wearing fresh uniforms for office hours; and like grade school boys when a classmate is called to the principal's office, the rest of the Detachment had been telling each other what had happened and making guesses about what the Lieutenant would do. Sitting at his desk now he felt that sense of power which comes when you know that during your absence you have been present: you have changed the appearance of an office and entered the minds and conversations of men.

He opened McKittrick's service record book, which told him that McKittrick's father was deceased, that he came from Davenport, Iowa, the address a route and box number

which made Dan think of a lonely house surrounded by
flat mud; he was at least partly right: McKittrick's civilian
occupation was described as *Raised corn and hogs on mother's farm.* He had left high school after three years, but
while on active duty had passed the General Educational
Development Test which the Marine Corps recognized as
a high school degree. McKittrick had listed hunting and
fishing as his hobbies. Dan closed the book and glanced
through the others, except Freeman's: two nights ago
he had read about Freeman in his platoon commanders'
notebook, and he still remembered it, because there wasn't
much to remember, so that finally the essential thing was
to connect the right face with the right information. Jensen was from Chicago, had graduated from high school
where he had lettered for four years in football and track.
After that he had gone to a trade school, studying auto
mechanics for two months. He had not finished the
course; for six months he had been a construction worker,
then he had joined the Marines. There were no hobbies
listed in his record book. Hahn's record was so bare that
Dan turned to the page listing parents and religion. It said
that he was a Lutheran, and that his mother and father
were alive in Haverhill, Massachusetts. The other page,
the one for personal information, merely showed what he
had not done: he had finished high school but had not
been an athlete, he had no hobbies, and his only job experience was working two months in his father's shoe repair
shop. Dan could easily have thought of him as a guard or
tackle, one who broke training but was mean and primed
for Friday games; he could not imagine Hahn sitting in

the stands, responding to cheerleaders or even the score. He especially could not picture Hahn bent over someone's worn-out boot.

He was rising from his desk to call Tolleson when two bells sounded on the loudspeaker and Tolleson came in and said:

"Is the Lieutenant ready?"

"It's time," he said. "Bring 'em in."

He sat down again, facing the door, and waited. They came single file, Hahn in front: he marched up to the desk, then right-faced and went to the bulkhead, left-faced and halted. His eyes had not met Dan's, but Dan had watched him all the way, knowing he had him now, no lies, no snow job this time. Jensen and McKittrick were next, then Freeman: they stood facing him, abreast, Hahn against the bulkhead on one side, Freeman's leg touching a desk on the other, and McKittrick and Jensen squeezed between them. Tolleson shut the door and stood at ease behind them. Dan opened the *Manual for Courts-Martial* to the page Tolleson had marked with a paper clip and, with a bored and near-scornful voice, he quickly read Article Thirty-one aloud. They broke their formation to bend over the desk and initial the unit punishment sheets, declaring that they understood their rights under the Uniform Code of Military Justice. When they were at attention and abreast again, Dan read the charge from each sheet. All were the same: disorderly conduct, and the specifications were simply: *did, on or about 16 November 1956 create a disturbance in the Marine Barracks aboard the USS* VANGUARD. Looking up at them, pausing at each man's face, beginning with Hahn and ending with Freeman, he said:

"How do you plead?"

He was watching Freeman when he said it; but it was Hahn, to his left, who answered:

"Not guilty, sir."

His head jerked toward Hahn, then he was on his feet and he struck the desk with his fist.

"What's this left field crap, Hahn? If you want me to interrogate like I did this morning then I'll by God do it but you're pissing me off."

"Begging the Lieutenant's pardon, sir, but I wasn't interrogated this morning."

"Well, Hahn, I'm sorry I left you out of the Goddamn office party. But since you're standing there looking so innocent, I'll refresh your memory: Freeman and your buddy McKittrick here admitted it this morning, and that's all I need. So forget about this sea lawyer business and face your Goddamn punishment like a man."

"Sir, Pfc McKittrick and Private Freeman were not warned of their rights under Article Thirty-one, sir."

Dan sat in his chair again and looked up at McKittrick. After a moment, he said quietly:

"How do you plead?"

"Not guilty, sir."

He looked at Freeman, whose stare went past and above Dan, to the bulkhead. "And you?"

Freeman did not answer: Leaning toward his profiled face Dan slapped the cover of the *Manual* and Freeman's eyes blinked.

"I'm talking to *you*. Freeman!"

"Not guilty, sir."

He leaned back in his chair.

"All right," he said. He looked at Hahn's stolid face; then at McKittrick, tight lips and angry defensive eyes like a man in a fight; then Jensen, short and compact, and appearing as calm as if he were merely standing sentry duty. Then he looked at Freeman.

"First Sergeant," he said. "Send them all out except Freeman."

While Tolleson gave the command to about-face and march out, Dan was already on his feet, circling his desk and going to Freeman; he stopped inches from him, watching Freeman's pale cheek and one blinking eye until he heard the office door close. He glanced at Tolleson and said:

"Type a confession for Freeman's signature, and start it off with: 'Having been warned of my rights under Article Thirty-one, UCMJ, I do hereby voluntarily make the following statement.'"

"Aye sir."

Dan waited until Tolleson was sitting at the desk to his left, directly behind Freeman; he waited for Freeman to hear the paper being rolled into the typewriter, followed by the rapid dull clicking of keys, the ring of the bell, and the carriage sliding fast to the right again, banging. Then he said: "Turn around and look at me, sea lawyer."

Freeman right-faced. Just as he finished the movement Dan brought both hands up from his sides, palms out, slapping Freeman's chest and closing on his shirt pockets; then he spun, jerking Freeman completely around and pushing him with one smooth unresisted drive across the office, and slammed his back against the bulkhead, then held him pressed against it. Freeman was limp and, as he held him, Dan could see the entire scene: the troops outside the office turning suddenly to the door when they heard Freeman hitting the steel bulkhead; Tolleson spinning in the swivel chair, his mouth opening in worried but approving surprise; and himself, his head thrust forward, his cheeks flushed, his white-knuckled hands twisting Freeman's shirt. Then he released him and stepped back.

"You're going to sign that," he said. "And no more of this Article Thirty-one bullshit. And I'll tell you why: because I plan to give you people three days' bread-and-water. That's *all*."

Behind him, he heard Tolleson typing again.

"That's why those unit punishment sheets don't say a Goddamn thing, Freeman. Because that offense is too serious for office hours: it ought to draw a special court. But it's not, Freeman: I'm going to handle it myself, right here today, because I'll be Goddamn if I'll let four grab-assing little *boys* for crying out loud screw up the reputation of this Detachment. Do you understand what I'm saying?"

Freeman's mouth opened but he did not answer.

"Are you going to cry, Freeman?"

He shook his head.

"No, sir," he said, his voice high in his throat.

"Do you understand what I'm saying?"

"Yes, sir."

"Then get in the ball game. Freeman. You know you don't have to sign this confession: you can request mast with Captain Howard and tell him—" now he mimicked a child's whine "—Lieutenant Tierney laid *hands* on me. But if Captain Howard hears about that business last night, it'll be out of my hands and you'll be facing a special court. So you lose: you play ball with Hahn and you'll get the bat shoved up your ass."

Tolleson had finished typing. Dan took the confession from him and read it, then looked at Freeman.

"All this says is that you and Hahn and Jensen tackled McKittrick, while he was a corporal. The First Sergeant has left out the rest of it. Because, Freeman, this confession goes on file too and we're covering this thing up. Now come here and sign it."

He laid it on the desk, placed a ballpoint pen on top of it, and watched as Freeman left the bulkhead and picked up the pen and signed his name.

"Sign all four copies," he said.

He went behind his desk and told Tolleson to bring in the others. They marched in, Hahn leading again, and Freeman moved over to give them room. When they were facing him, Dan left his desk and stood in front of Hahn, looking up at him.

"Hahn," he said, "it's a shame that in order for me to save this Detachment's reputation I have to save you. Because you're not a Marine, Hahn. You're not even a man. You lie. You lie so much I doubt if you can tell when to believe yourself. You're a bully: and to me that means you're yellow. *Yellow*, Hahn—" Hahn's lips began the bare trace of a smirk, and Dan was about to scream that old line he had heard in movies but had never heard in the Corps: *Wipe that grin off your face*; but he paused, held on, and continued coldly: "—Course you don't think so. You think you're a real man. Well, Hahn, I can only go on the evidence. Look to your left, Hahn. Co on: look at your buddies—" Hahn turned his head "—These are the guys you lead around with this manly courage of yours. McKittrick there is a tall man, but he's not as strong as you: you've got thirty-five or forty pounds on him. Jensen is strong but he's short—he's not over a hundred and sixty-five pounds, Hahn. And there's Freeman. He can't even whip me."

Hahn looked forward again; now his lips had straightened, the smirk vanished before it had formed. His eyes, though, were still defiant and confident.

"Those are the men you bully, Hahn. Oh: but I shouldn't forget your actual fights. Last summer you and Jensen tore up a couple of sailors. That was a fine show, Hahn. They were skinny little kids and they were drunk. But it's mighty funny, Hahn, that for a big man you don't have any guts. There's a boxing smoker on this ship every once in a while and some of the troops get in there and fight sailors. But not you. No, because that would take guts: you'd have to get in shape so you could last three rounds. You're getting flabby around the gut. And worst of all you'd have to get in there and fight a man your size. He wouldn't be drunk and he wouldn't be a ninety-eight-pound weakling—and all those people would be watching Hahn fighting someone as strong as you and maybe in better shape than you. You'll never fight in a smoker, Hahn, because that just scares the piss out of you."

Hahn's cheeks colored; Dan watched him for a moment, then spoke softly:

"You know, there's a young doctor on this ship—Doc Kellog—and he happens to be studying psychiatry. I think you ought to talk to him, Hahn. Because there's something wrong: all those lies, all that bullying—Everybody knows there's something wrong with a bully. You're running scared from something, Hahn, and I'm starting to worry about you. So maybe you should talk to that doctor while you can do it free of charge. You think it over, Hahn, and if you decide to get help I can arrange it for you—" Dan leaned over the desk and, as he was picking up Freeman's confession, he said "—when you get out of the brig." Then he straightened quickly, spinning toward Hahn again, and cried: "Because that's where you're going right now!"

Hahn's body jerked, stiffened in recoil, and his eyes blinked as, in a loud voice, Dan read the confession, then dropped it to the desk and in the same loud voice of the parade field he went on: "The *Manual for Courts-Martial* calls what you did last night lewd and obscene acts and you can get a special court for it and if you plead not guilty down here or if you let the word get out on the mess decks or anyplace else, Captain Howard will hear about it and you'll find yourself in real trouble. *Now* how do you plead: *all of* you."

Starting with Hahn, they all pleaded guilty. Dan sat at his desk and, in a detached voice, he sentenced them to three days on bread and water. Tolleson marched them out and turned them over to the Corporal of the Guard who sent them, with a chaser, to the dispensary where they would get pre-confinement physical examinations. Tolleson had left the office door open and, knowing the troops in the classroom would be glancing in at him, Dan pushed his chair back from his desk so he could get one foot up on it; then with his handkerchief he dusted the glossy toe of his shoe. Tolleson came back and closed the door.

"Well, sir, I guess the Lieutenant outfoxed 'em."

"I guess so."

"Lieutenant sorta stuck his neck out with Freeman, sir."

"Maybe. But I've got a long way to go in this man's Marine Corps, First Sergeant, and I can't be worrying about it every time I do something. Now let's get all the troops into the classroom and when the sentries come off post at sixteen hundred I'll talk to them too: I want to tell 'em what's going on, so they'll keep quiet."

"Aye aye, sir."

Dan gave Tolleson a few minutes to get the troops assembled, sitting on benches; then, picking up his swagger stick, he left the office and went to the front of the classroom. The barracks was quiet. Far above him he could hear jets landing. From somewhere he heard the echoing ring of pounding metal. His eyes swept the troops' faces; then he leaned slightly forward. In a voice that was urgent and low, at times almost a hoarse confidential whisper, he told them the truth: that he had just covered a serious offense, and he told them why he had done it, and asked them to keep it quiet.

Chapter Four

As I TOLD you two nights ago, Dan wrote, *I need and love your letters as much as I need and love you. They're all I have. I've been through all kinds of hell since I took over, problems I've never heard of before, and I've been playing it all by ear. I'm still not sure whether I've done anything right. The worst day was today, and this afternoon when mail call sounded I hustled to the barracks. But there* was *no letter and that's thirteen days. Khristy, darling, you can't be that busy—*

He stopped writing, laid his pen down, and stood up: enclosed by beige overhead and bulkheads, a bunk made neatly by a Filipino steward who also cleaned daily, so even the lavatory below the medicine cabinet was kept glistening white, no yellow crusts of soap, and the grey metal wall locker was dusted, and the green rubber tile floor shone dully under electric lights. Then he went to his wall locker and took out his stuffed greying-white laundry bag; taking a laundry chit from a drawer, he filled it out at the desk, continuing his letter in his mind, scolding her.

He stuck the chit in the laundry bag and tossed it into the passageway, which had disturbed him when he first saw it five and a half months earlier and which now he disliked, as a man ashore dislikes driving each day from home to work through a barren strip of land. Now the passageway was lighted with red lights that gave the beige bulkheads a ghostly almost noncolor and the green deck a darkness which reminded Dan of the black ocean far beneath his feet. He sat at his desk again, but did not write.

Certainly she loved him, for she had told him so on that first and last night when she was entirely his, after all those nights when she had withheld herself, though in a way he had to admire: no teasing, none of that adolescent preintercourse workout, then home to the showers. She had finally given herself not in car-seat half-clothed desperation, but with predetermined commitment, perhaps even her idea more than his, a result of some consideration by her heart—or, she might say, her psyche—so he hardly doubted that she had meant for that night to begin a new phase in their lives. But if that was true, then how could she coldly refuse to write as often as she had the time? Or, more accurately, how could she fail to give herself the time? Fidelity was by God more than keeping your legs together.

Which he did not even worry about, assuming that with the several college boys who dated her she was as firm and controlled as she had been with him. He had, in fact, while dating her, become so accustomed to her friendly expression of what he called love—though she had never named it—that her proposition (which he decided it was) had surprised him into a momentary but quite real impotence.

Looking back now, he could see that she had probably already decided before she jumped from the pier and suggested the bar at the south end of the beach; that jump was like a preparation for the final impulse required to make love to him. So was their walk down the beach: holding hands, they had walked urgently into the darkness as if in flight, not talking much, so that Dan could hear her rapid breathing. His own breath was quicker but he tried to hide that, taking only short and silent breaths which he could not control until they had been sitting for three or four minutes inside the bar, a low-ceilinged place situated at the end of a row of beach cottages close to the sea.

They sat on a straw mat and found places to stretch out their legs under the table, two feet high, which held their pitcher of beer. Their backs rested against the wall. Khristy removed her shoes, emptied them and brushed off the sand, then brushed sand from her stockinged feet, then from her hands. She left the shoes off, looked around at the moving, talking, drunken-looking people who filled the bar, made a face as if she had swallowed something intolerably bitter, then smiled and took his hand.

"So here we are," she said.

He only heard *are*. Jazz was coming too loudly from a pair of stereo speakers, one at each side of the small room, the rhythm section from one, the brass from the other, and Dan felt that he was in a space between a divided

orchestra. Young people swirled before him, not dancing, just moving from table to table or bar or rest room:
a boy with white duck trousers and a blue shirt tucked
in and opened to the waist, showing a sunburned and
blond-fuzzed chest; others in bermuda shorts and polo
or T-shirts or no shirts at all, some with near-pretty and
effeminate faces, others with incessantly moving smooth
jaws who seemed to be delivering incomprehensible
and ultimate speeches, and athletes of a couple of years
ago who struck the barstool poses of Western badmen;
among them moved girls like shadows, who apparently
had expended money on neither cosmetics nor comb and
brush since leaving puberty; girls who Dan imagined were,
though not technically, in some strange way virginal. He
rose and like a slow-motion broken field runner went to
the bar for another pitcher of beer. He waited for the bar-
tender—a young man with crew-cut red hair and a large
T-shirt-covered chest and belly—to break away from the
two men or boys he was talking to at the curve of the
semicircular bar. He looked at the wall behind the bar, but
there was no mirror: only a harpoon suspended by wire.
Above him, a large fishnet hung from the entire ceiling,
like a camouflage net over a gun pit.

When he was sitting on the floor with Khristy again,
he pretended to take a notebook from his pocket, looked
at it, then looked at her.

"Are you Miss Khristen VandeBerg?"

"Yes, sir."

"Colonel VandeBerg's daughter, ma'am?"

"I'm afraid so."

"Well, ma'am, I have no jurisdiction over dependents; irregardless, I should inform you that this place is off-limits for service personnel."

"I know. Marijuana peddlers."

He leaned back against the wall.

"I didn't know you knew," he said.

She was grinning at him, and he didn't know whether he wanted to kiss or scold her. When they finished half the pitcher they had to get rid of some of it, so they went outside and followed an arrow-shaped sign down a rough boardwalk to a single and unlabeled door. Khristy knocked and a young man said: "Uno momento, friend." They stepped off the walk and went all around the bar, in the sand, but there was no other door. When they got back to the rest room a girl was going in.

"*That's* cute," Khristy said.

"Phony. I'll just go around the corner before I bust."

He walked down the sloping sand, turned a corner into the shadows, and with his back to the sea he urinated against the wall, looking from left to right and over his shoulder when he remembered that only a couple of weeks ago he had passed the word to his platoon that if they got caught pissing in public they would have to be registered in California's lewd person category. He stood there longer than he wanted, joined to the spot by his urine stream and thinking of himself as a scout for the tide, soaking the wall and sand it could not reach. When he was finished Khristy was still inside the rest room; or he thought she was and, after a while, he knocked lightly.

"How intimate," she said.

"It might not have been me."

"I could tell by the hesitant knock."

She came out smiling and they went back to their table, Dan half-expecting it to be taken along with the half pitcher of beer he had left as an emblem of occupancy before they went outside. But both table and beer had been left alone. They sat drinking and holding hands, not trying to talk over the music which was drums and the sounds of jungle birds.

Dan was thinking this was his last night with Khristy for about a year and even then it would be touch and go, he would be under orders to a school or a security barracks or recruiting duty, certainly not Camp Pendleton again; for according to the normal career plan he would spend his last year as a lieutenant and his beginning years as a captain out of the Fleet Marine Force, where the combat units were. So the only thing was to marry as soon as he got off sea duty, or he might be sent to the East Coast and never see her again or, worse, run into her at a Marine Corps Birthday Ball some tenth of November at Quantico, perhaps, where so many officers finally returned either as mstructors or students, and he could see her now: five years older with perhaps a throatier voice and crinkles at the corners of her eyes, laughing beside some dress-blued captain to whom she had pledged her life. But now he could not even think of marrying her: images of their wedding at Camp Pendleton chapel, he in blues and Khristy in white leaving under shining Mameluke swords held by stiff but smiling officers, champagne and food at the Colonel's quarters—all these faded and he could only think of tomorrow, seabag and suitcase in his car trunk, pressed uniforms hanging in the car, as he drove alone up the coast. He looked sadly at Khristy, who mirrored his expression, and she said:

"The trouble with us is this is all we see."

She gestured toward the people sitting on the floor around them.

"Because we're service people, we're just like tourists: all we really know is the Base. We never know anything about towns except their prices and whether they're friendly to service people, and we see the surface: creeps like these people and restaurants with vulgar regional decor—and that's all. You know what I remember about Virginia? Quantico's an ugly commercial cold little street and Highway One is dangerous. So when I think of Virginia I think of the Iwo Jima monument at the entrance to the base and that long beautiful road past the golf course with trees turning orange, then you get to the snappiest MP's in the Marine Corps directing traffic. That and the officers' quarters and the stables and the swimming pool. I'm so glad I go to UCLA. You talk to people there about California, and it's like talking about a different state."

He nodded his head to show that he agreed; but he did not say what he felt: that giving up what you did, and being aware that you were giving it up, was to a lesser degree like knowing you were leaving tomorrow to go live aboard a grey ship: it made you feel the bravery of sacrifice, toughly committed as you were to an elusive ideal which was so often obscured by paperwork, by fat incompetent officers who could not even claim to be mercenaries in the more romantic sense, by old Staff NCO's who you realized had soldiered for twenty years because they were afraid to try anything else—so as you followed orders from service town to service town, as you rose punctually five days a week to shave and get into uniform, you felt that you were one of the few people in the United States blessed with a profession offering dissatisfaction which you alone could transform into satisfaction by squaring away whatever number of troops you were fortunate enough to command. He did not tell her that: he felt about it, loved it, too strongly to argue, to encounter even a fleeting grimace from her lips.

They left then, back down the beach where the fog was thicker now but not low, and the sand and dark water and white breakers were unobscured; above them, to the right, Oceanside's lights were dull and the backs of buildings dark grey in the fog. It was a long walk up the beach and they could have gone by the road, but they didn't bother to think of it; they walked very slowly, his arm around her, neither of them short-winded this time, and Dan had forgotten the sanding of polish from his shoes. He stopped several times to kiss her, finally holding her as they were about to climb onto the pier they had jumped from earlier, and she said:

"Would you run off with me? Right now?"

"Sure. Where to?"

"Reno. We can get married and then we can go over the hill and live in Canada or Mexico."

"Why not? Let's go."

"All right."

She turned away and placed both hands on the pier; he was going to help her, but she swung one leg up and pulled herself onto the pier before he had even touched her. He swung up after her—no more gracefully, he noticed—and they held hands walking up to the gravel parking lot. In the car she sat close to him. They drove up the main street, turned on the road to the Base, and Dan slowed at the gate long enough for the MP to see his officer's bumper sticker and salute them through. Neither of them had spoken since getting into the car. As he turned up Rattlesnake Canyon, making them about two miles from the BOQ where he lived and three miles from Colonel VandeBerg's quarters, Khristy said in a quiet voice:

"Are you packed?"

"Yes."

They reached the top of Rattlesnake Canyon.

"I've never seen where you live," she said.

He could almost determine the instant when his palms turned cool on the steering wheel, his throat and mouth dried, and his loins seemed to dissolve and painlessly fall away.

"You can," he said.

She did not answer. He passed one turn-off toward the BOQ before making up his mind; at the next corner he turned, and by then he was all right so he had to restrain himself, slow down and take the turn in second gear so he would not impart his passion to the cylinders, spoiling his silent rapport with Khristy by making a tire-squealing roaring plunge to the BOQ. He drove as if he were returning, rather preoccupied, from work. His body cooled, slowed, for only a moment as he opened the door to the corridor, hoping it was empty, which it was. She had still not spoken. They went slowly down the corridor, not even their hands touching, and into his room: she did not see it after all, for it was dark when they entered and still dark when they left, after she had surprised him again by proving to be a virgin, and after she had finally told him more than once, more than a dozen times, that she loved him.

Khristy's ardor had paled only once, when he asked her to marry him, and her entire body had seemed to cool as his palms had on the steering wheel, and she had said: *Let's don't even talk about it till you get back from sea duty. I want time to check out my psyche—*

ONE OF THE troubles of being at sea was they could always get you: problems which, ashore, would be saved until morning were thrown at you over telephones, discussed in staterooms or offices, and their solutions probed after or dictated until Taps at ten o'clock or even later. So with his work done for that day, his shoes polished for the next one, his laundry ready for morning pickup by the steward, Dan was about to return to the letter, but he did not. As he picked up the pen his phone rang: it was Commander Craig—the Gunnery Officer, his superior in the chain of command, the stepping-stone or barrier between him and Captain Howard—and Commander Craig told him, gruffly as always, that he wanted to see him.

Commander Craig's stateroom was actually two rooms: the first, which Dan entered after knocking sharply on the door, was furnished with a large metal desk and three leather-cushioned easy chairs; the second, which he could partially see through a door, contained a bunk which should have been called a bed even by Navy supply men, and a shower. Dan stood until Commander Craig told him to sit down; then he waited while the Commander finished whatever paperwork he had found to do after dinner.

Commander Craig wore starched but wrinkled khakis, with nearly grey oak leaves on the collars of his shirt; a limp khaki grease-stained cap with a dull black visor and gold braid, long tarnished green, was on the back of his head, the way only very young boys wear their baseball caps. Because he spoke loudly and often, it was known throughout the Gunnery Department, as well as in other segments of the ship, that he had spent most of his career on destroyers and, to him, the sky had nothing to do with being a sailor; he hated airplanes, pilots, and the ship—which he called a Goddamn floating bird farm. He had been in the Navy for almost thirty years, had greying hair, sunken and sometimes twitching cheeks, and a lean body that looked more tired than fit; he would never be promoted. Probably for that reason he had the reputation of a man who never sweated anything. There was a rumor claiming he had once told the *Vangaurd*'s executive officer—a pilot—to shove it up his airdale ass. Dan thought the rumor was exaggerated, but he chose to believe it anyway.

"Okay, Danny Boy."

"Yes, sir."

"Skipper tells me he got confinement orders today on four young Marines."

"That's right, sir."

"I figured he wasn't lying. He wants to know how come you locked 'em up."

"Disorderly conduct, sir."

"What did they do? Fart?"

"Well, sir, they were what you might call disorderly."

Commander Craig took off his cap, scratched his scalp with the same hand that held the visor, then replaced it.

"Look here, Sonny Boy. I don't give a shit what you do down there as long as the job gets done—savvy? I furthermore don't give a shit if the Skipper don't sleep at night. But I give a shit so big you couldn't walk around it about my sleep, and Jesus Christ up there with the silver birds on his collar wants to know something before he goes nighty-night with his pecker in his hands, and I'm his Goddamn messenger boy. So let's get this over with and I'll get them birds off my back and go to bed."

Dan was looking at some shapeless point on Commander Craig's cap, and thinking that when a man was twenty-five years old he shouldn't be sitting on a rear end which tingled as it had when he was a boy waiting for a spanking from his father.

"Well, sir," he said, and now he was looking at Commander Craig's lips which seemed little darker than his yellowish cheeks: "I guess I left off the specifications on purpose. It's the first time I've been in charge of them, and I was embarrassed I guess—"

"Okay okay: why did you lock 'em up?"

"For silent contempt, sir."

"Jesus Christ."

"Well, it wasn't exactly silent—I was giving a class and they were talking and I told 'em to knock it off and they—you know: kind of grinned and grab-assed a little—"

"I don't want to hear all that crap. Why didn't you put that on the confinement orders?"

"Because, sir, like I said, I was embarrassed and I didn't want anybody to read about it—the Captain, the Legal Officer . . ."

"Jesus—little boys I got to fool with. All right: go on home now. I don't know what the Skipper'll think, but I know Goddamn well he ain't going to like it."

Dan said aye aye sir and good night sir and left, his body still waiting for that spanking. He was not at all relieved by the success of his lie; when he undressed in his room and hung his uniform in the wall locker he glanced down at the leather-encased Mameluke sword they had given him at Basic School and, feeling that he could never again be scornful of a cowardly officer, he got into his bunk and smoked two cigarettes in the dark before the relaxation of sleep began in his legs and spread upward until finally only a space in the top of his head was still functioning, telling again that doubly shameful lie to Commander Craig.

NEXT MORNING TED Freeman woke in fright, his body tensing and his heart pounding until he connected the voice and loud banging of wood on steel with the turnkey, who was moving up and down in front of the cells, striking the flat-barred doors—steel grating, really—with his nightstick and shouting: "Reveille! Reveille! Outa the sacks, prisoners—"Ted got up quickly, turning his back to the door to protect his eyes from the fluorescent light of the white passageway. He knew that it was five-thirty, that if he were standing in the hangar bay three decks above him, or on the flight deck high above that, he could see only the pale beginnings of dawn.

Thinking of heights of decks and compartments above and below the brig made him realize, too suddenly, that he was trapped inside a huge structure of steel and machinery which was floating on inconceivable depths of water, and that if something happened, a collision with another ship, for instance (there might be thick fog topside, or a blinding storm: he had no more idea than he would if he were in a grave), or if there was a fire in the hangar bay, with all that jet fuel the airdales dripped on the decks, and those planes loaded with bombs: if anything like that happened he would be solely in the hands of this turnkey whom he knew to be as young and uncertain as he was. It would be the turnkey who would have to keep his head and unlock the cell and get him and the others up the ladders, to the fantail where he could at least see the sky while he waited for a lifeboat in the charge of some petty officer or officer he did not even know. He bent over and folded his rubber mattress at the middle. There was no bunk: only the mattress and a mattress cover, without sheets or pillow; he had one blanket and now he neatly folded that and placed it squarely atop the mattress. Then he put on his utilities and boots and sat on the mattress.

His fear at being trapped had already passed, as if his mind had discarded it for a more important trouble. Ted was thinking that on this same deck but about three hundred feet forward, the rest of the Detachment were sleeping and would be for another hour. In the darkened berthing area, they lay motionless under blankets so it seemed that it was not only the man but the entire bunk which breathed or snored. They lay sleeping just as they would if he were there in his bunk. When reveille sounded they would get up: some quickly, from disciplined habit which he admired; others lying there for a few minutes, then groaning and pushing away the blankets and dropping to the deck, landing on unprepared feet and ankles. They would put on shower shoes and walk slowly to the head—though, as with quick bunk-departers, there were always those who went briskly to the head, got the faucets and mirrors first, and already had lathered their faces and begun to shave by the time more normal people filed in. But one thing held true for everyone: there was little talking. They would start their day like that, spending the rest of it doing their ordered tasks, just as they would if he were still following Captain Howard about the ship. Those fifty-one Marines, including Burns, would go through this day just as they would if he were dead.

He rose from the mattress and went to the door. Both hungry and thirsty, his throat dry from sleeping open-mouthed, he asked permission to speak, then told the turnkey he would like to eat, with the same expectancy he might have had if he were requesting a vaccination; for he was thinking of cold orange juice in a tall glass and hotcakes and bacon and eggs all on one mess tray, the yolk moving thickly toward the edge of the stacked hotcakes, squares of butter melting within and on top of the stack, as he ate the eggs and some of the bacon, then sopped up the yolk with one of the hotcakes before covering the rest with maple syrup and following each sweet-dripping bite with a long swallow of cold milk; then hot black coffee and a cigarette. The turnkey handed him an unsliced loaf of bread, an aluminum pitcher of water, and a thick white glass mug, then locked the door again.

Ted sat on the mattress, the loaf of bread in his lap. It was from the ship's bakery, which was located directly above the Marine barracks. The Detachment had befriended the bakers; it had been easy to do, for sailors apparently liked being adopted by Marines, being treated as a special clique of sailors which was spared the general scorn for the Navy. In return, some Marine came down the barracks ladder every day with a couple of hot just-buttered unsliced loaves of bread: he would drop them on a table and the troops would crowd around it, burning their fingers as they gouged large hunks from the loaves. The loaf Ted held on his lap was not stale, but it was cool and unbuttered.

He drank some of the water, quivering in slightly nauseated recoil as he felt it course downward and spread in his stomach. On his bitter morning palate the water was foul, and he set the pitcher on the deck thinking of cold juices: orange, apple, grape, even grapefruit, even tomato.

He thought of those oranges so abundant in chow halls that on some days you ignored them, did not even see them, and on other days you peeled one and ate it on your way to the barracks (in his mind this barracks was in the sun and on the land of Sea School: bright casual days when he had never seen the inside of a brig); or you stuck one in your pocket, then put it in your wall locker to eat later. Oranges were what you got in Christmas stockings at grade school parties, and in your own stocking at home because they filled it so well for so little money. If he had one now, he thought, he would not even have the patience to peel it: he would bite through the skin and suck its juice.

He carried the bread, three-quarters uneaten, and the pitcher of water to the door and waited until the turnkey returned from one end of the passageway, opened his door, and took them. He was grateful for one thing: he had not had enough of a breakfast to make him want a cigarette.

There were five sailors in the brig and they had been moved into the last two cells, clearing the first four so each of the bread-and-water prisoners would have a cell to himself. The sailors were in the passageway now, standing rigidly in column; then a chaser came down the ladder and took them up to a sponson deck for calisthenics. From there they would go to the chow hall, then to some part of the ship which they would clean.

Ted sat on the mattress again. He was not hungry anymore, and he did not want to smoke: with a sense of fresh strength he knew he could live the next two days of his life without good food and cigarettes. He did not feel trapped either: as confidently as someone planning a holiday, he knew the *Vanguard* would not sink or catch fire while he was in the brig. And he wasn't concerned about the Detachment going obliviously through their day, talking about him—if at all—in the hardened tones of survivors, of young men who said and wanted to mean it: *Semper Fi means bring up the ladder, boys—I'm aboard.*

He could live two days or the rest of his life with that knowledge too.

Rising from the folded mattress he went to one bulkhead, then the other: Hahn was in the cell to his left, Jensen to his right, but he could not hear them; then he realized that what he had listened for was some sound of suffering. He thought of Hahn hanging himself with his web belt from one of the steel I beams overhead. But with as much rage at another human being as he could feel right then—which was not much—he assumed that Hahn was standing in his cell, glaring out at the turnkey like a caged panther.

That brought him to his final awareness and he had to sit down again, for he could not bear it: the only person in the world who loved him without qualification was Jan and she was farther away than ever now, in more trouble than ever now, while he was locked up between two people like Hahn and Jensen—Ted Freeman, whom he had known all his life as a good boy, rarely punished at home or school, never even questioned by so much as a traffic cop, a good boy who had always been a target for abuse, as though after the first bully got to him he had gone through boyhood with a mark that offended even the least sadistic and made them kick him for what he was. He had tried to please teachers without alienating classmates, so that his grades in high school were repetitions of C's which for happier students meant Casual but for him meant Conformity; he had tried to please his contemporaries, had cursed and drunk beer and smoked and gossipped about lost cherries when they did, had refrained when they did, had feverishly changed loyalties, tastes, clothes, haircuts as soon as—from his customary distance—he had a chance to see the shifting weathervanes of the crowd. Above all, he had been good. Of course he could do nothing else: he had never had the social power to be unkind any more than he had had the physical power to be a bully; he had never been able to bewitch one of those ostensibly hesitant and fearful and innocent girls, to return to the boys with his trophy-stained car seat. He was conscious of that too. But the point was, he had been good.

And now, for all that and nothing more, he sat in a cell between two of the dirtiest, most heartless boys he had ever known, and in the cell past Jensen's was McKittrick whose very name brought the nausea of revulsion to his stomach: a hatred of something base, of something terribly weaker than any weakness Ted had ever been accused of. He had gone before the Lieutenant as one of them, his name had been recorded in the Unit Punishment Book along with theirs, he had gone to sick bay, standing naked beside them, with no way at all to explain to Doctor Butler that he was different.

Suddenly his heart quickened. He stood up, his fastest motion of the day, remembering when the chaser took them to sick bay and Doctor Butler had come in, looking stern: but when he saw Ted he had been surprised. Ted had seen it in his eyes, and the Doctor had paused in front of him and said gently:

"What are you doing here again, Freeman?"

"Sir disorderly conduct sir."

Doctor Butler had gone over to the corpsman's desk and looked at the confinement papers, then turned again, his face a little puzzled and stern too now, but his voice still the same:

"It doesn't say what you did."

Ted was trying to think of an answer but Hahn did it for him.

"Sir we were kind of fighting sir."

Doctor Butler had looked at Hahn for a second or two, then told the corpsman to start the physical. He had not spoken to Ted again.

But he had known. It was as plain in his face as the look of surprise and disappointment in that civics teacher's face—Mr. Gary—when he had caught Ted passing his test paper to Karl Lutring so he could copy it.

Ted went to the steel grating door and looked at the turnkey sitting on a high stool at a podium four feet away. The turnkey was writing in his log; then he glanced up, saw Ted's face, and asked what he wanted.

"Sir nothing sir."

He returned to the mattress. He had to work out the process, remember the recourses he had heard about but had never used: request mast, evasiveness while talking to those who stood, by rank, between you and the man you wanted to see; he considered the sea-lawyer part of it too: his rank taken away without even the chance to tell his side of the story—the whole story—and without being warned under Article Thirty-one; the Lieutenant throwing him against the bulkhead (but when he thought of telling Doctor Butler that, he was ashamed: he would let that one go). He would tell the rest, though, all of it—

Then he began to see a new hope, a chance not only to leave the brig and those three completely rotten people he did not deserve to be with, but a chance to win back everything he had been screwed out of: his unit punishment sheet taken out of the file and destroyed, the offense he had not committed crossed out of his record book, his rank restored, and a clean record with a shot at corporal when Captain Schneider got back. He would request mast with Captain Schneider too, just to make sure his slate was clean so he would be considered for promotion when he became eligible in March.

Now March itself took on a new sound. He saw himself hurrying down the packed after-brow from the ship to the Alameda pier, Jan having pushed forward to wait for him at the foot of the brow, and on his green sleeves not the single red chevron of a Pfc but the two chevrons of a corporal: an NCO, a man of rank and a man with a future too. His mind skipped backward to the Sunday afternoons aboard ship when Burns had taken him into the Detachment office and shown him some of the things you had to know to be a clerk: Ted had sat there learning about filing systems, a bit shameful of this secret initiation into a soft military specialty, but over the shame he had experienced a sense of confidence which was always absent when he worked on his correspondence course in squad tactics, bent over the usual drawing of a hill with one treeline going up to its flank, knowing the probe called for a single envelopment, but thinking of how it really was, removed from the relative comfort of a ship: unable to see himself as a corporal telling one fire team to lay a base of fire while he led the other two fire teams up that treeline to assault the hill. Burns had said the Detachment could send him to clerk-typist school when his sea tour was over, and after the school he'd go somewhere as a company clerk: the right-hand man of the First Sergeant and XO and CO, going out to the field only when there were big exercises and the whole company went out; it didn't matter how much the guys harassed you for not being a crunchy, you still had the best of all jobs. It was a good field for promotion too, and though he, Burns, was not staying in the Corps, if he were he'd stick it out as an admin man—

With all these reversals, victories, seeming to rush through his very blood and heart, Ted rose again from the mattress, went to the door, asked the turnkey for permission to speak, then said he wanted to request mast with the ship's Medical Officer. The turnkey was the first in the chain of command to ask him why.

"Sir personal reasons sir," he replied, with nuances of anger and determination in his voice, surprising even himself. As the turnkey phoned the Detachment and told the assistant brig warden, a corporal, Ted thought—without defining whom he was referring to and in how many ways—*Semper Fi: fuck 'em all.*

It took the rest of the day, whose intervals he spent wanting a cigarette and pacing his cell except when he paused for more bread and water, to see everyone: a succession of increasing ranks, beginning with the assistant brig warden who came to his cell; then the brig warden, a second-hitch corporal soon to be a sergeant, who also came to his cell; the First Sergeant, and for that he was taken by chaser to the barracks; and finally, toward evening whose approach he knew from waiting, having surrendered his watch upon confinement so that he measured time by the relief and posting of a turnkey every four hours, he saw the Lieutenant. This trip also involved a chaser-escorted march to the barracks, his eyes feigning obliviousness of the passing men he saw more clearly than he ever had before: sailors who smirked or stared, some of them fearfully as if they were guilty of undetected offenses, and the Naval officers who glanced sternly at him, officers he hated; but, even more, he hated being a prisoner, forbidden to salute them.

So he did not see Doctor Butler until early that night, after the evening meal, and by then he was tired. Or at least his body was. All day long his only communication had been to repeat the request, then his answer to their inevitable question: *Sir personal reasons sir.* By the time he entered Doctor Butler's office he was as ready to talk as he had been that morning.

"HE TRUSTED ME too," Doc Butler said, then over the loudspeaker the bosun's whistle sounded and Dan automatically looked at his watch, and they both leaned forward,

arms on their thighs and knees, and gazed at the car-
peted deck of Butler's stateroom or their burning cigarettes which neither of them smoked while the Protestant
chaplain, a stout pleasant-faced Baptist, spoke the evening prayer over the loudspeaker: "Oh heavenly Father,
in Thy name we have finished our day's work. We have
handled planes on the flight deck and in the hangar bay
for our brothers who fly them. Some of us have stood far
above the ship on the signal bridge, in Thy sun and wind.
Some of us have worked in the heat of the engine room,
out of our brothers' sight, but always in *Thy* sight, oh Lord.
Some of us have worked in the galley, cooking for our
brothers and even cleaning their trays as Your Son washed
the feet of the apostles. We have manned radios and radar
and other modern equipment which give even more glory
to Thy ever-glorious name. And we have rested too. We
have written letters to loved ones, we have talked with our
friends at chow, we have had bull sessions over coffee; and
now our fellowship is ending for the day, our games of
acey-deucy are over, and silence is about to fill this great
ship. As the *Vanguard* takes us over Thy dark sea tonight,
we pray that You keep us in Thy hands, oh Lord, that we
may enjoy our well-deserved rest and wake tomorrow to
perform our many duties in Thy name, oh Lord: Ah-men."

The bosun's mate then announced Taps, lights out, and
the smoking lamp is out in all berthing spaces.

"But I've been in these cases before," Doc Butler said,
"and the only thing to do is call in ONI."

"No! Come on now, Major, haven't you ever heard of
circle jerks in Boy Scout camps?"

"This is different."

"It *isn't*. Look: I *know* these troops. Freeman's a good kid and the other three aren't worth the powder to blow 'em up—but they're *not queers*."

Butler looked at him for a few moments, then smiled briefly, understandingly, as he had been doing for the past thirty minutes, and said:

"How do you know, Dan?"

"Because I know these troops."

"Not that well. There's nobody on the ship qualified to handle this, including me."

Dan stood quickly and began walking back and forth so that he was always looking at Butler with turned face, in passing.

"How 'bout Doc Kellog? He's a shrink."

"Oh, hell: Kellog's no psychiatrist. He's *going* to be one when he gets out."

"Then how come he interviews all my Marines getting security clearances and asks 'em those Mickey Mouse questions about did they ever kill a cat when they were little boys?"

Butler shrugged.

"Somebody's got to do it."

"Jesus. Somebody's got to do this too—according to *you*—so why can't Kellog?"

"That's not the way to handle Undesirable Discharges."

Dan stopped.

"Young Private Freeman is *not* getting an Undesirable Discharge. Major, he *told* you what they've been doing to him down there. I'd have jumped McKittrick too."

"We'll have to leave that up to ONI and the Skipper."

"Hell with *that*. Freeman's a Marine and what happens to him is up to me and the Commandant of the Marine Corps—and it's not about to get as far as the Commandant."

Doc Butler smiled again, even paternally this time.

"Why are you fighting it, Dan?"

"Because I gave those four Marines my word."

"Your word wasn't that important when you talked to Commander Craig last night."

Dan thought of Commander Craig sitting in the wardroom and telling the gathered laughing commanders and lieutenant-commanders of his stupidity.

"I guess everything that happens on this bucket gets talked up at the wardroom—" he paused "—this too, I guess."

"I'm talking to *you*, Dan."

"All right: but at least I snowed the Gun Boss to save those four troops."

"Why don't you sit down and have a cigarette and relax?"

"I can't. I got more problems than you do."

"You're not going back on your word. It was Freeman that let it out, not you."

"But don't you see? He didn't know what he was getting into. What did you do: just sit there acting like Daddy Chaplain while he talked himself into an Undesirable Discharge?"

"Something like that. *He* came to me, Dan."

"Jesus."

Then he stopped and sat down.

"Did you warn him under Article Thirty-one?" he said quietly.

Butler's face paled, then quickly colored again.

"That's beside the point."

"Like hell it is."

He stood and picked up his cap and swagger stick.

"Like hell it *is*," he said.

Looking at the cap and stick, Butler said:

"Don't go off half-cocked and get yourself in a sling."

Dan moved toward the door, then stopped and faced Butler again.

"Listen, *Doctor*: everything you heard is inadmissible at any kind of court or hearing."

"Dan, you're talking through that Marine hat. You know and *I* know what's happened, and you've got a signed confession from Freeman down there in the barracks."

"That's right, Doctor Butler, but those confessions don't say a Goddamned thing about what you think is a homosexual act. That was part of my decision too."

He put on his cap, holding its sides so he would not touch the spit-shined visor that came over his eyes, exactly two fingers above his nose.

"And I'm going to stick by it," he said.

"You can still back off."

"No sir, Doctor Butler, I'm sorry but I can't."

When he walked out Butler was calling him back but he shut the door and went down the passageway with strides that were near running; he approached the ladder going down to his room, then passed it without slowing and went on through the mess deck, turning right and snapping a salute to a posted sentry whose saluting motion he had seen but whose face he had not. He went through two more hatches, then descended, his feet pounding on the steel ladder, into the brig.

"Let me into Freeman's cell," he said, his voice high as he strained to control it. As soon as the key turned in the lock Dan jerked the door open and stepped into and past the turnkey who was trying to dodge him. He slammed the door behind him, saw in the darkness Freeman starting to rise, a white T-shirt and light hair, from the dark shapeless blanket and mattress near the bulkhead.

"Get up!" Dan said, whispering, because if he let his voice have any sound at all he would have shrilly awakened the entire brig. Quickly Freeman was on his feet, the white shorts and legs visible now, standing at attention beside his mattress. In two steps, Dan was in front of him, smelling his stale odor which was indistinguishable from the odors of the cell that seemed to have sweated with every prisoner it had contained. Still he whispered hoarsely:

"God *damn* you, Freeman, you're in so deep I don't know if I can pull you out, I ought to—" he even raised the swagger stick like a club, held it tightly there, the stick too thin and delicate in his grip, his hand and arm wanting more weight and size to swing; then he lowered it and Freeman's eyes left the stick and focused on him again "—Doc Butler, your friendly Goddamn chaplain, wants you investigated as a *queer:* he wants you to get a U-*Dee,* Freeman—a Goddamned U-Dee." He stopped now, listening to his own rapid breath. Then tears filled his eyes and he said: "Goddammit, I *lied* for you, Freeman!" and he raised the swagger stick again and swung it against the bulkhead, his rage increasing when it struck, thinking of what it would look like now: he had a vision of forever carrying that stick marked by this night. He spun away and left the cell, pounding up the ladder without a glance at the turnkey.

He did not look at his swagger stick until he reached his room. About four inches down from the top, where it had struck the edge of a steel shelf, there was a deep white cut shaped like a football. He rubbed it with his thumb, then laid it on his desk beside his letter to Khristy which he had meant to finish tonight but had not, for after chow he had waited, doing nothing at all, having asked Doc Butler to call him when the request mast with Freeman was finished. Now he folded the letter, remembering why he was writing it as he might have remembered something which had been very important, when it had occurred a year ago. He did not undress for a while. Then he did, because it was something to do, hanging shirt and trousers on a wooden hanger, buttoning the shirt all the way up. He got into bed and pulled the covers to his chest and smoked. There were footsteps in the passageway and a knock on his door; turning on his side, he looked at the door for a second or two, then said:

"Come in."

Doc Butler had the large book with him, the *Navy Regulations*, holding it with two fingers marking the place. He sat in a chair and lit a cigarette, then got up again and took an ashtray from the desk, and returned to the armless straight-backed chair, leaning forward with the book awkwardly in his lap, the ashtray and cigarette in one hand and the other still inserted into the book.

"I brought you something to read."

"Why don't you put it on the deck? I know what it says."

Doc Butler put it on the deck, stooped forward, his fingers lingering between the pages even when he had released the book. Then, as if the fingers themselves were reluctant, they slowly came out and the book closed. Doc Butler straightened in the chair, a bit short of breath, and Dan both scorned and pitied him for being a Naval doctor approaching middle-age, harassed so late at night, so far from home. Then he was only scornful.

"It says that all such cases will be referred to the ONI," Butler said.

"This isn't one of those cases."

"What would you call it?"

"Childish grab-ass."

"Good word."

"Another thing: you're after Freeman too. If it was only the other three— No: I still wouldn't, because they're not queers. But I already told you Freeman left before this hanky-pank. He took off."

"He's still involved."

"Doc, if you're going to try to get Freeman a UD, after what that kid's been through, you might as well get me one too."

"You don't mean that."

"Oh, yes. I'm so committed on that, you wouldn't believe it."

"What do you think Raymond would do?"

"Same Goddamn thing I'm doing. And Captain Schneider would also tell you to stick to medicine and keep your nose out of the discipline of the Marine Detachment."

He paused, stopped his eyes from going to the deck, and forced them at Butler's face.

"Which I guess is what I'm telling you."

Butler picked up the *Navy Regulations* and rose; he looked at Dan, some anger in his face but not much— mostly that friendly and now paternal hurt expression again that not only outraged Dan but scared him too, made him feel he was looking at the precursor of his defeat.

"Dan, I'm trying to help you. This thing *is* medical now, it's my responsibility. I have to go to the Skipper with this—"

"—Pretty shitty of you—"

"—but I'll wait till tomorrow. You sleep on it. I'd rather you went in yourself. But if you don't, I will."

"Then that's the way its going to be," Dan said, rolling, turning his back, pulling the covers to his shoulders, talking to the bulkhead: "Because as far as I'm concerned— and I believe I'm still Acting CO of this Detachment— the incident is closed."

He lay with his eyes open, looking at the bulkhead inches from his face, waiting for Butler to leave. Finally Butler said: "You sleep on it, Dan," and walked out. The door hardly made a sound when he shut it.

Chapter Five

HE GOT OUT of his bunk and turned out the lights at the desk and lavatory, then got into the bunk again, his stateroom lighted now by only the small reading lamp above his head. He set his alarm clock for six-thirty. It was now eleven-ten.

At eleven-thirty he considered calling Tolleson to his room, but did not for he knew exactly how it would be: Tolleson, as ignorant of homosexuality as he was, cursing Freeman, Butler, and the entire Navy. Just before midnight he half rose, pushing the covers back; then he lay down again. There was no use seeing Alex either. Alex could only give him legal advice, and he already knew about that: if he held on, refused to be scared or bluffed, and if the troops kept quiet, he could win. He rather doubted the troops could get through an interrogation by a man from the Office of Naval Intelligence; he had never been involved with them, but he had heard that they rarely failed to break a case. Usually they got confessions as well. But that did not overly disturb him. For one thing, even if the troops broke—which he thought they would whenever he allowed himself to think about it—he felt that an ONI investigator would agree with him: it was all a matter of grab-ass caused by the restlessness of young men at sea. Most of all, though, he did not worry about the troops' ability to survive an investigation, because this was not the important thing—what mattered was whether or not he would fight.

With fatigued but nervous post-midnight clarity, he knew he was not afraid of them. He could stand before Captain Howard like a commissioned Hahn, could refuse to answer, could plead Article Thirty-one for the troops and himself as well. If the troops—Freeman, for instance—confessed, then he would be in trouble. But at three in the morning he knew, as certainly as he knew anything, that it was not his career or his life that mattered: it was today. He could take anything they did to him: getting through this day and the ones to follow, without cowardice, without lisloyalty to the troops, the Detachment, and the Corps, would be worth the price.

He was hesitant, though, for another reason. Knowing it took as much guts to admit you were wrong as it did to fight, he lay in his bunk, opening a pack of cigarettes, and tried to recall anything from his own experience like what had been done to McKittrick—and, worse, apparently with McKittrick's cooperation. He could not. There had been things on night bus trips in high school, when the baseball team was returning from a game. But all these things had one common factor: no one touched anybody else. Toward four o'clock he was trying to imagine himself as a nineteen-year-old boy, full of sap and dirty-minded anyway; but he could not see himself doing that to McKittrick or having it done to him.

He thought of Burns going to the head to puke, of Freeman running away when he saw what the joke was turning into: Freeman, who obviously was not queer, sleeping with and impregnating a girl whose photograph and letters excited Dan, and even made him jealous.

So possibly it was true that something was wrong with the other three. They didn't look like queers, but people said that half the actors in Hollywood were queer, and none of them were the fat, wavy-haired, whiskerless, girl-ish brand of human you would expect. And if they were queer, then by Cod his first duty was to drum them out of the Corps. He thought of the Iwo Jima monument in Washington, and the Marines who guarded it: those tall strong young men in blues, standing there as living testimony of the tradition which had existed long before Iwo Jima and would always exist, all those Marines from 1775 until now joined by Admiral Nimitz's words cut into the monument: *Uncommon valor was a common virtue.*

That fusion of the discipline and courage of the past with the present and future too, was more important than anyone and everyone on the *Vanguard*; it was the lie come true, worked into truth every day by perhaps only a hand-ful of dedicated officers and troops—all that was needed, really—and he would sacrifice anyone, including himself, to keep that truth alive.

There was no place in the Marine Corps for queers.

The worst thing that could happen would be the discovery that Hahn, Jensen, and McKittrick were indeed—if incredibly—homosexuals; and they would be undesirably discharged. Freeman was clean. As for himself, he would be in trouble for covering up an incident which should have been reported, and for lying to the Gun Boss. But that was all right too.

It was nearly four-thirty now and Dan was so tired that he gained no emotional reward for deciding to face the Captain and admit that he had been wrong.

His meeting with the Captain occurred at eight-thirty that morning, after two hours of sleep and a breakfast he had felt he ought to get down. Doc Butler went with him, looking fresh, and still acting kindly; it was Butler who, after they had poured coffee from a hot silver pitcher, told Captain Howard that Dan had something to say. So he told the entire story, his voice unnaturally high: he silently blamed this on lack of sleep. He talked for a long while, without interruption, looking from the encouraging face of Butler to the inscrutable nodding Captain, and several times his voice broke. As he spoke he felt that names— Hahn, Jensen, McKittrick, and especially Freeman—were becoming merely that: names spoken in the official aura of the Captain's cabin, names linked with perversion, the ONI, Undesirable Discharges. He began talking about those names, inserting into his narrative *a good trooper; a fine Marine; a good sentry; a good orderly, as you know, sir;* he found some praise for each of them, even Hahn, whom he said would be a good man in combat. Then, as he was finishing, he suddenly began to cry, as he had not cried since he was a boy: he had no more control over his body than he would if he had been throwing up, and his face went into his hands and he heard with amazed despair the volume of his jerking sobs; and finally, to explain to someone if only himself, he moaned into his hands:

"Oh Goddamn. Those Goddamn stupid little boys."

But it was not over: not this meeting, nor this day, nor this week. He knew that and, when he could, he blew his nose and wiped his face, glancing at Doc Butler whose voice he had heard a long time back, it seemed, telling him: *That's okay, Dan, that's right; just let it all out, boy.* When he was settled with a cup of coffee, they began the process. He hardly listened as Captain Howard phoned the ship's Communications Officer and told him to come to the cabin. Then Captain Howard, sitting at his desk, faced Dan.

"Of course you know where you've gone wrong: you've mishandled a serious case, you've lied to your superior officer, and you almost aided and abetted four homosexuals on my ship. It's only fair to say that I'll take this up with you later on. Right now there are other things to do."

He had spoken so gently that Dan's consciousness was barely penetrated. It was not until a few minutes later, walking alone to the barracks, that he realized Captain Howard had said four homosexuals, while Butler had sat there, quietly watching. He went on to the barracks, feeling that he had consumed nothing but coffee and cigarettes for the past twelve hours. By the time he reached the office and told Burns to get out, his face looked so tormented that Tolleson pushed back from his desk and

stood up, his face beginning to change too as if from immediate contagion. When Dan told him, he said in nearly
a whisper: "The ONI?"Then hesaid it again, shaking his
head; then he began to curse until Dan said to have the
four prisoners report to the office. They were there in
ten minutes, standing puzzled before him; he told them
calmly that the word was out, that it had reached Captain Howard—he did not say that Freeman was responsible—then he sent them back to the brig to wait, and
told Tolleson to take them off bread and water when their
three days were up, but to keep them in the brig until the
investigation was over.

By certain standards of time, no one had to wait long.
A message was sent from the *Vanguard*, received on Okinawa, and answered that same day. Toward evening a
plane left the ship and flew to Okinawa. It came back in
late afternoon of the next day, carrying mail and an investigator from the Office of Naval Intelligence. During that
time Freeman, Hahn, Jensen, and McKittrick had drunk
seven pitchers of water and eaten nearly thirteen loaves
of bread. They had not smoked, they had not talked, and
they had slept little. Dan had spent about four hours with
Alex, telling him what had happened. Besides those four
hours he could not have said what he had done from the
time he informed the prisoners until four-thirty the next
day when he was called to the Captain's cabin to meet
the ONI investigator: a stocky man dressed in a grey suit,
a white shirt, and a dark grey tie. He stood up to shake
hands. Doc Butler was there too; they all had a cup of
coffee and chatted with the investigator, whose name was

Paulsen, about duty in the Far East and at sea. Dan rarely spoke. Instead he watched Paulsen; you were never supposed to know whether an ONI investigator was an officer or enlisted man, a sailor or Marine—but Dan thought he could tell if Paulsen was a Marine. He thought that would make a difference.

The bosun's whistle sounded and mail call was announced. A part of Dan jumped, and he glanced at the door; then he looked at Paulsen again and after a moment or two he was all right. He tried to think of Paulsen's long, wide, dark-whiskered face and large interested eyes under a Marine barracks cap. Finally he gave up, knew he would never know anything at all about this man, would never hear of him or see him again. Captain Howard was standing now.

"Mr. Paulsen, would you like some chow before you get to work?"

"Yes, sir." He grinned. "I believe my stomach's settled from the flight now."

Captain Howard and Doc Butler chuckled; Dan smiled, watching Paulsen and wondering if this too was subterfuge, if perhaps the man had been a pilot himself.

"I'll have some brought in here," the Captain said. "It's probably best not to show you to the entire wardroom. Mr Tierney?"

Not knowing whether he was supposed to stay, Dan said: "Yes, sir."

So four trays of food were brought in and, when they had eaten, Captain Howard told Dan to find some place where Mr. Paulsen would have privacy. Dan took Paulsen to his own stateroom, cleared the desk for him, and emptied the ashtray.

"This kid Freeman," Dan said. "He's a good boy. He's got his fiancée knocked up back in the States: fine girl, she'll be showing soon—"

Paulsen was watching him, no expression except interest, and Dan averted his eyes because he could not think of what he had begun to say. He was very tired again, and he blinked his eyes and rubbed them, hoping Paulsen would see how worried he was, how much he cared for this kid.

"That's the orderly?" Paulsen said.

"Right."

"Captain told me about him. Why don't I see him first, then I'll call and let you know who to send in next."

"Fine."

Dan wrote his office phone number on a desk calendar, then phoned Tolleson and told him to send Freeman up to his stateroom. Tolleson said right away, sir, he had a chaser standing by in the brig. That small touch of readiness, of order, gave Dan his first slight satisfaction of the day. When he hung up he looked at Paulsen, but did not know what to say, so he left.

Tolleson was waiting in the Detachment office. As Dan shut the door he saw the single letter on his desk and recognized Khristy's handwriting. He sat down, picked it up and hefted it, then dropped it on the desk.

"Shit," he said.

"Right, sir. He might find out all *kinds* of Goddamned things about this Detachment."

"Jesus: poor Captain Schneider—"

"It's gonna tear him up, sir."

Dan nodded. He had Khristy's letter in his hand before he knew it, then he dropped it again.

"I wouldn't be surprised if we lose office hours. Captain's pissed off about the way I handled this."

"The way *we* handled it, sir. I guess I advised the Lieutenant wrong."

Dan shrugged.

"I'd have done it anyhow," he said. "I just wish I'd followed up and sent Freeman home."

He spun his chair to face Tolleson.

"Goddamn, First Sergeant. If they give that kid a UD—" He stopped.

"Sir, the Lieutenant's had a rough time and he ain't made a wrong move yet. Freeman should have kept his mouth shut."

Tolleson went to the door.

"Well, sir, if the Lieutenant needs me I'll be slopping down some o' that garbage in the chief's mess." Then his eyes softened as they did when he smiled, though his face was serious and there was in it a certain tenderness which reminded Dan of Doc Butler. "Don't worry, sir. They ain' queers. Cut the top off a Marine's head and all you'll see inside is little beer cans and pussies."

Dan raised a hand in half-salute to him as he left. He sat there for several minutes, thinking of Freeman being trapped by Paulsen's calm manner, before he picked up Khristy's letter again and slowly opened it:

Darling Dan:

I've thought about everything I'm going to say in this let-
ter for a long time, in fact since I first met you at that Com-
manding General's reception, so you probably have already
sensed some of the things I'm going to say. For instance, I've
always fought loving you. I think you knew that. Judging
from the way I feel right now, I didn't do a very good job.
But even that last night was more goodbye than anything else,
even then I meant it that way. I hope it wasn't a dirty trick.

I've been walking around the campus all day, and for
days before that, for months, and I've been thinking how lit-
tle my life would change if we were married. There would
be you, but the honeymoon would end and you'd put on that
Marine green again and we'd settle down. We'd live in places
where I lived as a child, where I waited for Santa Claus and
the Easter Bunny and a fairy to buy my lost tooth. You'd go
to the same service schools my father went to, the same duty
stations, and we'd go to the Birthday Ball every year, and the
officer clubs, and battalion and regimental parties, and I'd
hear variations of the same old sea stories from protégés of my
father and his friends. I'd have your children in Navy hospi-
tals, maybe even where I was born: good old USNH Camp
Lejeune, N.C. Our children would grow up in riding stables
and officers' swimming pools and Base movies. They'd go to
Base schools or they'd be those service kids who start school one
year and are gone the next. We'd have to tell a daughter who
was going steady that we were moving across the country
again.

And you, my darling trooper. Oh, and you. Within this
decade Marines will probably be fighting again somewhere.

You'll be a captain, a company commander, and I can see you now, maybe with a rough brown beard and with all sorts of gear strapped around you instead of a woman's arms. You'd have to check foxholes and fields of fire and clean your pistol before you could even read my letters, much less answer them. And all that time I'd be reliving my life. Danny, I don't want to relive my life . . .

IN THE REMAINING paragraphs she assured him that she had, and did, love him. He read it through, to her name at the end, then went into the classroom and got a cup of coffee from the percolator, nodding at the Corporal of the Guard; then he returned to his desk, closing the office door again, and read the letter a second time.

He could not put shape, form, to his loss. He felt it, his spirit barren and salted, but he could not see images of it. He saw his career she had summarized, saw himself as a lonely captain inspecting defenses on bare and rocky terrain. But he was unable to focus on Khristy's absence; it seemed impossible that she would not always be there, either loving him on stationery or in his quarters.

He stepped out to the classroom and refilled his cup; when the Corporal of the Guard said he was about to make some more, Dan found that he could not reply. Back in the office he replaced the letter in the envelope and stuck it under his shirt. Then he busied himself with coffee and cigarettes while he waited. He was angry only once, when he remembered all the Japanese girls he had refused. In just over an hour Paulsen phoned and said he thought he'd like to see McKittrick now. Dan called the brig and told the turnkey to send McKittrick to his state-room. He did not realize how solemn his voice was until the turnkey echoed his tone.

After a while Tolleson came in and they waited to-gether, through McKittrick's interrogation, then Jensen's; half an hour after the evening prayer and Taps, Doc Butler phoned and asked how it was going.

"He's with the last man now. Hahn."

"Okay, Dan. I'm sacking out."

"You are?"

"You should too."

"Not me, Doctor."

When he hung up, he said to Tolleson:

"That son of a bitch."

It was close to midnight when Paulsen phoned to say he was finished.

"What's the word?"

"Three of them confessed to homosexual acts in the past. They were the passive party. In San Francisco, for steak dinners, five bucks—stuff like that. Hahn, Jensen, and McKittrick. They used to go to a queer bar on liberty."

"What about Freeman?"

"No past homosexual experiences."

"What about the other night? He say anything different?"

"He left when the sexual business started."

"Will you stay there a minute so I can talk to you?"

"Sure."

Then he told Tolleson.

"Well, sir, that's nothing new."

"What isn't?"

"Marines've always got liberty money from queers so they can afford a woman."

"They'll have to go: those three."

"No loss, sir. Lieutenant ought to sleep good tonight."

As he reached the passageway above the barracks, he touched Khristy's letter through his shirt. He went quickly to his room, entering a smell of cigarette smoke like the lingering scent of spoken confessions. The written confessions were lying on his desk, and Paulsen—without coat and tie now—let him read them. Most of Freeman's was concerned with what Hahn, Jensen, and McKittrick had done to him since he joined the *Vanguard*.

"Do you think they're queer?" Dan said.

"Nope."

"Will that go in your report?"

"We just investigate. No opinions."

"Have you investigated queers before?"

"Too many."

Dan looked at the other confessions. They were written in longhand, and he thought of those three illiterate boys biting their tongues as they put words on paper. They had awkwardly used medical-sounding terms to describe what they had done, several times, in San Francisco.

"UD's—right?" Dan said. "Because of San Francisco."

"I guess that's what it'll be."

"And Freeman's clean."

"The only thing you could charge him with is assaulting an NCO, which would be stretching it. He's probably the only one you should have charged with disorderly conduct."

Dan nodded. He was touching Khristy's letter again. When Paulsen left, he took out the letter, opened the envelope, then stopped with his inserted thumb and forefinger closed on the letter. He released it and put it in the drawer, on top of the letter he had started two nights ago. He got a single sheet of stationery from a box on the shelf, dated it, and printed in block letters:

> AS THE SAYING GOES, IF THE MARINE
> CORPS WANTED ME TO HAVE A WIFE
> THEY WOULD HAVE ISSUED ME ONE.

He signed it, then went up to the post office and mailed it before going to bed.

WHEN HE WOKE he still had not had enough sleep, and in his mind he was talking to Khristy, telling her he had tried to make the right moves and it looked like he was breaking into the clear now, Freeman was clean, which was what counted, and that made his original decision to cover up the whole thing one-quarter right. Then he was fully awake, his loss tangible now, and getting out of bed and unbuttoning his shirt from its wooden hanger, then changing his mind and deciding to wear a fresh one, he could see her: some night she would lie in a motel bed, a diamond ring and a wedding band on her finger, her psyche all checked out; and perhaps the bastard would even ask who had taken it and she would say *horseback riding* or she might say: *A Marine, on our last night together*. He did not know which he preferred.

Now he was dressed. But he did not leave yet; he phoned Alex and told him what Paulsen had found.

"Then Freeman's okay," Alex said.

"Yes. Thank God something's working out." As he was leaving, his phone rang.

"Morning," Doc Butler said. "Skipper wants to see us at nine."

"Looks like you're in the chain of command now."

He could hear the grin in Butler's reply:

"Looks that way."

"Well, I waited up last night. Hahn, Jensen, and McKittrick have had passive homosexual experiences in San Francisco. Freeman's clean."

"We'll see."

"Paulsen said so."

"I only work here, Danny."

"You do more than that."

He hung up and went to the wardroom, eating creamed beef on toast at a table of junior officers, whose presence ruined whatever little pleasure he could have got from his favorite breakfast, a meal he had eaten heartily in peaceful days, at Quantico and Camp Pendleton, when trucks had brought it to the field early in the morning and it was steaming in green metal food containers when you got out of your sleeping bag and quickly dressed against the chill. He looked at the officers' faces with near hatred: smooth, happy, untouched—or if they seemed unhappy it was of no more importance than the homesickness of a boy at camp. Not one of them was a commander of troops. Not one of them had to face the Captain today. And not one of them had to worry about the future of an innocent boy who had knocked up a pretty red-haired girl. When he left the wardroom he was whistling "Somewhere Over the Rainbow."

In the passageway he saw Alex, steady, smiling, his moustache rising with the corners of his mouth, his cap on the back of his head, and his belly seeming to delight in its nascent spreading beneath the wrinkled khakis.

"Stand by," Dan said.

"What's the word?"

"I smell blindness in upper echelons."

"I'll be in my room after chow."

Frowning, Alex shook his head and went on to the wardroom.

At five minutes before nine, Dan met Butler at his stateroom, then they went up the escalator, Dan feeling that tightening in his rear. With his thumb he was rubbing the cut in his swagger stick.

Again they poured coffee from the silver pitcher. Then Captain Howard, sitting at his desk, pointed at the papers in a thin stack beside his coffee cup.

"Mr. Paulsen has given me the confessions and I've read them. Not with much surprise, I might say. I've seen this too many times at sea."

He glanced at Butler, who nodded once, then sipped his coffee.

"Now," the Captain said, "that's step one. The next step is up to you, Mister Tierney, and I'll tell you how to do it. You will give each man one of two choices: they can either sign a statement accepting a UD, or face court-martial for homosexual acts. I'll have the legal officer prepare the statements in the proper form. The men will sign them and we'll fly them off the ship. All this can be done today."

He looked at his watch. Doc Butler finished his coffee and returned the cup to the tray holding the pitcher.

"Just a minute, sir," Dan said. "Did I understand the Captain to say *each* man?"

"That's right."

"Sir, Freeman is innocent. Paulsen said—"

"Paulsen's business is not to say. Freeman helped them undress McKittrick."

Dan sensed again that futility of dealing with names in the Captain's cabin: especially now, when the names had become signatures on confessions elicited by an ONI investigator.

"That doesn't make him a queer, sir."

"It makes him something. He's been involved in this stuff for a long time in that Detachment of yours."

"Involved? He was forced, they bullied him—"

"Then why didn't he report it?"

"I guess he was afraid to, sir. The Captain knows these kids: they don't want to be informers—" He paused. "I guess he was ashamed to tell about it too. *I'd* be."

Captain Howard looked at his watch again.

"Mister Tierney, I'm getting damned tired of your stubbornness. To a certain point, I admire your feelings for your troops. I'll even say I wish my junior officers had some of it. But I've passed that point. I have duties on the bridge in fifteen minutes for air ops—that's what this ship is for, Mister Tierney. Now I'm telling you to go down to that barracks and handle this, with the proper procedure this time, and I want those men off my ship as soon as possible."

"Where's Paulsen?"

Captain Howard stood up.

"Mister Paulsen is on his way to Okinawa. And this meeting is over. You go do as you're told and report here at thirteen hundred. I'll have statements ready for signatures then."

Without answering, Dan walked out, leaving Butler. He almost ran to Alex's room, but managed to stop long enough to knock—you did not burst in on a man at sea.

"Saddle up," he said. "That bastard wants a clean sweep."

Alex was sitting at a desk cluttered with magazines and books. He took off his glasses.

"I thought so," he said.

"*Why?* Jesus Christ, it's all there in the statements if he'd open his eyes."

" 'Professionalism is our business.' "

"What?"

"It's a motto painted over a hangar at Alameda. Broken down, it means screw you. Look at it their way."

"What do you think I am?—five foot nine of walking shit?"

"Try it for a minute. Doc Butler—let's say he went along with you. Then let's say Freeman goes to another duty station and surprises us all by turning out to be a queer. They investigate him and they find out that Butler decided he was all right. Bad for Butler."

"Jesus—you don't believe Freeman's going to turn queer someday."

"Course not. He'll go home and marry that girl. But we've got to familiarize ourselves with the enemy's motivations. Now, the Captain. It'd be worse for him. Suppose he forgot about Freeman, just let it drop. Then suppose we pull into port someday and Freeman gets caught doing hanky-panky with a young sailor. Another ONI investigation. The Captain has a one-year tour on the *Vanguard*. He's the fourth skipper she's had, and every one of the other three has made admiral. He doesn't want two ONI investigations, especially for the same man."

Dan moved a piled uniform from a chair and sat down.

"Can we beat it?"

"Good chance with Freeman. The others are through, but I'll defend them anyway."

"All of 'em?"

"The book says they have the right to counsel, and to appear before a board of three officers."

"Alex Price, you're a good tough son of a bitch."

"They don't bother me. I'll be a civilian in a few months, if this bucket doesn't sink. Howard'll crap all over you, though. Can you take a bad fitness report?"

"Jesus, Alex."

"Okay, friend. Let's gird for battle."

"Let's."

Then he went to the barracks, where Tolleson was waiting in the office.

"Captain Howard wants me to threaten these Marines into refusing their rights to a board. He wants 'em off the ship today."

Tolleson did not even curse. He stood there with his mouth open, and Dan realized for the first time that, with the exception of Alex, he was entirely alone now. Tolleson would be no help. Defense counsels, field boards, legal infighting: these were part of that world which Tolleson neither comprehended nor wanted to: the world of officers' clubs, mess nights, investigations, decisions, courts-martial—always involving officers. For the rest of the fight, Tolleson would be there to encourage, to listen to the progress, to curse, and to solace. That was all.

"Let me see the *Personnel Manual*," he said. "Then get those Marines up here."

"Aye aye, sir."

Dan had spoken curtly, so now he added in a friendly tone:

"Mr. Price is going to defend them. We'll request a board."

Tolleson got the manual from a shelf, then found the page concerning Undesirable Discharges. Dan sat and read it once quickly, then a second time, more slowly, then a third. He did not want to have to read it to the troops.

But just before they came in he felt that he could not face them. He opened the book again, wanting to use it as a prop, something to fix his eyes on. He looked up at Tolleson, who was watching him.

"I hate to tell those kids," he said. "Even Hahn doesn't rate this."

"I know, sir."

When the chaser knocked on the door, Dan closed the book and nodded at Tolleson. He let them in. They stood abreast before him, then Dan rose, told them to stand at ease, and came around the desk and sat on its edge, as close to them as he could be, looking in turn at each man's face: Hahn, McKittrick, Jensen, Freeman.

"The word isn't good," he said.

He paused, breathed once.

"Captain Howard wants each of you to get a UD."

His eyes lowered then, and he bent over and took his pack of cigarettes from his sock, offering it as he straightened.

"Here. Your brig time's over."

He passed his lighter around, then lit one for himself.

"Now: you can either sign a statement waiving your rights and accepting a UD, or you can take advantage of your rights. The book says you have right to counsel, to appear before a board of at least three officers, and to call witnesses and make a statement on your own behalf. My friend Mr. Price has offered to serve as counsel for all of you. I'll give you time to think it over. If you want my advice I'd say take every right you can get."

Hahn nodded. He was the only one who looked more determined than afraid.

"I can't say what will happen, but I have a few ideas. You, Hahn—McKittrick—Jensen—will probably get UD's: because of that business in San Francisco. The book's pretty clear on that. But I'd fight it anyway. Freeman, you have a good chance, since there's no evidence against you except that bit the other night."

"So you men think it over. Meantime, we'll prepare release orders and at least get you out of the brig. Are there any questions?"

"Sir," Hahn said. "I don't need to think it over. I want counsel and a board."

"Okay. Anyone else?"

McKittrick and Jensen said yes, sir; Freeman licked his lips and finally got out his answer too.

"All right. I'll inform Mr. Price and the Captain, and I'll let you know if there's anything new. You ought to stand by in the barracks for Mr. Price. Any more questions?"

They shook their heads. Hahn came to attention, clicking his heels, and the rest did too.

"That's all," Dan said.

Tolleson opened the door as they marched out, then sat at his desk, the *Manual* open beside his typewriter, and began typing their requests.

At precisely one o'clock, after lunching with Alex, Dan was outside the Captain's cabin, returning the orderly's salute, then going past him and knocking, without waiting to be announced. He went in and this time did not sit down. The Captain, sitting at his desk, had not invited him to anyway. Doctor Butler sat to one side of the Captain's desk, half-facing Dan, who stood at ease.

"Sir, they want counsel and a field board."

For the first time Captain Howard's face colored, and his voice was high, unnatural, as if it had not been raised for months.

"Goddammit, what are you doing? Losing control down there?"

"I'm not losing control, sir. I advised them of their rights as provided by the *Marine Corps Personnel Manual*."

"Mister Tierney, I specifically instructed you to get

them to waive their rights. I told you I'd have those state-ments prepared for their signatures—" He was on his feet now: he tried to scoop up the typed statements from his desk but they slid away from his fingers, separating into a disorderly row of originals and carbons; so he pointed at them— "Here they are. Now you tell me no one's going to sign them. Why?"

"Because, sir, they have a right to be heard."

"Mister Tierney, I want these statements *signed*. I *told* you how we handle these cases on this ship and there will be *no exceptions* for your Detachment—" he lowered his voice, still firm "—which will not be yours for long, I can assure you. Now you go tell those men they will either face a court-martial or accept a UD."

Dan looked at Butler, whose face was a mingling of surprise and—yes: he saw it, drew from it—admiration. He turned to the Captain again; he was not even stand-ing at ease now, one foot ahead of the other, his hands on his hips.

"No, sir," he said. "I can't do that."

"I'm *tell*ing you to."

"Sir, I'm not paid to railroad troops into UD's. The Cap-tain knows they have rights, sir."

"Mister Tierney, we've spent enough time on this, and in about two minutes I'm going to be highly pissed."

"Goddamn, sir—" he had not said it loudly, had nearly breathed it pleadingly, but Captain Howard's face colored again "—three of 'em don't have a chance, but Freeman does. He doesn't rate a UD, sir. The Captain knows that man—"

"—I know enough about him to get him *off my ship*—"

"—Yes sir. As for the other three, sir, they're going to have to go through life trying to get jobs with a UD. They've got to fight it, sir. Jesus—I'd fight it with everything I had: board, counsel, letters to Congressmen for crying out loud. Wouldn't *you*?"

The Captain sat down. He slid the typed statements together into a stack, then picked it up and tapped it on the desk until it was neat again.

"Mister Tierney, I'm getting damned tired of having a junior officer interfering with the way I choose to run this ship. There will be no board. Those men will sign these statements and they will pack their gear and leave this ship by plane at sixteen hundred today. They will go to Okinawa and await transportation to the States where they will receive their discharges."

"Well, sir, let's look at it this way: they know their rights, so they can't be snowed. They've requested Mister Price as their counsel and he's agreed. And by now they've signed requests to that effect."

He paused. The Captain was glaring at him as no senior officer had ever done, no sergeant during his officer candidate training. But he was not frightened. He could not see, hear, beyond this moment, and would not have wanted to if he could.

"So you see, sir, there's no way in hell they can be refused their rights."

The Captain had been slouched forward in his chair, his arms resting on the statements. Now he tensed and struck the desk with his palm.

"All *right*, Mister Tierney. All *right*." He turned his swivel chair and worked the switch of an intercom near his desk.

"Orderly, get Commander Craig on the phone and tell him I want to see him."

Then he looked at Butler.

"I should have a doctor.'"

"Kellog?"

"All right. And I'll get another Regular officer."

He turned his chair again and faced Dan.

"They'll get their board, Mister Tierney. It will be to-morrow afternoon; Commander Craig is senior member. That's all, Mister Tierney."

"Aye aye, sir."

He came to attention; then he about-faced and walked out.

THE DIFFERENCE BETWEEN a court-martial and a field board is that the members of a field board already know a man is guilty. They deal with men who are considered a discredit to the service for any of several reasons: repeated minor offenses against the Uniform Code of Military Justice, refusal to pay debts, homosexuality, or lewd and obscene acts. The board does not give a sentence, as a court does; it merely hears the case, then makes a recommendation to higher command, either for the man to be retained on active duty or be given an Undesirable Discharge.

The field board ordered by Captain Howard was held a two o'clock the following day, a Sunday, in Commander

Craig's stateroom. A Marine orderly was assigned to stand outside the door and call in each man when Alex told him to. The four men waited down the passageway, around a corner, in the waiting room of the dental office which was closed for the day. They were dressed in fresh tropical khaki uniforms, with neckties; their web belts were scrubbed clean, the brass tips and buckles polished; their shoes were brilliant dark brown. They all sat on a couch, smoking as carefully as women so ashes would not spill on their uniforms; they faced a dentist's office and through its door Ted could see the chair, the light, and the drill. He remembered waiting to have three teeth filled—counted the years by looking at the outstretched fingers on his thigh—when he was sixteen. Waiting then had been much the same as waiting now. He shut off the nervous conversation beside him and considered that: as if somewhere beneath the shadows of his experience in dental offices, there lay some hope. Maybe that was the game, played over and over: you waited, with fear or excitement, and finally whatever you waited for happened and it was never as bad or as good as you had expected. Except pussy. He was quickly disgusted with himself for thinking in that term, and he corrected it: *making love with Jan.* Now he felt old. He had gone off to sea and become a man who could hardly talk anymore without profanity; he was indeed no longer a boy. He wondered if Jan would notice, if even when she burst through the crowd on the pier and ran to him, she would see something different about his face, would look at him curiously just before they lovingly collided.

Then Hahn was talking to him.

"How'd he get a confession from you?"

Ted shrugged, looked vaguely at the dental chair through the door.

"You didn't have nothing to hide, is that it?"

"I guess so."

"He kept calling me 'son,'" McKittrick said.

"Yeah," Jensen said. "I thought *he* was a queer. 'Have a cigarette, Leo.' Pretty soon I was waiting for five bucks—" He laughed, then as suddenly stopped. "Be good to see 'Frisco again," he said.

"I got to go home," McKittrick said. "Daven-fuckin-port. The farm. I'll say, 'Well, Mom, I'm home early. They just figured I ought to get my ass home and see you.' "

"You wouldn't be going if you'd kept your mouth shut," Hahn said.

"You didn't do so good yourself."

"He wouldn't have got one Goddamn word out of me if he hadn't said you guys already wrote it down."

"All right," McKittrick said. "You got snowed."

"Yeah, but you were the first one—Teddy-Baby don't count. You were the first one, then he had us."

"I told you, I never said nothing about you and Jensen."

"You didn't have to. After that, he knew."

"That's what he told me," Jensen said. "He already knew."

"You'd have told him too," McKittrick said to Jensen. "Goddammit, he sent the chaser for coffee, and we sat there talking about liberty in Japan and all that crap, then he started talking about 'Frisco, and we're sitting there laughing like old shipmates, then he says he used to play around with the queers when he was young—pick up money on Friday so he could get him a woman Saturday. Then he says at first he just tried rolling 'em and him and a sailor got hold of one and got both their asses whipped—"

"He was snowing you," Hahn said.

"No lie. Think I don't know that now? He says after that he didn't try rolling 'em anymore, he just went along with the game. Maybe it's true: I don't know."

"Sure," Hahn said. "Think he could be an ONI man if that was true? ONI would *know* about it."

"I don't know. Anyhow, so I told him about the time Russell got pissed 'cause that other queer was buying me drinks and they got in this Goddamn argument like two women. And Paulsen starts laughing and acting like a queer—no lie: he starts around the Lieutenant's room, shaking his hands and talking like a pissed-off queer and he says yeah, don't I know, don't I know. I remember he Goddamn said that: don't I know. Then he sits down and says hell, Bradley, if that's all you did why don't you write it down and we'll get this over with so everybody can get back to work."

Jensen chuckled.

"Mac," he said, "you just ain't cool."

McKittrick reached for a cigarette in his sock, paused bent over looking at the deck, and said:

"Shit."

Hahn stood up and walked to the bulkhead opposite the couch, then faced them—no, faced Ted, squinting at him, and Ted averted his eyes to the dental chair past Hahn. Then the orderly came in and said the board was starting and they wanted McKittrick first. McKittrick said "Shit" and jabbed his cigarette in an ashtray, leaving it smoldering as he rose and left.

Hahn was looking intently at the door now, and in that respite from his glare, Ted lit a cigarette. Alone with Hahn and Jensen he thought of the old riddle of the fox, the goose, and the sack of grain. But there was no grain: two foxes and he was the goose, not even a goose really, just a small—

"Mr. Price is cool," Jensen said.

"He better be." Then Hahn was looking at Ted again. "I ain't getting no queer discharge."

Ted found himself watching Hahn with pity: he was thinking of him and Jensen walking through the night of San Francisco, pretending they were glad to be out of the Corps, probably dropping into their old bar, laughing as they gulped the paid-for drinks and told the queers what had happened. Now Hahn's face, looking at Ted, changed too, became quizzical, and he said: "Ain't none of us God-damn queers. Not even Teddy-Baby."

"Guys at Dago used to do it," Ted said. "For easy money."

"Easy money," Jensen said, and Hahn began to pace, looking at the door McKittrick had gone through.

Ted felt closer to them, the comradeship you felt for your buddies in Boot Camp when you were all getting crapped on; but at the same time he felt cheapened, and he put his face in his hands as if he were tired, and thought of Jan.

He did not have to worry long, though, about being one of them. Less than an hour after McKittrick had left, he returned with the orderly, who said they wanted Jensen.

McKittrick's face was pale. He stood in the center of the room, smoking deeply, his slumped height making him appear entirely defeated. When Jensen had followed the orderly and shut the door, McKittrick said: "You little son of a bitch," and crossed the room, his hands reaching for Ted who jerked back on the couch. Then McKittrick spun toward Hahn.

"He *told.*"

Ted could not see his eyes but he knew there were tears in them; his heart seemed to drop and melt and flow coldly down through his legs.

"The sonofabitch told Doc Butler! At request *mast.*" Hahn crossed the room and stood in front of him.

"What did you tell him?"

His voice was low, hoarse.

"I don't know, I—"

"What did you tell him?"

"I told him what happened, that's all."

McKittrick stepped beside Hahn.

"He told them everything," he said.

Then he was leaning forward, reaching for Ted, one fist cocked, but Hahn stuck an arm across his chest.

"Wait. Mr. Price telling 'em that?"

"No. The Goddamn board already knew about it. *They* was the one's asking."

"What did you say?"

"I said we were just grab-assing with him and he never bitched about it or we'd have stopped."

"What about the other night? What'd you tell 'em?"

"I said we got carried away, that's all."

"*We*, huh?"

"Yeah."

"We."

"That's right. What do you think?—I look like Freeman or something?"

"Get out of here, Freeman," Hahn said.

Ted started to rise but could not because they were standing so close to him. Then Hahn grabbed his wrist and jerked him off the chair and shoved him toward the dental office.

"I don't want to see you—"

He kicked him, at the base of the spine, and Ted winced as he stumbled forward into the room. Without looking at them he shut the door, then faced the small room of silver equipment. He brushed at the seat of his trousers, limped to the dental chair, and sat down. He had lighted a cigarette before he saw there was no ashtray, so he flicked the ashes in his palm. Finally he looked around, saw a wastebasket, and got up and brought it to the chair and sat down again.

From the other room he could hear Hahn and McKittrick: urgent voices without meaning. Gradually there were longer spaces between the voices, until there was mostly silence. He tried to avoid looking at his watch, but it was no use: he read the time at least once every five minutes. He heard Jensen return, then voices, and the door closing again. So they were saving him for last. After a while he decided that Mr. Price was smart to do that.

He smoked long after inhaling bored him. Once looking at the drill and lamp above his left shoulder, he wondered what it was like to be a dentist, saw himself with an office some place near mountains and the sea but without

Washington's rain: maybe east of the Cascades, or down in Monterey. Jan wanted to spend their honeymoon in Monterey. It looked like, he thought, if a man could take apart and put together an M-1, a .45, a BAR, and a light .30, he could learn to work on teeth.

He heard footsteps in the other room, and his hands gripped the arms of the chair, his body rigid. But they were not coming toward him. For a while, the goose was alone on one bank of the river.

So, later, it was with more relief than fear that he followed the orderly—who had opened the door and looked strangely at Ted, sitting in the chair—down the passageway to Commander Craig's door, where the orderly stopped, knocked twice, and opened the door when someone in the room called: "Okay. Come on in."

Then Ted wasn't relieved anymore. The voice was Commander Craig's and it sounded too old, too official; he walked in, seeing no one but Mr. Price who motioned him to a single chair facing Commander Craig's desk. A Naval lieutenant he didn't know sat at one end of the desk; at the other end was Doc Kellog, who had interviewed him for a secret clearance, had even been friendly—though he probably remembered none of it. Commander Craig sat behind the desk. Ted looked up at Mr. Price and waited. Mr. Price asked him to stand and be sworn in. He stood at attention, raised his right hand, and answered in a voice that was not his:

"I do."

Mr. Price told him to sit down again. He sat stiffly, his hands touching in his lap, and answered Mr. Price's questions. In that strange voice he told them his full name, his service number, his present duty station. Then he told what had happened when they jumped McKittrick. Mr. Price made him start with him and Hahn and Jensen waiting for McKittrick. While he spoke he was wondering why he had to start there, why he couldn't say what happened before, couldn't even say Hahn and Jensen had been coming for him; and his panic went into his voice, shaming him. He reached the part about looking up from McKittrick's legs, then stopped.

"Tell the board what you saw," Mr. Price said. "In your own words: it's all right."

He told them.

"What did you do when you saw that?" Mr. Price said.

"I left, sir. I went to the classroom."

"Why?"

He hesitated, groping.

"I didn't want to be there, sir."

"Why?"

"I felt dirty, sir."

"All right: that's enough for now. Would you sit in that chair by the bulkhead, please?"

He got up, feeling onstage as he passed the board, and sat in the chair. The board was to his right now. He looked straight ahead, at a painting of a destroyer on the opposite bulkhead, near the door. Mr. Price was at the door now, thrusting his head out and talking to the orderly.

When First Sergeant Tolleson came in, he looked at Ted, then around the room until he found Mr. Price. While he was being sworn in, Ted wished he had been allowed to wait with the First Sergeant, wherever he had waited. He listened as the First Sergeant, speaking slowly and loudly, glancing alternately from Mr. Price to the members of the board, told of his performance as a Marine, of his fast promotion to Pfc, his chance to be a corporal. Then the First Sergeant was excused.

The Lieutenant came in next, wearing his tropical uniform with a blouse; and juxtaposed with the Naval officers, he looked more competent than Ted had ever seen him. The Lieutenant said the same things the First Sergeant had, except he added that he had been wrong to lock up Freeman for insubordination to McKittrick. He had found out later that McKittrick had been harassing Freeman in a personal way, which possibly didn't justify insubordination but certainly had a bearing on it. He said that only the sharpest and most reliable Marines in the Detachment were made the Captain's orderlies, and that Freeman was one of these. With a little more confidence and with experience at troop-handling, he said, Freeman could be a good NCO, a credit to the Corps.

Burns came in next. Last night, lying in his bunk, Burns had said he was sorry about telling the First Sergeant and the Lieutenant, but he surely didn't know at the time that anybody could think Freeman was involved too. Nobody, Ted had assured him, can figure out how people with rank will take something, and he shouldn't feel like it was his fault. Now, always looking nervously at Mr. Price, Burns told how Freeman had been snapping in on Sunday afternoons, learning administration, so he could get into a good career field. Then Mr. Price asked him about the night of 16 November and it was Burns who, losing some of his nervousness, even showing anger, told the board of Freeman's harassment that night, how they were coming for him with shaving cream and he—Burns—had been afraid to help; and how they had got Freeman and shaved him and painted him with Mercurochrome, that first week he was aboard (Ted wanted to shut his eyes, his ears—but Burns did not say what they had painted on his chest); he had felt sorry for Freeman, he said, and had asked him to go on liberty and that's where he met his girl.

When Burns was finished, and had left the room with twice the dignity he had when he entered, Mr. Price asked Ted to take the stand again. Then Mr. Price faced the three officers at Commander Craig's desk.

"I'm going to ask Private Freeman to make a sworn statement. I'm going to ask him to tell us everything that's happened to him since he joined the Marine Corps. Everything, that is, which fits into a pattern in his life, everything that has brought him here this afternoon—" he looked at his watch "—if it's still afternoon." All three of them grinned and looked at their own watches. "I'm also going to ask him *why* he joined the Marine Corps, why he decided a couple of summers ago up in Washington that he wanted to be—or ought to want to be—a Marine—"

Unprepared, Ted glanced down at his hands. Last night was one thing, talking to Mr. Price in his stateroom, Mr. Price laughing and even talking about himself, how he had screwed up so many times as an ensign or with girls or the high school football team—but here, in front of these solemn men in this room, that was another thing altogether.

"—By the time he finishes his statement, I think you will have seen a young man who, if anything, needs our help. I'm not so sure he even needs that anymore, but that's Doc Kellog's field, not mine. What you're going to see," he said, "is a scared kid trying to get along, trying to get through each day without being scared. He didn't always know what he was scared of, and sometimes he had to do strange things to get by. He had to swallow a lot and pretend he liked it. But I believe you'll see more than just a kid afraid of his own uncertainty, his own competence, and his imagined lack of it. I think some of you, maybe all of you, will recognize feelings that you've had yourself. At least that's true for me. You'll see timidity turning to fear, fear to cowardice, cowardice to hatred. But you'll also see a young man who—like all of us—kept trying to put all those pieces together and come out whole. Above all, you'll see a young man who is guilty of faults, not crimes; who lives with self-doubt, not perversion; who is not evil, but unlucky."

Now he faced Ted, his back to the board, and very quickly smiled and winked. He stepped to one side, profiled between Ted and the board:

"Private Freeman, what were you like in high school?" Ted had no idea what to say; but, with despair, he knew that did not matter: Mr. Price would draw it out of him, and he did. He began by asking questions about sports, popularity, girls—and soon Ted was looking at the carpet but talking, slowly, finding himself going farther back than high school even, for some reason telling of dreading recess in winter because so often the other boys would take his cap and play keep-away with it and he would spend the entire recess running from one boy to another, pretending it was a fun game. Mr. Price did not stop him; instead he questioned him, calling forth the names of grade school bullies—then abruptly said:

"Why did you join the Marine Corps, Freeman?"

"I wanted to be different, sir—"

Before he had time to regret saying that, Mr. Price asked him about Boot Camp and he was talking about his Drill Instructor and the night he lifted his wall locker in his sleep and, next day, he could not even lift it an inch; then another question and he was saying the Tijuana whore seemed so old, maybe she wasn't older than he was but she looked like it, and he'd been scared of a dose and— he shrugged his shoulders.

"That you wouldn't do well in bed with her?"

He was blushing at the carpet.

"Yes, sir. That's why."

Then it was all right again because he was talking about Sea School and how much he liked it after busting the hills at Pendleton, and he was just getting warmed up about Sea School when Mr. Price asked him when he first slept with Jan Thompson and he didn't want to answer that, it wasn't that he was mad, but you just didn't—

"On our third date, sir," he said.

"Were you uneasy?"

"No, sir."

"She loves you?"

"Yes, sir."

"Were both of you in love back then? Starting to be?"

"Yes, sir."

"You never felt uneasy with her, about anything at all?"

"No, sir. We always have a good time."

"She's pregnant now?"

"Yes, sir."

"Do you have a picture of her?"

"Yes, sir."

"Would you mind if I showed it to the board?"

"No, sir. I don't guess so."

He gave Mr. Price the photograph of her standing on the blanket in the lawn behind the apartment building, wearing her two-piece aqua bathing suit. Ted watched Commander Craig looking at Jan, nodding, and passing her to Doctor Kellog, who looked up from the picture and smiled at him. A smile was somehow forming on his own lips when Mr. Price said:

"How many times did Hahn, Jensen, and McKittrick give you the shaving cream treatment?"

"Three times, sir—Hahn and Jensen." Doctor Kellog reached over the desk and handed the picture to the Naval lieutenant. "McKittrick wasn't with them the last time."

"What else did they do that first time?"

"That first time, sir?"

"Yes. Your first week aboard. Tell the board about that first time."

Mr. Price was stroking his moustache. Ted lowered his eyes; the members of the board must be watching him now; then Mr. Price's legs moved out of his sight, returned, and Jan's picture was in his hand again. He put it in his billfold and sat looking at the billfold resting in his hands.

"Go on, Freeman," Mr. Price said softly. "The first time."

He began to talk. His eyes on the billfold, he told in detail how he had tried to stop them, and everybody was watching and nobody, not one of them, even said a word to help him, and he had hollered too until Hahn said to shut up—

"You hit him once, didn't you?"

"Yes, sir. Later on, the third time they did it."

"What happened then?"

"He slapped me a few times, then they gave me the shaving cream."

"All right. Back to the first time."

He had given all the details he could and now he had to go on to the Mercurochrome painting. He told that slowly, about Hahn painting his flesh where they had shaved him. Maybe that would be all. Maybe Mr. Price would let him walk out of here with that. But when he stopped talking, Mr. Price's voice came right in. His hands gripped the billfold now, twisted, squeezed. Then he told them what Hahn had painted on his body.

Now Mr. Price was talking to the board again and there was a pause and then Commander Craig said no one had any questions; and it was him again that Mr. Price was talking to, telling him he could leave now, he would not be needed anymore, telling him thank you.

He did not go to the dental office, or the barracks either. He walked aft, climbed two ladders, and was on the hangar deck. Through the large doors to either side of him the sea and sky were blue. He went between the parked bombers to the fantail, pushing the hatch shut behind him. Standing at the guardrail he smoked and looked out past the wake at the calm sea. The sun was low, the horizon already catching its gold and red. He felt nausea and realized it was hunger, but he did not go to chow. He would go later. Right now he only wanted to stand here as long as he could see the sky and sun.

Chapter Six

Toward sunset the *Vanguard* and her destroyer escort, spread near the horizons to port and starboard, made a slight change in course. She was entering her last phase of operations: for four days she would try to hide from attack planes of the Marine Air Wing at Iwakuni. After this defensive maneuver, the *Vanguard* would go to Iwakuni and spend five days in port.

At eight o'clock that night the air defense watches began. During normal air defense or general quarters drills, Dan's position was in the aft gun mount on the portside. But for these day and night watches, four hours on and eight off, he rotated with junior Naval officers from the Gunnery Department, manning what was called Sky II: a turret high above the ship, on the signal bridge. On this first night he had the midnight-to-four watch.

He tried to sleep at seven-thirty, but could not. There

were so many things to worry about that he lay there waiting for nothing in particular, simply for something to happen, if only the approach of midnight. So he was grateful
when, at nine-thirty, Alex came to his room, grinning but
asking if he wanted to sleep before his watch.

"I can't."

"I think we might have won," Alex said. He sat down,
and Dan pulled away the covers and sat on the bunk's
edge, his bare feet on the deck whose vibration was so
unobtrusive that his feet seemed to be hearing rather than
feeling it.

"I've just been chewed by the Captain: about twenty
minutes' worth. Says I handled that board like it was a
court-martial when it wasn't. Supposed to be cut and
dried. I also get the idea he's tired of junior officers in
general, you and me in particular."

"He said that, huh? What did you do in that board?"

"Everything I could think of: even his girl's picture in a
two-piece bathing suit—"

"—Good picture."

"Maybe it worked. When you deal with people who
think in cliches, you got to talk in clichés."

"And the Captain was pissed?"

"Was and is."

Dan left the bunk and started dressing, putting on utilities and boots.

"You going on a hike?"

"Might as well get dressed for the big hide-and-seek
game. I'm going to see the Gun Boss."

"He can't tell you the results yet. Captain's job."

"I know."

He looked up from lacing his boots.

"I'll try to read his eyes. Maybe he'll wink at me, I'm so well-loved on this ship."

He put on his cap and field jacket, and asked if Alex wanted to meet him in the wardroom for coffee.

"Okay. I'll go watch my peers playing Monopoly."

"Tell the sweet little things hello for me. Sometimes I wish all I wanted to be was a dumb ensign: never get chewed out, never chew anybody else—just walk around and smile and hope nobody messes up the routine."

He left and went to the Gunnery Office, but Commander Craig wasn't there, so he went to his stateroom. The Commander was at his desk, doing paperwork that would have been saved until the next day if the ship were in port.

"Jesus—all I've seen is Marines today. What do you want?"

Dan smiled at him.

"Sir, if we go to general quarters during this exercise, does the Commander want me to man the gun mount or take Captain Schneider's place on the signal bridge?"

"Goddammit, what commander are you talking about?"

"Commander Craig, sir—the Gunnery Officer of the USS *Vanguard.*"

Commander Craig's lips spread to one side, the grin of a man who is about to explain how badly someone has cheated you.

"Well, Danny Boy, that poor son of a bitch is sitting right here and he wants the Acting CO of the Marine Detachment to man that worthless gun mount."

"Very good, sir. Lieutenant Tierney will gladly comply with the Commander's wishes, and man that gun mount which couldn't hit a broadside cruiser."

He was starting to leave when Commander Craig leaned back in the swivel chair and said:

"We pull into Iwakuni, Danny, you transfer that kid Freeman. You get him off the ship."

"Transfer him, sir?"

"That's what I said. You know how to write orders, don't you?"

"Yes, sir. I can transfer him to a barracks ashore."

"Okay. You do that."

"Does that mean he's been cleared, sir?"

Commander Craig sighed and scratched his head.

"Someday I'm going back to destroyers. No airdales, no Marines. Sonny Boy, in all the time you've been in this room, have I said one word about that board?"

"No, sir. Not a one."

"That's what I thought. Now go protect this Goddamn bird farm from air attack or whatever the hell you're dressed up for."

"Aye aye, sir."

He walked to the barracks with long fast strides, enjoying the sound of his boots hitting the steel deck, their tightness on his shins, he had owned these boots since entering the Marine Corps, so they were well broken-in, although he had never oiled or saddle-soaped them, a precaution which allowed him to spit-shine them now as quickly as he could shine his cordovans. The distinctly Marine boots and utilities seemed a proper uniform tonight, when he was becoming certain that he and Alex had won; and, approaching the barracks, he was recalling cool mornings at Camp Pendleton when he had led his platoon to the field, setting a brisk pace over the blacktop roads and hard dirt trails.

It was Freeman who called the scattered troops in the classroom to attention. When Dan told them to carry on, Freeman relaxed but did not sit down again; he had been reading a magazine, alone at a table. Tolleson came out of his stateroom. Dan nodded toward the office, then stopped close to Freeman.

"Be tough," he said quietly, and followed Tolleson into the office.

"No word yet," he said. "But we've got some signs and wonders. The Captain reamed Mr. Price for doing a good job, and Commander Craig told me to transfer Freeman as soon as we pull into Iwakuni."

"Sir, these Goddamn swabbies can't tell us to transfer a Marine. We're under the administrative control of the Commandant and last time I checked there wasn't no sailors in that chain of command."

"I know that. But if they want him transferred, they must have cleared him—right?"

Tolleson's face showed the defeat of compromising victory and Dan wanted to comfort him for being the only real Marine aboard, the only man who saw one goal and one course to follow stubbornly.

"It's not a big thing," he said. "If they clear Freeman, it's worth giving up administrative control over one man."

"Sir, wouldn't the Lieutenant like to start a mutiny and take over this ship?"

"Okay: after the midwatch tonight. I wouldn't tell Freeman about this yet—and I'd also watch him: I've seen even him look happier."

"No sweat, sir. He's got that little redheaded piece Stateside. It's the other three that's walking around here like lost sheep."

"Think we ought to lock 'em up?"

"No, sir. I had a talk with all four of 'em, one at a time. Nobody's going off the fantail."

"Good man. I'm going to the wardroom now, then I have the midwatch at Sky Two."

"Aye sir."

In the wardroom Alex was sitting at a long table, watching four ensigns playing Monopoly. When he saw Dan he waved and moved to an empty table. Dan got coffee from the percolator and sat beside him.

"Gun Boss told me to transfer Freeman."

"Good. He was just in here, then he got a phone call and took off. I guess it's his turn in front of the Captain."

"Captain won't get to that old salt," Dan said.

" 'Shove it up your airdale ass,' the Commander said."

"That was to the XO."

"So they say," Alex said.

"Gun Boss will just sit there scratching his bald spot and thinking about destroyers. That's all he'll hear: destroyer engines. Won't hear a Goddamn thing the Captain says."

Alex raised his cup.

"To justice," he said.

"Save the toasts. We pull into Iwakuni, we'll first off get roaring-ass drunk. Then we'll get a hotsi bath to sober up.

Then we'll eat some sukiyaki and hot sake and get some nice clean soft pretty Jo-sans and we won't come back to this bucket till sunrise."

"What about the girl friend? *Semper Fidelis*, Dan."

"The girl friend has detached herself and become a separate command."

"Aw no."

"I'll tell you about it when we're good and drunk, just before the hotsi bath."

"You've had a great tour."

"Haven't I?"

They stayed in the wardroom until eleven-thirty, when Dan started climbing ladders, keeping track of his progress by reading numerals on the bulkheads: past the hangar deck, the flight deck, up into the island: passing the bridge, then the admiral's bridge, finally with burning thighs and short breath reaching the top, pushing open a hatch, and walking onto a narrow deck. A soft breeze cooled his face. He turned to it and breathed deeply, then looked down at the outlines of planes on the dark flight deck, and the shining black sea with a silver strip of reflected moonlight perpendicular to the portside of the ship; behind the *Vanguard* was a slow wake. The night was perfectly clear, more stars than he had ever seen in his life, and there was a bright pale full moon. He felt drawn into the immensity of the sky, lost in it, and he gazed straight up until he was dizzy; then he found the Big Dipper and North Star and looked out at the horizon, thinking of directions now, of the ocean as it appeared on maps, of islands and countries and continents. Holding the white guardrail he moved forward to the portside turret, opened its hatch, and said:

"Okay."

A lieutenant junior grade hurriedly climbed out.

"Nothing happening," he said, and was gone into the shadows.

The turret was small, shaped like half an egg. He sat behind a pair of binoculars attached to a port, adjusted their lenses to his eyes, then started his sweeps: focusing directly aft, then slowly rotating the turret a hundred and eighty degrees, studying the sky on the portside. At the end of his sweep he raised the binoculars ten degrees and started aft again. Through his earphones he could hear men in the radar rooms and port gun mounts far below him; two sailors were trying to count stars. After a while they stopped.

By the time he had finished half a dozen sweeps, Dan was simply looking through the binoculars at the sky; he was not searching for planes, which was an anachronistic part of his function anyway. His real job was to take bearings from the radar man if he made a contact, then to lock on the plane and direct the gun mounts. But that, too, as useless. If the Marines came tonight, they would strike at five hundred or so knots, and at most the guns would swing toward their general direction while the radar tried in vain to lock them on target.

Finally he opened a ventilation port beside him and, still rotating the turret, looked out at the sea. *Semper Fidelis*, he thought. Well, he had been always faithful to Khristy, had not been with a woman since making love to her last May, had decided next morning as he drove north that he had slept with enough women: as a farewell, he had recalled each of them with moods ranging from bitterness to nostalgia. There in the car, he had sung "Time After Time":

> *So lucky to be*
> *The one you run to see*
> *In the evening*
> *When the day is through . . .*

SO ON THE cruise he had felt no need to collect Japanese pelts, or ever again to love a woman because of loneliness. But he had kept faith with a lie. Immediately, he regretted that word. Not a lie, but an evasive tactic which he should have recognized. Then, looking out at the ocean, he knew that he had known all the time and had successfully repudiated that knowledge so it could not interfere with his purposes and dreams.

At ten past four he was relieved by an ensign, whom he asked bitterly if there wasn't still an order that reliefs of the watch should report fifteen minutes early. The ensign apologized with shame that Dan knew was caused not by his tardiness but his inability to reply with any sort of nerve. He descended the ladders and went through red-lighted passageways to his room, where he took off his boots and shirt but left his trousers on, so he would be prepared if general quarters was sounded while he slept. Months ago, during a four-day readiness inspection before the cruise, Burns had heard from a sailor that general quarters would be sounded at three next morning; he had slept in full uniform that night, including boots, but there was no alarm. It was finally sounded after reveille, while Burns stood lathered in the shower. Remembering that, Dan was able to feel like smiling, though he did not. He went to sleep.

Four hours later, when his phone shocked him awake, he was certain he had not slept at all but had spent the night involved in dreams that were too real. A Marine, the Captain's orderly, was on the phone. He said that Captain Howard wanted to see the Lieutenant.

This time Doc Butler was not there. Captain Howard was sitting at his desk, calm again, his voice detached.

"Night watch last night, Mister Tierney?"

"Yes, sir."

He was angry with himself for not hiding his weariness.

"Things will be normal again soon. I have the results of the board here." He nodded toward the papers on his desk. "The recommendation is that all four men receive Undesirable Discharges."

Dan was standing at ease in front of the desk; his hands came out from behind his back, gestured as if to wrestle with air, then dropped to his sides.

"Freeman too?"

"Yes. I will endorse their recommendation and forward it to the Commandant of the Marine Corps for final disposition. As Acting CO, you may also add an endorsement—"

"—I sure *will*—"

The Captain lifted his hand, then lowered it, picked up a pen, and continued:

"In the meantime, you will transfer those men to the Commanding General at Iwakuni for further orders and transportation to a transient barracks in the States. They can wait there for the Commandant's disposition."

Dan was shaking his head, sensing the impotence yet commitment of that gesture.

"Mister Tierney, there's a plane leaving at fifteen hundred. I want them on it."

"No, sir—not Freeman. I'm not transferring him out of my sight until I get word from the Commandant. I'm going to write—"

"You are *very* close to being placed under arrest. Now before that happens get out of here and write those orders."

Dan shook his head.

"Not Freeman—sir, the Captain *knows* that kid—he's been your orderly, for crying out loud. Why don't you talk to him? Would you do that? Just call him in and talk?"

"You're being foolish as well as insubordinate. I have no desire to talk with Private Freeman."

"Foolish. Jesus Christ—*fool*ish. How *can* you? How in the world can you turn your back and just railroad him out with a UD like a—"

"—That will be *all*, Mister—"

"—He's not a Goddamn *per*vert! He's a kid! Nothing but a good fouled-up little kid! Jesus Christ—you'll make admiral anyway, the fuckin' ship's not going to sink if he stays on it—"

The Captain was on his feet, circling the desk, stopping just in front of him, and Dan was ready to dodge a fist.

"Mister Tierney, you're under arrest. You are hereby confined to quarters. You are relieved of all duties except air defense and general quarters. Until Captain Schneider comes aboard at Iwakuni the First Sergeant will run that Detachment under the direct supervision of the Gunnery Officer."

Then he stopped.

"On what charge, sir?"

"Conduct unbecoming an officer."

"I'll instruct my First Sergeant not to write orders for Freeman."

"*I'll* write them. Now go to your stateroom."

"You can't. The Detachment is under operational control of the ship's captain; Headquarters Marine Corps has administrative control. And since I'm—"

Captain Howard turned to his desk and picked up the phone.

"If you don't leave *right* now, and go to your room, I'll call the Master-at-Arms and have you taken there by force."

After a moment in which Dan saw himself being led away by two sailors with brassards and nightsticks, he walked out of the cabin.

In his stateroom he phoned Alex; as he spoke he was aware that his voice, compared with Alex's incredulous anger, sounded tired and beaten. He cursed a little but it did not help. Alex said he was going to poke around the ship, and hung up. Then Dan called Tolleson to his room, and told him what had happened; by now his voice was so dull that he began to dislike it, and he thought of taking the phone off the hook, locking his door, and sleeping until tomorrow. When Dan finished, Tolleson said as long as the Lieutenant was writing a letter for Freeman he might as well write another endorsement because he was going back to the office to submit a retirement letter.

"Nineteen years and six months is enough shit for anybody," he said.

Dan nodded, picking up the phone again, having Freeman, Hahn, Jensen, and McKittrick sent to his room. They came in as he knew they would: expectant but without hope. He admired their reaction. As he faced them and spoke with the litttle intensity he could muster, Tolleson standing somewhere behind him, he could see in their shifting eyes revisions, plans—by the time he was finished, parts of them were already off the *Vanguard*. Even Freeman looked as if somehow he would survive. When the other three left, Dan told him to stay for a moment. Tolleson stayed too.

"I don't have to tell you you've been screwed," he said to Freeman. "Those other three didn't have a chance to begin with. I'm going to write the Commandant today and ask that he retain you on active duty. I'll write as good a letter as I can. But you can do something too. I've never told a Marine to write a senator before, but that's exactly what you ought to do. You've got that Senator Magnuson and if he starts asking questions, he'll shift the sand under some people's cages. The *least* you could do is make a few people wish they'd acted like men. I'd say you also have a damned good chance of being cleared. So you write it tonight at Iwakuni. Send it airmail—" He took a piece of his stationery and wrote the name and address. "Here. The copy of the investigation won't leave the ship till tomorrow, because it'll take me that long to write a letter. And don't be afraid to write this letter. They can't touch you. Course you could never stay in as a career Marine, because you wouldn't get past a promotion board after bitching to a senator. But as it stands, you can't stay in anyway. You write to him."

"Yes, sir. I will."

Freeman was looking at the stationery; then he put it in his billfold.

"Mention my name. I don't think they can get me for being a witness."

"Yes, sir. Thank you sir."

"Another thing. If this doesn't work, do you have any plans? Making a living, I mean?"

While Freeman answered that he had no plans except getting married, Dan felt something which, because he took pride in honesty, was rare for him: that whisper of guilt preceding a lie, though he was about to say what he suspected was the truth.

"Well—try to look at it this way. It's not the end of the world. We tell troops a bad discharge will ruin their lives: they won't get jobs, they won't get into college. I tend to doubt that. A hell of a lot of people on the outside don't care about the service, one way or the other. And I'd be willing to bet that very few people doing the hiring and firing ever ask to see your discharge papers."

He paused. He had not kept Freeman here for this, had meant only to suggest the letter to Magnuson—or per-

haps simply to tell of his own letter to the Commandant—
but now he was like someone desperately giving toys to an
ill, suffering child. Aware of his disloyalty to the Marine
Corps and himself, he wished Tolleson were not there.

"So I have an idea you can make out even if you get the
UD. But I don't think you'll get it anyway. When a senator
farts, generals inhale deeply. You write to Magnuson."

"Yes, sir. Tonight, sir."

When Freeman was gone and Tolleson was about to
leave, Dan asked if he were actally retiring and Tolleson
said no, sir, he couldn't retire until his overseas tour was
up anyway: he'd stick out this Goddamn tour and go back
to the infantry where the Marine Corps was. Dan said he
was ready for some of that good duty himself.

Then he started working on the letter. By eleven
o'clock, time for watch-standers' lunch, he had finished
a draft. But he was not satisfied; trying to foresee the
reaction of some colonel at Headquarters Marine Corps,
he went through it, crossing out adjectives, phrases, sentences—everything which implied righteousness. He
knew better than that. With one bar on your collar,you
did not even suggest that the ship's Captain was wrong:
you pretended to be merely relating facts about an enlisted man whom the Captain had not had the oppor-
tunity to observe. You wrote as if you were objectively
performing one of the duties of the profession: not
defending a man so much as informing your superior
officers of certain circumstances which you were aware
of because you worked closely with him. A reader at
Headquarters Marine Corps must conclude that Cap-

tain Howard, because of the size of his command, quite understandably could not share these insights.

So he left that first draft on his desk and went to lunch, planning to work on it again that night. After lunch, on his way to the ladders going up to the signal bridge, he met Commander Craig in the passageway. From a distance of ten paces he saluted, and spoke with a cool formality that he normally used only when greeting strangers who outranked him.

"Good morning, sir."

Commander Craig averted his eyes and saluted flaccidly in return.

"Going up on watch, Danny?"

"Can't go anyplace else, sir"—looking straight ahead, passing him.

He climbed to the signal bridge, then stood at the guardrail, his cap in his hand because of the wind, until he could fully open his eyes to the day. Several large white clouds moved with the course of the ship, passing it. The ocean glared, appearing hot. He relieved the officer in the turret and slowly moved it, fore to aft and back again, but he did not look through the binoculars; he had not adjusted them to his eyes.

Sitting in Sky II, the only place he was free to go, earning his pay by performing a senseless function as part of a complex but inadequate air defense system, he smiled at the absurdity of it. He knew the Captain had acted on impulse, and he wondered what feeble ruse the Captain would think of to free him from arrest. Being court-martialed was out of the question. It was bad for the officer

corps, cost too much in terms of the troops' respect and
certainty; so an officer's punishment usually took a more
expedient form. The Captain might give him a letter of
reprimand, hurting him when he entered the promotion
zone next year. But many good Marines, as a direct result
of their virtues, had been in frequent trouble. He remembered a lieutenant-colonel once, in a leadership class, saying if you had been in the Corps ten years and still weren't
a colorful character you'd never be a field grade officer. Of
course Dan had known that was not true: he had already
seen too many field grade officers who exuded inconspic-
uousness as some nervous women exuded motherhood.
Yet he had believed it was partly true, the colonel's plea for
individuality a proof in itself.

That leadership class had been in Basic School where,
he could still recall with pride, he had been the Honor
Man of his class, having consistently maintained for
eight months the highest grade-point average for work
in the classroom and the field. It was a goal he had set
for himself during the first week, as soon as he discovered that such a goal existed. He had studied nightly,
had purposely gained competence without annoying his
classmates, for he had never forgotten that his profession was one which, above all, involved men. He disliked
martinets as much as he disliked their slovenly, ineffec-
tive opposites; and while he absorbed his education, con-
verted words from manuals into rules he could follow
by instinct, he remained a humble noncritical compan-
ion even to those lieutenants whose professional short-
comings and noncommitment actually pained him, as if

their presence in the Corps somehow blighted his. He was doing more than just being friendly. He was waiting. His function was not to chide Reserve officers, but to lead troops, and he impatiently stored his energy for the time when he would leave Basic School and join the Fleet Marine Force, where he could impress his standards and ideals on those troops he longed for.

As Honor Man he had received two awards: a regular commission and a Mameluke sword, and he had left Basic School with a conviction that he had found his destiny in a world of action. He did not consider war a necessary part of that world. He could have a satisfactory career without ever encountering an enemy, and he did not think of combat as an accumulation of corpses nor as an end in itself, but as an abstract test of how well he had lived each day, how well he had trained himself and his troops. Since he could judge that for himself, he did not need to be tested, and he was able to fulfill himself with the knowledge that he and every man under him were ready for the most demanding of duties. He thought football coaches and baseball managers probably felt the same; but there was a difference: he had gone further than they had. While they worked with skillful athletes, he trained and led every sort of man who decided, for his own reasons, to join the Corps. Each of these men became a measurement of his effectiveness as a leader. For he could not rest until he knew that everyone under his command was able to do anything that had to be done, whether it involved a flamethrower or the delivery of a message. Therefore, he could never rest, and he liked that too.

This was his attitude when he had left Basic School, and three and a half years later it remained as untarnished as the Mameluke sword he had been awarded: a ceremonial heirloom from First Lieutenant Presley O'Bannon. He liked to recall that O'Bannon—a colorful soul, it was said—had been given the sword in 1805 by the rethroned ruler of Tripoli after O'Bannon had led a force of Marines, mercenaries, and Arabs against that ruler's enemy; that, in spite of this, O'Bannon was not promoted to captain, so two years later had resigned. Years after O'Bannon's award, the Marine Corps had adopted the Mameluke sword as its own. Now every Marine officer knew who Presley O'Bannon was.

If, then, Captain Howard gave him a letter of reprimand, he would not be the first good Marine to become a victim. Certainly the Commandant and future promotion boards would be able to read the truth in his case.

Shortly before three o'clock the *Vanguard* turned into the wind. Looking at his watch, Dan stopped the turret and half-rose from his seat, his face to the open ventilation port. On the flight deck a small propeller-driven plane was being pushed to the catapult.

He had forgotten. His impulse was to leave the turret, run down the ladders and onto the flight deck, if only to exchange salutes and handshakes and wish them luck. Now he saw them, moving away from the island in scattered file; their hands were pressing on the tops of their barracks caps, their faces turned from the wind, their bodies leaning under the weight of shouldered seabags. Freeman was the last to board. He stood beside the plane, looking up at the hatch, a small green figure against the silver fuselage. He swung his seabag to the deck. Then he released his cap, took the seabag in both hands, and with an effort that Dan could see from his distance, he lifted it. The wind caught his cap and took it, his head turning aft, watching, as he stood with the raised seabag. Someone took his bag into the plane and he ran: he had covered about ten yards when he stopped and watched the cap rolling and leaping the last few feet, over the portside. He looked around at the sailors on the flight deck, and glanced upward at the bridge; then, lowering his head, he jogged to the plane and climbed through the hatch.

When Dan was relieved from the turret at four o'clock, he started writing the letter again. He wanted to sleep but he did not have time: the next two watches were the dog-watches, from four to six and six to eight, and he would be in the turret again at eight o'clock. He had written a page when the Captain's orderly phoned and said the Captain wanted to see him in his cabin.

As he went up the ladder he felt that he could be whipped now: he was tired, he had lost Freeman, and there was nothing else that he felt like fighting for. If Captain Howard was going to attack the independence of the Detachment, start handling Marine disciplinary cases himself, then Captain Schneider would have to fight that. He would concentrate what energy he had on Freeman's letter, and he would go through the motions of air defense. When the ship reached Iwakuni he would tell the story to Captain Schneider, then he and Alex would go on liberty.

He waited for the orderly to announce him; when he

entered, Captain Howard was standing behind his desk, holding a small yellow sheet of paper. He waited impatiently as Dan formally reported, standing at attention three feet from the desk. Then he told Dan to stand at ease.

"I have sent this message to the Commandant of the Marine Corps."

He was holding it across the desk now and when Dan simply looked at it, trying to imagine the Commandant receiving a message which apparently had something to do with him, the Captain said: "Here. Read it."

Without moving his feet he reached out and took it. The words were printed in pencil:

> REQUEST IMMEDIATE TRANSFER IST. LT.
> DANIEL F. TIERNEY 065524 USMC FROM
> THIS COMMAND. INCOMPETENCE AND
> CONDUCT UNBECOMING AN OFFICER.
> LETTER OF REPRIMAND FOLLOWS.

He read it again; then for a while he merely looked at it. Finally, his eyes still on the message, he said:

"A clean sweep."

It occurred to him to drop the message on the desk but that required energy he did not have; so he handed it to the Captain. He could look at him now.

"Since you'll need to go about the ship to check out, I am taking you off arrest. I suggest you start packing and checking out as soon as possible."

"Yes, sir."

"In these cases, orders generally come by message. I expect them in a couple of days at most. You will certainly be departing the *Vanguard* upon our arrival in Iwakuni."

"Yes, sir. Is that all, sir?"

Captain Howard shook his head.

"Your letter of reprimand will be ready tomorrow. Among other things it will mention your handling of the incident, lying to Commander Craig, and your insubordinate outbursts in my cabin. I'm telling you this so you can plan your statement, if you choose to write one. You will also get a change-of-duty fitness report. It will be unsatisfactory and you can enclose a statement with it too. So there are a lot of things to be done. You are restored to command of the Detachment, but if anything unusual comes up, you will consult with Commander Craig before taking action. I also expect you to perform your duties in connection with our exercise with the Marine Air Wing."

"Yes, sir. Is that all, sir?"

"That's all."

When he returned to his stateroom, he thought of calling Tolleson, but decided not to. Tolleson had been through enough lately, was becoming marked by a look of futility; and, besides, Dan had no time for impotent cursing. He did not have time to phone Alex either. He went to the wardroom and ate quickly, speaking to no one—he could not even have said who sat at his table—then he worked on Freeman's letter. When it was finished—clear, objective, subordinate—he just had time to bring it to Tolleson for typing before he climbed the ladders again, to the turret.

Since afternoon the wind had diminished. Before entering the turret Dan watched a cloud slowly cover the moon, bright and full again. For the entire first hour of his watch, he sat without moving the turret. When he found himself having an imagined dialogue with Khristy, he let it continue, telling her about Freeman as she listened, sitting opposite him at a cocktail lounge table, drinking a martini. He paused to reflect on that: how he always thought of her in the surroundings of their dates, or that one time in his bed. He would never be able to think of her at a kitchen table, say, or reading a magazine on a couch in late afternoon. He tried placing her in a living room he had never seen, but he could not do it; so he brought them back to the cocktail lounge and talked to her again. For a while her face showed little. But gradually her lips tightened, her eyes started to squint—then she broke in and said he was right, oh didn't he see? Couldn't he? *They* were wrong: the Navy, the Marine Corps—all those men narrowed down to one purpose: victory in combat, yet their final purpose was subject to grander complexities on higher levels, trickery of politics, interests of nations, lies, lies, *lies*. Inhuman: what they were doing to Freeman, what they did to thousands so they could take a piece of land, an island—some bloody place that happened to be of tactical worth. Then he said no, as long as there had to be armies, there should be a Marine Corps, because they were the best. And no matter what the government used it for, the Marine Corps was people. Men became professional Marines not because they had to but because they could: they chose a way of life that followed a clear-cut truth, politically neutral in a world of changing enemies. Why, a Marine—with his detachment from home, money-making, and politics, and his devotion to an isolated and insulated truth—was the man with most liberty in twentieth-century America. The professional neither lived nor fought for governments, but for courage, endurance, honor, duty—

He stopped the converation. Looking out at the sea he was disturbed that his talk had shifted from Freeman to an argument about the ideas he lived by yet rarely voiced. He tried to start over, to conjure Khristy and the cocktail lounge, but he was looking at the flight deck, estimating the now darkened spot where Freeman had been standing when his cap blew away, and he was too alert for daydreams. He was wondering how the Captain's message had been received at Headquarters Marine Corps; there was no way to find out how badly damaged his professional reputation was; he could get an indication from the type of orders he received, but that was all.

He had been in the turret for nearly two hours when the hatch behind him was jerked open and, turning, he saw in the darkness Alex's face and shoulders. He took off his earphones.

"I'm being shanghaied from the ship," he said.

"What?"

"With a letter of reprimand and unsatisfactory fitness report. Transfer's being arranged by message."

Watching Alex's face as it jerked back, he felt the pleasure of having delivered a shock. Then Alex said:

"How would you like to bust the *Vanguard* wide open?"

"Show me how."

"I just got hold of Doc Kellog, because he's been flying most of the Goddamned day. I asked him what I did wrong and he said I must have known I didn't have a chance when they already confessed homosexual acts in San Francisco, passive or not. So I said no, I mean with Freeman. And he said what the hell did I want—a promotion too?" Alex paused. "The board cleared Freeman."

Dan dropped the earphones and climbed out, standing on the signal bridge and looking at Alex in the moonlight.

"Wait a minute. He's off the Goddamn ship, they flew him off this afternoon—"

"That's not the point. Point is, the senior member is the only one who signs the recommendation of a field board. The Goddamned point is—"

"Commander Craig."

"Right: the old salt, the old no-sweat—"

"Jesus Christ, what could the Captain have *told* that bastard!"

"You tell me. What do captains tell commanders in this Goddamned outfit: they tell 'em to change the recommendation of a board and sign it and these ball-less wonders change the recommendation and sign it. *That's* what happens."

"Okay. Okay: I've got two statements to write and there's going to be one screwed-up Captain when I'm through. By the time Freeman writes to Magnuson and I write the Commandant there won't be anybody getting promoted around here."

"Magnuson?"

"Freeman's senator. I told him to write tonight."

"Well, now: we may see a little justice yet."

"Revenge. But I won't be here."

He was thinking of an investigating officer from Headquarters Marine Corps arriving on the ship. Since a Navy captain was involved, the Marine would probably be a senior colonel, maybe even a brigadier-general.

"Would Kellog testify?" he said.

"He wouldn't start anything, but I'm sure he'd tell the truth at an investigation."

"Well, he'll get the chance—I'll guarantee you that."

Alex stayed with him for a while longer, neither of them mentioning Dan's transfer, then Dan got into the turret again. He began planning his statement and as he wrote it in his mind, he pressed his eyes to the binoculars and swept the sky as if all of them—Captain Howard, Commander Craig, Doc Butler—were out there, for him to find and destroy.

When he was relieved at midnight he knew exactly what his letter would say: much simpler to write too, no dodging the truth as he had in the recommendation for Freeman. The honest simplicity of his next day's work allowed him to sleep well. He woke at seven, thinking of Captain Howard up in his cabin: saw him wearing pajamas and a robe, shaving with an electric razor and thinking of evading Marine air now that Freeman and Mister Tierney were taken care of. By the time Dan had finished shaving he was angry, impatient to start his letter; it would have to wait, though, for he had the eight to twelve watch in Sky II.

But he did not stand that watch. As he was climbing the last ladder to the signal bridge, his breakfast-filled stomach protesting, general quarters was sounded. He turned and started down the ladder before he had time to curse. Then he did, aloud, to the bulkheads. He had three minutes to get from the top of the ship down to the hangar deck, then across it and aft to the gun mount. Then condition Zebra would be set: hatches closed all over the ship and no one was supposed to open them until the drill ended. He ran down three flights, holding the handrail, swung onto a landing and stopped: the ladders below him were crowded with sailors, pushing upward. He started down, pressed against the handrail so that for moments he could not move. One of the sailors jammed against him said:

"Wrong ladder, sir."

"I know," and gripping the rail he jerked himself down, broke through, reached a landing and was halfway down before he was jammed again, stupid and enraged: probably every sailor on the ship knew there were two ladders in the island and during general quarters you used one to go down and the other to go up, just as port and starboard passageways were used for going aft and forward. But he had no idea where the other ladder was.

He went on, pushing sailors, further shamed when they turned angrily but, seeing his bars, said nothing. The bosun's mate announced over the loudspeaker that condition Zebra would be set in two minutes. Dan reached another landing, bumped into a commander who looked surprised, then annoyed: "Wrong ladder, soldier." "Right, sir—" When he got to the hangar deck there was one minute left. "Circus—" he said and ran, dodging between planes: across the hangar deck, aft, through a compartment where a damage-control crew in helmets and life jackets waited to close the hatches, up another ladder—an empty one—and finally, out of breath, onto the sponson deck beneath the gun mounts. He climbed a ladder to Mount 8, ran over the catwalk to Mount 6, and climbed into its large grey turret. A Marine in utilities stood watching an instrument panel, as if he were actually bringing up rounds from below-decks. Dan moved past him, climbed into his seat within the plastic bulb, put on earphones, and received manned-and-ready reports from the gun crews.

A Navy lieutenant was taking Captain Schneider's place on the signal bridge, asking for reports in a high nervous voice. Dan told him Mounts 6 and 8 were manned and ready. He heard Commander Craig's voice and thought of him talking into the phone on the signal bridge, looking at the sky, his cop-out digested by now. Then the lieutenant cried, "Air action port!" and the guns jerked and swung toward the horizon and Dan saw them: a formation of silver A4D's coming in low, the sun at their tails.

His gun mount swung and jerked again as the radar operator below-decks tried to lock on. The lieutenant screamed, "Action port! Action port!" and Dan, having no function now but to pass on orders, watched the Marines closing the distance from horizon to ship, five hundred knots and three hundred feet above the water, their noses rising as they approached the ship, then flew over it ahead of the extended crash of their engines, the lieutenant now: "They're over the ship!" —and Dan yelled into the phone, at the lieutenant and Commander Craig on the signal bridge, at anyone else on the whole ship who might be listening to that circuit:

"Good! Good! Sink the sonofabitch! *Sink* it!"

As if watching it from a distance, Ted waited for the nausea to spread upward from his legs which had suddenly cooled. He had not touched his beer in the last ten minutes; now he did, pushing the tall Asahi bottle farther away. The cold reached his stomach and he loosened his collar and tie: he was no longer conscious of Amiko's hand resting on his leg, just above the knee.

What bothered him most was not that, on his first night in Iwakuni, he was drunk in a whorehouse with Hahn and Jensen and McKittrick. It was more: the entire evening seemed to be the story of his life.

They had landed at Iwakuni after dark, carried their seabags across the airfield, and Jensen had said: "Dry land, guys." No one had answered. They had reported in to the Officer of the Day, a tall Marine first lieutenant with a blond moustache shaped like the gold pilot's wings he wore over his left breast pocket. On the plane, Ted had dug a garrison cap out of his seabag, and now he clutched it in his fist at his side; standing beside the others, their barracks caps with shined visors held smartly under their left arms, he felt that the rectangular wool cap in his hand was a conspicuous indication of his character. The lieutenant read their orders, and said they had missed chow but there was a slop chute where they could get sandwiches and beer. He seemed to consider their case for a while, then added that he saw no reason why they couldn't go on liberty, no matter what kind of discharge they were waiting for. He did not ask them what they had done to get the discharge. He gave them liberty cards, told them to be cool, there would be a Stateside hop in a couple of days, and sent them to a barracks with his clerk, whose plump body and long oily black hair worked on Ted's shame until he had an impulse, as they climbed the barracks steps, to collar him and say that no matter what it looked like, he was a good seagoing Marine. Going down the corridor he said:

"Soft duty."

He had not spoken for some time and his throat needed clearing. He did this as Jensen asked what he had said.

"Soft duty in the Air Wing."

The clerk looked back at him, smiled, and shrugged. He took them to a squad bay where a few Marines were putting on civilian clothes, gave them four bunks at the far end, and left. None of the Marines spoke to them; soon, in pairs and threes, they were gone. Jensen said he was hungry.

"Let's hit the beach," Hahn said.

Ted had taken off his blouse, hung it in an empty locker, and was lying on a lower bunk. He would wait for them to leave, then go to the slop chute for a hamburger. On the plane they had been friendly enough, or at least not unfriendly, and he thought that was because his sharing their punishment made him less of an informer, perhaps not one at all. Still he wanted to avoid them. More important, he had to write those letters: first to

Jan, who had not heard from him since last week when he had told her the Lieutenant knew she was pregnant but could not send him home because of regulations. He looked forward to writing that letter: he would be able to tell everything and she would know he wasn't lewd and obscene, that he did not deserve an Undesirable Discharge. His letter to Senator Magnuson would be much the same. He had never in his life written a letter of any importance, had never used mail to change the way things were. In fact, he had rarely changed anything by his presence either: not like this, revenge, and also getting back what he had lost.

Jan would at least be happy that he was coming home. He would tell her that if he won, he would probably go to Stateside duty; if he lost, he would start looking for a job. Either way, they would get married, and Jan was making money now—so actually there was nothing to worry about. It wasn't nearly as bad as it had seemed.

But as he was lying there, the others had put on their caps and Jensen had said:

"Let's go, Teddy."

"No thanks. I got to write my girl."

"Come *on*," Hahn said. "We'll beat the letter to the States."

He had got up, put on his blouse and cap, and followed them out, thinking of what he might have said: that he wasn't hungry, or he felt sick, or he was tired. But as soon as Jensen told him to come with them, he had known he would go. He was unable to refuse invitations, even one like this: whenever someone asked him to go some place, to do something, his mind emptied and he could never think of a reason why he should not accept. These three had picked on him as long as he had known them, at a time when he thought everyone—including himself— had outgrown physical harassment; they had been ready to beat him up during the board and although they had left him alone since then, they surely did not like him. Nor did he want them to. He knew all this, knew that Hahn's telling him there was no use writing a letter was not a plea for his company, but a form of attack, as if Hahn could not tolerate his making a decision on his own. Still he had walked with them to the slop chute, chuckling at their remarks, solemnly nodding his head when they cursed the Lieutenant and Mr. Price and the ship. At the slop chute they changed their money to yen; hoping if they lingered they might not leave, Ted suggested a beer.

"What do you want to stay on the Goddamn base for?' Hahn had said. "You waiting for the Lieutenant?"

"Piss on him. I just need a beer."

But apparently no one had heard: they were leaving, and he followed. A Japanese taxi brought them to town, where for a while it was all right, drinking the first beer fast, then ordering again and talking to the hostess, soon unaware of the others except for their voices. He bought the hostess drinks because this was his last night in town, he would stay aboard the base from now on, and he might as well get rid of the yen. Sometimes he did not talk to the hostess, but watched the other people in the bar: sailors and Marines in uniform, the Marines probably from a ship because the Iwakuni Marines were allowed civilian clothes. You could tell the seagoing Marines by their haircuts anyway, and he was beginning to feel superior to every one of the long-haired civilian-clothed Iwakuni Marines in the bar until he remembered why he was there; he found himself glaring at Hahn, and shifted his eyes before Hahn saw him.

"Fly lice," Hahn was saying, and Ted said to the hostess beside him:

"Me too. Fried rice."

He heard McKittrick and Jensen ordering fried rice; then he shook his head.

"Make it sukiyaki. And bring some chopsticks."

She nodded and went to the bar, a short pretty girl with a high voice like music, long hair knotted on top of her head, and wearing a blue silk kimono which felt to his hand like a delicate responsive part of her body. He watched her placing his order, lit a cigarette, and poured beer into his glass with the casual preoccupied motions of a man who has lit cigarettes and poured beer in a thousand bars of a hundred lands while waiting for native women to bring him strange food. Before she got back to the table, he rose and went to the rest room, stepping without effacement around standing Marines and sailors and girls. The rest room was large enough for two men but only one could urinate, and a sailor was doing that, so Ted waited behind him, a little to one side, his back to the wall. The sailor was one of those who took a long time, braced with one stiffened arm at the wall, his head lowered to observe the whole function. He shook and milked afterward too, his head turning once to look at Ted: a wide reddened face that was at the same time amiable and antagonistic, depending on whether you looked at his numb smile or his drunk eyes.

"Just a minute, bellhop," he said, and went back to his business as if alone again. Ted was thinking he could shift to his right and bring down a chop to the base of the skull. Or he could wait until the sailor turned, pretend he didn't want trouble, step toward the urinal and quickly knee him in the groin. There was also the solar plexus to consider. In Boot Camp they had said if you hit a drunk man there he would vomit every time. The sailor turned and, without looking at Ted, walked out. As he urinated, his body trembled and he wished with all his fast heart that the sailor had given him a chance. Returning to the table he looked around for the sailor, found him sitting at the end of a booth crowded with sailors and girls, and walked by, his jaw set, waiting for a remark which he would answer with a sudden chop to the throat. But he passed unnoticed.

He sat beside the girl at their table which was between the booths, out in the middle of the floor, so there was always someone skirting them or standing nearby, and Ted prepared himself for the first one to spill beer on him. He gazed with insolence at people in booths and saw himself telling Jan: *He was a big guy, but I caught him off guard;* on the table, his right hand straightened for a karate blow.

He saw himself as a corporal—and not a clerk either—but leading a rifle squad up a hill at Camp Pendleton. No one would ever know that he could have done that. Even

Jan would say she believed he could do anything, but she wouldn't really mean it, for he was different with her and she didn't know this side of him. He had nearly completed his correspondence course and he knew the answers. That was the secret: while everybody else stood around, it took one man to spot a treeline or draw going up to a flank, establish a base of fire, and execute a single envelopment. Or, if there were no other approaches, it was hi-diddle-diddle-up-the-middle with a frontal assault. Those were the only two movements a squad could use. A platoon could go into a double envelopment or a penetration; turning movements were for regiments and above. COCOA was the key word for terrain appreciation: critical terrain, observation and fields of fire, cover and concealment, obstacles, and avenues of approach. The four phases of offensive combat were MACE: movement to contact, attack, consolidation, and exploitation. He had been looking scornfully at a profiled, oblivious Marine in civilian clothes, probably a grease monkey. Now his eyes swept boldly over Hahn, Jensen, and McKittrick. The dumb bastards, *he* should be leading *them. Hahn*, he would say, *You open your fat mouth one more time you're going to see the Skipper.* I'M *running this squad.*

When the food came they started into their fried rice, using forks; then Hahn, at the opposite end of the table, stopped with his fork halfway to his mouth and watched the hostess filling Ted's plate with sukiyaki from the pot. She gave him a bowl of rice, another bowl with a raw egg in it, and a pair of varnished chopsticks which he carefully arranged in his right hand.

"Look who's going Jap," Hahn said.

Ted did not answer until he had taken rice with the chopsticks, dipped it in egg yolk, and got it smoothly into his mouth.

"Hell," he said, chewing, "that's chow-hall rice you're eating. If you want to eat native, go all the way."

"The old salt," McKittrick said. "Who taught you to use chopsticks? The Lieutenant?"

"Right," Hahn said. "Lieutenant kept him back this morning and said he sure was sorry old Teddy-Baby was getting a UD, and they sat on the deck and ate with chopsticks."

"Ate what?" McKittrick said.

Before Ted had thought about it, he said:

"I thought you were the one knew all about that." McKittrick pushed his chair back, ready to stand.

"I'll break your Goddamned jaw, Freeman."

Ted took a piece of meat, watching more than he had to the chopsticks closing on it, then chewed and swallowed before he said:

"What are you pissed for? We're all getting thrown out, aren't we?"

"Shut up, Freeman," Hahn said.

Ted shrugged and began eating, his eyes on his plate except when the hostess asked if they were going to make trouble, and he turned to her and said quietly that they were already in trouble, but those three guys were too stupid to know it. But, he said, he wasn't going to be in trouble long. She smiled as if she understood.

That smile of hers seemed to follow him for the rest

of the night. When they finished eating, Hahn, Jensen, and McKittrick stood and put on their caps and he did too, though no one had spoken to him, and walking with them on the sidewalk he realized that possibly he could have stayed, then caught a taxi to the Base. It was in the next bar that he began to get drunk, talking again to the smiling lips of a hostess, and when some time later he was in a third bar with a third hostess, he felt that he had spent two days looking at a woman's smile. All this time, since Hahn had told him to shut up, he had not spoken to them; or, if he did, he had said so little that it was the same as saying nothing at all. When he talked—less and less often as the evening advanced—he talked to a hostess. Every time they rose to leave a bar, he thought of sitting there and letting them go; but not knowing what he would reply if one of them said to come on, he quietly went along: having too many beers in bars which he could not remember except as a merging of one continual noisy room and the smile of a hostess, strangely broken by walks of a couple of blocks, or taxi rides. Finally he was at the whorehouse, sitting at a table with those three and their girls and with little Amiko whose face was prettier than when he had first seen it, though he still had not thought of changing his mind. When she had come to sit by him, perhaps an hour earlier, he had told her what he had not told Hahn and Jensen and McKittrick in the taxi.

"I buy you drink," he had said. "But no bed. Go home to Stateside girl, maybe couple days."

She had smiled.

"We'll see about dat. Maybe you change your mind."
She had laid a hand on his thigh. It was still there, but in
place of the discomforting warmth, his leg was now cool.
He pulled at his tie again, though its knot and his collar
were already pressureless against his throat. Then someone
shook his forearm on the table; he looked to his right, up
McKittrick's arm stretching past the girl between them.
McKittrick had his glass of beer lifted in a toast. They all
did, even the girls.

"To a UD," Hahn said.

His face reminded Ted of the sailor whom he vaguely
recalled from the rest room of the first bar: grinning, and
so numb that you imagined his skull awash with alcohol,
his consciousness drowned.

"Toast, Goddammit," Hahn said.

Ted's hand touched his beer bottle; its tepid surface
made him swallow, and he withdrew his hand, shaking
his head.

"Might not get one," he said.

Jensen chuckled and lowered his glass. The others still
had theirs raised.

"To a UD," Hahn said, looking at Ted, and Jensen
picked up his glass and raised it with the others—
Amiko too (he could see her lifted then disappearing
glass out of the corner of his left eye)—but Ted's hands
lay on the table.

"And why won't you get one, Teddy-Baby?" Hahn said.

Ted focused on him, at the end of the table. All night
Hahn had been sitting at the head of a table, sending his
voice down it like static in Ted's mind as he had groped to

understand what he, Ted Freeman, was doing in this suspended drunken hiatus, so far away from Jan, so far away from all that he deserved. It occurred to him that Hahn would fold if you kicked him in the balls.

"I'm going to write to Sen'tor Magnuson of Washington. Lieutenant tol' me to."

Jensen grinned and started talking to his girl again. McKittrick said something that Ted did not hear.

"He told you that, huh?" Hahn said.

"Yep. Got to write it early tomorrow and send it airmail." He opened his mouth to laugh but nothing happened, as if the climbing nausea would not allow it. So he forced a sound like a laugh, and said: "He tol' me when sen'tors fart gen'rals *inhale*."

Hahn was talking to him. Ted pushed his chair away from the table, told Amiko he would be right back, and as he was leaving the only thing he heard was Hahn's weirdly excited shout:

"I want to see that letter!"

He weaved between crowded tables, sidestepped a Marine in uniform at the rest room door, the Marine's haircut dully registering on his mind as the mark of a seagoing man, and he lowered his eyes in shame at his pale face, his loosened collar and tie. He made it. For five minutes, which seemed as long as the evening had been (he even thought he recalled and somehow relived each swallow of beer and bite of sukiyaki as it left him), he was helpless. He thought dying must be like this, your body turned against you finally, doing things you couldn't resist—and he felt wretched, no better than a muttering wino on a dark street. As with the loneliness of love, he thought of himself sleeping in the barracks, his letters to Jan and Senator Magnuson already in the mailbox for tomorrow's plane. In some future time he was sitting with Jan in the living room of a strange host, nursing a (he was sick again) beer and saying calmly: *I don't drink much anymore.* No matter what happened after his letter to Senator Magnuson—and he would write those letters tomorrow, if it took hiding in the Base Library—he would change. *I'll never get drunk again*, he told Jan; then, trembling and gasping, almost went to his knees.

Once they reached the States, he would never see Hahn and Jensen and McKittrick again. Maybe he would not write to Senator Magnuson, just take his discharge and start a life of his own in Oakland, or that place near the mountains. What place?—His stomach doubled him over, dry heaves now, and he waited for it to give him peace. Monterey, or east of the Cascades: two places he had never been. But he would write the letter, not to stay in the Corps so much but to show them on the *Vanguard*. Shift the sand under their cages, the Lieutenant had said. To show everybody. He did not immediately know who everybody was. Then he did: they were the people back home, or wherever they were now, boys and girls who had spurned him or barely noticed him. *You remember Ted Freeman? Well, get this: he's in the MaRINE Corps now and he's married to this great-looking—I always thought he was cute but he was so shy—*For some reason the girl was that cheerleader, the older girl with long dark hair, who was said to be putting out; a girl he had never spoken to. He replaced her with the faint image of a girl he had managed to date on those times when the whole class did something together—picnics, dances—and it took more nerve to stay home than it did to go. He had not thought of her in a long time; with pain made easily bearable by the demands of his stomach, he realized that she never thought of him either. His body jerked double, shivering, and he sobbed at his futility to resist it.

Before leaving, he washed his face, buttoned his collar, and adjusted his necktie. He stepped out and was struck by light and sound which threatened and halted him. Then he moved into it. When he sat down Amiko said, with sweet concern that both soothingly and disturbingly dispelled the isolation he had felt in the rest room:

"You been sick, Ted-san?"

"A little."

"I get you something."

She wore a green silk kimono which pulled tightly at her hips as she walked to the bar, coming back with ginger ale for him and a drink for herself. After she was settled and smoking one of his cigarettes, her hand returned to his thigh. He looked at the bottle of beer, thinking of how warm and flat it was, and pushed it farther away. Then Hahn was standing at the end of the table.

"Upstairs, men."

Ted lit a cigarette and then merely held it after feeling that first breath of smoke on his throat; he pretended to be unaware of Hahn's girl standing and looking at the other girls. Amiko squeezed his leg.

"We go upstairs now?"

He glanced at her and shook his head. They were all on their feet, except him and Amiko; one of the girls spoke in Japanese and Amiko shrugged.

"What's the matter, Teddy-Baby?" McKittrick said. "Can't get one up?"

"Jesus, I had one up since I come in here."

"You going to stay down here and play with it?" Hahn said. "Maybe he's going to write a letter with it. It's about the right size."

He took a ballpoint pen from his trouser pocket and held it up, while the girls laughed and Amiko's hand moved down between Ted's legs.

"No lead in his pencil," Hahn said. "No pencil. Leave on ship. Forgot all about it."

Amiko's voice penetrated the giggles and laughter:

"No, not true. He bring to Iwakuni. To *Am*iko."

Her hand moved again and Ted grabbed it.

"Jesus Christ, Teddy-Baby," Hahn said.

He was turning to leave.

"I don't want to catch anything, man. I got a Stateside shackup."

"You sonofabitch kid," Amiko said; to him it sounded like a scream and, his eyes on her angry face, he thought everyone in the place must be staring at him now. Her hand was gone.

"I *clean*. You ——"

"Ssshhh: okay. A joke, huh? I know you clean. Very pretty girl. We go topside, okay?"

Her face softened and, before he knew it, her hand had gone to his leg and moved up.

"You sure?" Amiko said.

"See?" Hahn said. "I told you."

"Too much beer," he said to Amiko, hardly hearing his own words for the laughter. "I be okay. You see."

"*Ho*-kay."

She rose, took his hand as Hahn said something about letter to senator, and looking straight ahead and feeling that he was the only one in the place who was going upstairs with a whore, he followed them. At the small landing they were briefly squeezed together, so Ted's back was pressed against the cool brick wall. Then Hahn and his girl started up, and soon Ted was ascending behind Amiko whose kimono slipped up to expose her calves, for the stairs were as narrow and steep as a ship's ladder.

When she closed the door of the bedroom at the top of the stairs, the first thing he felt was silence: Hahn's voice gone, the others too, faded down the hall. She was standing in front of him. Maybe now he could refuse. But he thought of her screaming at him, saying she was clean, cursing him, even forcing him to pay—and the others hearing it and grinning in beds down the hall. She unbuckled his blouse, and he asked her to turn out the light. When she got back to him in the dark, he was turned away, standing on one leg as he took off his trousers. She did not touch him. He heard the kimono rustle from her shoulders and, naked, he went past her and lay in bed, on his side. As she got into bed, he started to reach for her but did not; then she was close to him.

"Poor Ted-san drink too much. Here: you take it easy."

He tried to raise his head against the nausea which was coming back; but it ebbed, was gone, as her hands moved.

Well—Maybe he would be all right. She was his second woman, and a man certainly rated at least one more before he got married. Jan had probably had more—Probably. For too long he had been saying that. He had no idea what a virgin was like (deprived of that too) but he knew she had not been one. Although he had heard that many young girls lost it in other ways. But Jan had been so easy. If she had been a virgin it might have been different; as it was, though, he deserved this—He was surprised. Why, there was no difference at all, and she—now he remembered her name—Amiko could have been Jan. But after a while there was a difference, and Amiko finally asked him.

"Soon," he said. "Too much beer."

He saw himself asleep in the barracks, his letters mailed. Then Jan was sitting in her apartment, watching television. She looked up at him when he told her he was sorry, her face neither angry nor disgusted, but disappointed. She had waited so long, dressing carefully to hide the growing child from the people at work, from her parents: she must have tried to avoid them, made up excuse after excuse when they asked her to spend a Sunday in Stockton. He thought of those Sundays when her parents drove to Oakland: Jan wearing a loose dress, forcing herself to eat, throwing up with both faucets turned on and the toilet flushing as repeatedly as it could. He saw her with strained smile and voice, forcing her eyelids to stay open and her eyes to remain fixed on whoever asked about her boyfriend on the ship. All that time she was the only one in the world waiting for him: she had stood all that, had never mentioned abortion in those early months when it would have been possible, had never doubted (he assumed, hoped, then knew) that what she wanted was to live with him: a young kid who didn't even know his way around San Francisco—or any other place, for that matter—who hardly ever liked himself unless he was with her, who was not even a man, so that here he was, tired and beginning to soften, Amiko hardly moving now, when all he had to do was simply get home, walk into the apartment and squeeze her while she talked and cried and pressed her head against his jaw until it hurt—

He heard voices down the hall. Someone was finished, or maybe all of them, and they would go now. He was ready to stop, had reached the point where, without shame, he could explain to Amiko what was already obvious, then go back to the Base. But he did not stop. He decided to wait: give them enough time to get downstairs, see that he wasn't finished, then leave him. Until then, he would continue with Amiko. And that was what he was doing several moments later when the door opened and light from the hall crossed his legs, followed by Hahn's voice:

"You getting seconds, Teddy-Baby?"

And Hahn's girl:

"No, no—you no go in there."

But over his shoulder, poised as he was, Ted saw Hahn, Jensen, and McKittrick step into the room. One of them shut the door.

"Don't stop now, Teddy-Baby," Hahn said.

Someone crossed the room, and Ted was sitting near Amiko's feet, on the edge of the bed, when Hahn turned on the light. He got up quickly and went for his clothes.

"What did I tell you?" Hahn said.

Amiko started cursing him. With his back turned he dressed, Amiko cursing still and Hahn and McKittrick and Jensen saying things he knew he would hear at night for the rest of his life. He buttoned his shirt, pulled on his trousers, and carrying his blouse, cap, and tie, started for the door. McKittrick was blocking it, but he didn't care. Before he reached the door, he turned to look at Amiko, tears glistening as she knotted the belt around her kimono, screaming at Hahn:

"Why you do dat, you sonofabitch mean bastard—"

Ted faced her.

"That's right," he said. "That's what he is." He looked at Hahn, who was grinning.

"Just like the Lieutenant said: he's yellow."

Hahn moved close to him.

"That right, Teddy-Baby?"

Hahn stiff-armed his chest, pushing him backward.

"Show me, Teddy-Baby."

Ted had the blouse over one arm, his cap and tie held in that hand, and he knew that if he dropped the clothes he would be just as committed as if he had raised his fists. McKittrick was still at the door, Jensen a few paces inside the room; either one could stop him. But if he got his knee into Hahn—and that knee was telling him now to move forward, get within range—maybe they would be too surprised to grab him before he ran out the door. Hahn shoved him again; Amiko, who had been quiet, began her loud repetitive cursing; and Ted waited for the next time Hahn closed the distance between them. But when the moment came his legs refused, or he refused them, and after that shove he was near the door, hearing quick climbing footsteps under Amiko's voice. A stocky Japanese man looked past McKittrick's shoulder, into the room; then he went downstairs again.

"Let's go," McKittrick said. "He's calling the Shore Patrol."

"So *what?*" Hahn said. "What can *they* do?"

Jensen said something about a UD. Then Hahn pushed Ted with both hands and he went backward, glancing off McKittrick, into the hall. Now Hahn was at the door, the other two just behind him but still in the room, and Ted shouted:

"What are you trying to *prove?* Here—"he lifted his right arm, bent at the elbow, tightening his bicep "—*feel* it. You can beat on me all day and it won't prove a Goddamn *thing.*"

Grinning, Hahn felt his bicep, then Ted jerked his arm down to his side again.

"You're right, Teddy-Baby: I guess everything you got is tiny."

"At least I just stick mine in women, you queer sonofabitch."

He saw the swing beginning in Hahn's face and a slight shifting of his weight, and he was bringing up his left arm when the fist struck his jaw, lifting him, sending him backward against the wall, then onto his hands and knees: looking at the floor, he wished he had been knocked out. Incredible that anyone could hit so hard. He gathered his blouse, tie, and cap, then stood up. Hahn put his left hand behind his back.

"Come on, Teddy-Baby. One hand."

Ted slowly shook his head.

"You'd eat shit, wouldn't you? I'm going to do it again, Teddy-Baby. Watch it, baby, it's coming—" Hahn was bobbing and weaving in front of him. There must be words, some way he could stop this; then he saw it coming and ducked to one side so it struck him near his left eye, knocking him to the floor. He lay on his side, considered staying there until someone lifted him to his feet. Then he got up. Somewhere beneath his dazed pain, his limp weight, he thought that just for Hahn to see his face would be enough, that surely he looked like the most helpless, the most pitiful—Hahn slapped him.

"Cut it out, Hahn," he said.

Hahn's right hand was moving again, and Ted got his arm up in time to block it, but Hahn slapped him with his left.

"Don't *slap* me, Hahn!"

McKittrick and Jensen were in the hall now. Then Amiko came out and ran past Ted, down the stairs, and watching her he slid his feet closer to the stairs. Two strides and he could be running down them.

"Come on," McKittrick said. "You can't make him fight."

"Fuck you," Ted said.

Hahn slapped him, harder than before. Jensen and McKittrick were far enough to Hahn's rear; he could easily make the stairs, and if he could use surprise, could get his knee up there real hard, then he could be downstairs before Jensen or McKittrick moved after him. Real hard: drive them right up into Hahn's throat, send that big sonofabitch to the floor, paralyzed. He half-turned, his left side to Hahn, and said:

"Fuck all you guys: I'm going."

As Hahn stepped forward, Ted spun to meet him, his knee coming up fast; but Hahn saw it, twisted his hips, and caught it on his leg. Ted had only an instant to wish he had never tried that before Hahn's fist, coming around with the full weight of his untwisting body, hit his chin and drove him straight back, falling to nothing, to the stairs, sliding down head first on his back, his vaguely conscious mind clutching the duration of his fall as something peaceful, saving, an ultimate respite—

He did not know whether his eyes were open. Voices above him spoke in Japanese, then he heard a familiar one but could not recognize it. He was aware that he was lying on his back, his legs stretched out, his arms probably at his sides; but he could neither move nor feel his arms and legs. Cold was all he felt, and absolute weakness: he did not want to move or be awake to hear those voices above him, one of them shrill as a hovering bird. Then he felt the blood on his neck: from some wound he could not locate, it was spurting warmly at regular intervals. At first, like a child wetting the bed, he gave himself up to its pleasant warmth on his cool skin. Then he was afraid.

When he woke again, his fear was waiting for him like the pain of illness; whatever remained of his consciousness searched for the bleeding and found it: a pulsating flow of blood at the back of head, but still he could not feel the cut. Then he heard the siren—rather, allowed it to enter his mind now that he had finished looking for the source of his bleeding—and he looked up at the dark head and chest of a man, who was speaking guttural Japanese. Now he felt the man's fingers pressing the side of his throat and, with a gasp that he was too weak to make audible—as if some very small part of him in his chest, the only part he was aware of now, had taken that startled breath—he knew he was dying.

Either his eyes or head moved to the right: he saw a long bright ribbon of neon signs, thought of the word *Iwakuni*, and had no recollection of why he was here. He had one clear thought: nothing in the entire world mattered except Jan, for she loved him and her hands would cover her grieving face, and he knew that he should not be here, he had done something irrevocably wrong. Now he felt the vibration of the engine, as if he were sinking into the floor of the ambulance, merging with it.

Chapter Seven

STANDING IN FRONT of Captain Howard's desk two hours after the Marines had attacked and theoretically sunk the *Vanguard*, Dan read a copy of the message from the Commanding General of Iwakuni; the original had been sent to the Commandant of the Marine Corps. In the language of telegrams, the message said that Hahn, Jensen, and McKittrick were being held for investigation concerning the assault and battery of Pvt. Theodore C. Freeman. It ended with: *Freeman critical condition USNH Iwakuni fractured skull*. Looking at Freeman's printed name, Dan saw him chasing his barracks cap down the flight deck. Then he looked at Captain Howard.

"He was your orderly," he said.

He dropped the message, watched it fall slowly and settle near a thin stack of papers; on the top one, he saw his name.

"Is that my fitness report and letter?"

"Yes. You may read them now, if you like. If you'd rather wait—"

"Might as well. Everything else happens at once around here."

He read them quickly, standing with his weight on one stiffened leg. "That's not me," he said, and tossed them on the desk. He picked up the message and looked at its last sentence.

"Mister Tierney, I know you don't want my advice, but I'll give it anyway. You notice your fitness report says that with more experience you might develop into a good career officer, provided you gain some maturity. But I'm beginning to wonder. It looks to me like you've given up. You're acting like some of my disgruntled Reserve officers. I was informed of your poor leadership this morning. What you said over those phones is inexcusable from an officer. It's harmful to the morale of the men—and you say you're concerned about their welfare."

"Good old Gun Boss: doesn't miss a chance."

"There are other officers on this ship besides Commander Craig."

"That's right. There's Doc Butler and you."

"Mister Tierney, another indication of your poor attitude is that I have to remind you, a Marine officer, that you have not said *sir* since you came into this cabin."

"Shit. Freeman's dying."

He tossed the message toward the desk, saw with satisfaction that it fell short, and walked out. He went to his room and sat down with pen and paper. But he did not begin his statement. He would write to Jan first, get her address from the brig mail log, and there was no use writing that letter until—When he realized what he was waiting for, he left his room. In the passageway he stopped. He went back into his room, phoned Tolleson, and said to meet him on the sponson deck where physical conditioning was held.

On his way there he approached the dispensary passageway, turned into it, and knocked loudly on the door marked *Medical Officer*. Then he pushed it open, slamming against a desk, and two chief petty officers turned from the coffee percolator but he did not see them: across the room Doc Butler sat behind his desk, and Dan pointed his swagger stick at him:

"If I sign a statement that I'm a habitual masturbator, will it ruin your Goddamn career?"

He stepped in far enough to grab the doorknob, watching Butler's surprise changing to embarrassment, not anger; then he left, slamming the door.

Tolleson was waiting on the sponson deck; the sea was calm and blue again, and Dan wished he could wave his swagger stick, changing blue to grey and black, lapping waves to water crashing against the hull. They saluted, then stood by the guardrail while Dan told him about Freeman, the changed decision of the board, his letter of reprimand, unsatisfactory fitness report, and transfer.

"Sir, if I went berserk and shot that Goddamn Captain, how many years would I get?"

"About what Hahn will get, if it was him and they find him guilty: ten years."

"Well sir. I'd be forty-eight then—it might be worth it."

Dan was thinking that in ten years he would be thirty-five; by that time you were supposed to be a major, a year or so from lieutenant-colonelcy and the command of a battalion. For a while he was quiet. He could think of nothing he wanted in ten years except to be a major, an executive officer of an infantry battalion.

"How are the troops?" he said.

"Confused, sir. I ain't passed much word 'cause I can't keep up with it."

"Get them together in the classroom, and I'll talk to them. In about fifteen minutes. First I want to tell Mr. Price about Freeman."

"Aye aye, sir."

Alex was not in his room. His office was somewhere in the island, and to find it would take more time than Dan felt he had, so he phoned from Alex's room. He spoke quickly, only slowing down when he realized he was delivering pain so fast that Alex could not vocally react to it. When Alex asked him to go to the wardroom for coffee so they could talk about his statement to the Commandant, Dan said it would have to be later because right now he had to meet with the troops.

"They need drawing together," he said. "I've been so fouled up lately that I forgot about them."

He left Alex's room, turning into a passageway that went by the Gunnery Office, and thought of stopping to tell the Gun Boss that an innocent boy was dying in Iwakuni. But it was a fleeting thought, as if only from habit, and he kept on to where he was going: the troops.

They came to attention, rows of them standing in front of benches; he paused at the foot of the ladder, behind them: their shoulders and backs were straight, some wearing pressed tropicals for guard duty, others in starched green utilities; all had crew cuts, the backs of their heads nearly shaved. He moved around to their front, stepping past Tolleson who stood at the rear, and told them to sit down.

"The smoking lamp is lit," he said.

About three-quarters of them reached into socks or utility shirt pockets for cigarettes. His swagger stick in one fist, he put both hands on his hips. Looking at their faces he saw them walking out of the Chosin Reservoir, pinned down in the surf at Tarawa, holding at Guadalcanal, fighting their way inland at Iwo Jima; he thought of them wearing bowl-shaped helmets and overcoats in Belleau Wood, saw them marching past the reviewing stand at his retirement parade, none of them knowing how each marching step pulled at his heart, while gold bugles and scarlet drums glittered in the sun—

"First of all," he said, "some information. Pfc McKittrick and Privates Freeman, Hahn, and Jensen appeared before a board of three Naval officers. They were represented by counsel—Mr. Price—" He spoke louder, watching the troops but talking to Tolleson really, showing him the approach he had chosen, the only approach there finally was "—After a long hearing, the board recommended that these four Marines receive Undesirable Discharges." He lowered his voice. "In the cases of Hahn, Jensen, and McKittrick it was for passive homosexual acts in San

Francisco—in other words, they went with queers for money. Keep that in mind if you end up broke on liberty. Also, the incident that occurred here added up against them. Private Freeman was cleared by the ONI of any previous homosexual experiences. *However*, because of that grab-ass the other night, he was found guilty of lewd and obscene acts. You all know how Captain Schneider, the First Sergeant, and I feel about that particular Marine. We made him an orderly for the Captain of this ship. But the discipline of the Chosin Reservoir is not formed on the football fields of America—" He paused, regretting an allusion they would not grasp "—it is formed right here, on this ship, every day. Or on the hills of Camp Pendleton. Or the boondocks at Camp Lejeune. Or whatever duty station where Marines are. What sets us apart from our sister services, and I mean sister—" they glanced at each other, wearing smiles "—is discipline and a brave tradition that goes back to the first young hard-charging Marine who enlisted at Tun's Tavern in 1775. Those things—discipline and tradition—must be enforced. Even when it seems unfair."

He looked over their heads at Tolleson, standing with folded arms, his face nearly as interested as theirs.

"We are part of a whole," he said. "Just like a bolt is part of a rifle—" that disturbed him "—or a shortstop is part of a ball club. And every Marine, every one of the one hundred and seventy-five thousand of us, must carry his load, submit to discipline, enforce traditions, fit smoothly as part of the whole. Now: back to Freeman. His case was a little different from the others, so as his Acting CO I felt obliged to write the Commandant and recommend that he be retained on active duty. Whether or not he's cleared is not the main thing. What's more important is that the regulations we live by are being upheld. As long as—" glancing at Tolleson's face, quizzical now, he suddenly remembered where Freeman was "—as long as each of us upholds these regulations the Marine Corps will continue to be what it has been and is: the best fighting organization in the world, the organization you joined.

"There is more about Freeman. Captain Howard received a message this morning stating that he is in the hospital at Iwakuni. He has a fractured skull and his condition is critical. Hahn, Jensen, and McKittrick are being held for investigation at Iwakuni. Freeman was apparently beaten up—" They were turning to each other, or twisting around to look at a friend; some began to whisper.

"You people knock it off," Tolleson said.

When they were all facing him again, Dan went on:

"I'm as concerned as you are—maybe more—and I'll let you know as soon as I hear any word."

But he realized that wasn't it: few of them were actually concerned. Today and perhaps tomorrow they would go through phases of emotions which they would consider pity or outrage; but most of all they would be interested. Something new had entered their lives, and his timing of the announcement was overshadowing those things he had felt before speaking, those things he had to say.

"Now. Those are the only announcements I have. I wanted to talk to you for another reason too. I want to congratulate you and thank you for a job well done during the air defense exercise. Since I spent my watches on the signal bridge, I wasn't able to be with you in the gun mount watches. I know it was a long boring duty. Soldiering often is. We wait and we wait and we wait. But that's part of discipline too. And when the waiting's over, Marines are ready, just as you were when general quarters sounded this morning. Course we didn't shoot the planes down—" they started grinning "—but we *could* have. Or I should say you could have. I suppose there are some sailor officers aboard who have a low opinion of this ship. Because this morning when I hollered sink the son of a bitch, they thought I was referring to the *Vanguard*—" he smiled back at them "—well, I've called this ship a few names now and then, but it happens that this morning I was talking about those A4*Dee's*."

He had them now: they didn't know whether or not he was telling the truth, but they would believe him anyway; and those who doubted yet still believed him would feel they were in collusion with him, that they were joining him in some victory over the rest of the ship. He leaned forward, his face serious, and waited until their smiles were gone.

"And I'll tell you something: if the Navy would throw out this obsolete radar and let you Marines fire those guns manually, you'd have shot down some A4D's."

He stood erectly again.

"I believe that, because you're Marines."

He scanned the faces in the first two rows.

"And it's *your* Marine Corps."

He looked at the next two rows of attentive believing faces.

"You're the troops: the ones who make the Corps what it is."

His eyes swept over all of them.

"And I'm glad to be in it with you."

Before he had taken three steps, Tolleson called them to attention. With his eyes straight ahead, he moved past them and Tolleson, up the ladder.

He did not see Alex until lunch. After the other junior officers had eaten and left, they stayed and drank coffee and talked for a while about Freeman, trying to imagine what had happened; neither Alex nor Dan thought Freeman had actually fought with anyone. They guessed he had been beaten up for telling Doc Butler. Finally it was Alex who mentioned Dan's statement to the Commandant.

"I can't think about it till I get word on Freeman," Dan said. "You're sure Kellog will tell the truth?"

"No doubt about it. I'll tell you something else: Commander Craig will too. He won't lie to an investigating officer."

"So that leaves Captain Howard."

"And he'll have to tell the truth."

"That'll be new," Dan said. "I just hope they don't bring me back as a witness."

"Wouldn't it be worth it?"

"I wouldn't set foot on this bucket to watch him get stripped of his rank and drummed out. I'll read your letters about it, in some quiet duty station on land. Wherever that'll be."

He was wondering where and what that duty would be when the next message came, in late afternoon. Cap-

tain Howard phoned him at the Detachment office and
told him Freeman had died. Dan looked at Tolleson, who
read his face; then Dan pointed to the classroom and
Tolleson nodded and went out. Captain Howard said the
ONI had a signed confession from Hahn, saying he had
knocked Freeman down a flight of stairs in a Japanese
tavern. There would be a general court-martial. Iwakuni
would inform Freeman's parents and arrange for his body
to be shipped home. Dan said "Yes, sir" and "Thank you,
sir" and hung up.

The troops were waiting on the benches. He only spoke
long enough to tell the few details he knew; but even in
that short time, Freeman's name in his throat began to
sound dead. As he talked, he watched the troops leaning
into his words. Their faces were serious rather than sad.
Burns seemed most upset of all: he was staring between
his knees at the deck. When Dan said the ONI had a
signed confession from Hahn, Burns looked up, his back
straightening, his face vengeful, triumphant. One man
half-raised a closed fist, thumb pointing up, to a friend.
Another elbowed the man beside him, and nodded. There
was not one face which did not show at least approval.

"I'm sure you can count on justice," Dan said, and dis-
missed them.

In the office he copied Jan's address from the brig mail
log, keeping his back turned to Tolleson; without knowing
why, he wanted to be alone. Then he went to Freeman's
bunk. It had been stripped of sheets and blanket; the un-
covered pillow lay on the black rubber mattress. The shelf
where Jan's picture had been was empty, the small lockers

open, containing nothing save a fresh layer of dust. When he left the berthing area and went up the ladder, he was trying to find a reason, not for Freeman's death, but for his life. He had hardly begun to live, had been swept along by various forces; and had died, leaving nothing but a nameless child and a girl whose life he had altered.

In his stateroom he phoned Alex; when he heard Alex's voice he could recall Freeman again as he had been able to before telling the troops of his death. He said "Alex?" his eyes closing on that slender kid who had been cursed with a pretty face and a small penis, and he thought of how Freeman's heart must have swelled and pumped when Jan looked at him, touched him, wrote him a letter—with his eyes still shut, he said:

"He's dead, Alex. They killed that Goddamned little boy."

Then he was crying. He hung up, his head dropping to the desk, his arms folding under his forehead. He saw all of Freeman's life as he had known it, each memory jerking his body, hurting his throat: when he remembered throwing Freeman against the bulkhead, he moaned. He had done it too, had exposed and used Freeman's weakness to be at Hahn in the only way he could—but more: in Freeman's scared eyes there was something he had to deny by attacking it. Yet no one in this world should ever have laid a hand on Freeman. *The last time I saw him his cap blew over the side and the sailors laughed.* He thought of Jan waiting in California for something to happen, Freeman to find a way to get home, or—when she would be seven months' pregnant—for the ship finally to return.

She would probably not even go to the funeral, add to its grief her swollen body; she would not have those last hours with his repaired face, would forever be without the finality of ceremony and grave. Then he was thinking of Khristy, and now his tears were for her.

After a long while, realizing he had missed the evening meal, he climbed to the sponson deck. The night was clear and warm. For the second time in a couple of hours he felt that Freeman only existed in the past. Freeman's involvement in his future was the letter he would write to Jan tonight, and his statement to the Commandant tomorrow. Both finally, by God, the truth. And it was about time. There had been too many days when he had fought with ghosts, all of them lies.

But as he looked down at the black waves, he was reminded of death. No matter what Jan knew or did not know, Ted Freeman was dead. She would have the baby alone, saddened and ashamed; and sometimes, feeding it, she would see Freeman's face and weep. But there were things in her favor: since she had started loving him, he had been away more than he had been with her. She had waited for letters and his return. Now she only had to stop waiting. A terrible wrenching grief, yes; but she would make it. In a couple of years, or perhaps less, she would remember him as the young boy she had loved, father of the child on whom she would gradually focus that love. Pretty girls married, and certainly she would too, probably claiming the truthful lie of widowhood. While now she loved her past with Freeman and their future together, in time she would love his memory alone.

THE LIEUTENANT • 235

As he raised his eyes from the water to the clear sky of stars and moon, it occurred to him that there was no reason to make her memories painful. If Freeman had already written her about the Undesirable Discharge, he was helpless to shape her future. But he ought to follow his own course, on the chance that she knew nothing. To add outrage and pity to her grief was senseless: he would write that, while on liberty in Iwakuni, Freeman had— He tapped his swagger stick on the guardrail. Unless she went to the funeral, she would not even know how he died, would be spared the images of Freeman's beating. He would tell her that Freeman had fallen down a ladder aboard ship. He would write the letter tonight, but would mail it from Iwakuni, several days after Freeman's body had been sent home. He felt that he was cheating her, for she might have wanted to attend the funeral; but he was certain that this was the best way. To live, she hardly needed the truth.

His orders arrived by message next morning while he was at the barracks. A sailor from the Gunnery Office delivered them and Dan smiled at Tolleson.

"Looks like the Captain and the Gun Boss are using delivery boys now."

"Maybe they got conscience problems, sir."

He unfolded the message. It told him to stand immediately detached from the USS *Vanguard*, to report to the Commanding General, First Marine Air Wing, Iwakuni, for further transportation to the continental United

236 • ANDRE DUBUS

States where he would report, with thirty days' delay, to the Commanding General, Second Marine Division, Camp Lejeune, North Carolina, for duty in the Second Force Service Regiment. He closed the door and sat down.

"FSR," he said.

He gave the message to Tolleson.

"Well, sir, I'd say they had a quota to fill just about the time the Lieutenant's name came up."

"I'm being shanghaied."

"I wouldn't look at it that way, sir."

"*Jesus*—FSR isn't even the Marine Corps."

"Well, sir, like the Lieutenant was telling the troops, it's the bolt in that rifle."

"Come on, First Sergeant: you've seen officers get shanghaied before."

"Yes, sir. This is the first time I've seen it happen to a good one, though."

Dan picked up his swagger stick and sighted down its length.

"Maybe when the Commandant reads the Lieutenant's statement, he'll change his mind."

"I doubt it."

"I guess that's right, sir. There ain't no way in hell to fight city hall."

Dan stood up, looking at the cut in his swagger stick.

"I don't suppose anybody carries one of these in the FSR."

"Probably not, sir."

"I guess I'll go pack."

His letter to Jan was lying on the desk in his stateroom, already stamped and sealed. It was a thick letter, most of it

telling her what a good man Freeman had been, on board
ship and ashore. He had faked a knowledge of Freeman's
liberty habits, implying what he suspected: that Jan was
the last girl Freeman had made love to. He had almost
told her he regretted not sending Freeman home when
he had the chance; but he decided that, too, would only
add to her pain. He put the letter in his overnight bag. He
would mail it before leaving Iwakuni, and the whole thing
would be over.

Now he saw it clearly: Freeman was indeed finished. If
anything, the board's recommendation for his discharge
would be entered in his closed record book. Officially, he
died on active duty.

He read his orders again. When he had received orders to sea duty he had felt that somehow his name had
made an imprint on Headquarters Marine Corps: they
knew who he was, what he was going to become, and they
had given him a duty commensurate with his worth. Now
they had changed their minds and, with shame, he imagined them sternly speaking his name as they took him
away from the infantry, the troops, and sent him to a duty
where he could do neither bad nor good: Force Service
Regiment, when they dumped Reserve lieutenants with
poor attitudes, old ex-enlisted captains who had no future
except doing their jobs every day while they waited for the
twentieth year, majors and lieutenant-colonels who were
not given the command of infantry units because earlier
in their careers they had not been at the right place at
the right time or, being there, had not seized the promise
of the day. He would be with all those retread veterans

and misfit Reserves, working in a supply or maintenance unit, wandering among warehouses or garages or welding shops, a useless man among technicians. And the troops: he had seen them at Camp Pendleton, duck-tailed, soft, as unmilitary as the most casual sailor. They worked in shops or warehouses five days a week, were inspected rarely and leniently because no one expected them to look like Marines. In trucks and jeeps, they went to the field perhaps once a year when the entire division had an exercise; in the field—my God—they set up shower units for combat troops, established maintenance areas far behind the lines where they could work on vehicles and weapons. He had to grit his teeth when he remembered that they even had an ice cream platoon.

And the Marine Corps was relatively small: you never went to a duty station without running into an old friend. That was not all: people kept track of each other through *Navy Times* or *The Marine Corps Gazette*, and his friends would know that he had been ordered to the *Vanguard* (they would have envied that) and, after half a tour, transferred to the Second Division. At least the *Gazette* would only say: *From USS* Vanguard *to 2nd Marine Division*, and his friends would assume his duty was with the infantry. Still, in offices and clubs, they would be shaking their heads, wondering why Dan Tierney got orders so fast. Also, he could not complete a two- or three-year tour with the FSR without seeing old friends: giving them explanations which they would only partially believe, for everyone who was shanghaied or relieved or reprimanded always blamed the Old Man. Their eyes would shift with embarrasment for him as they listened: once in a while they would grant him a soft curse directed at the Navy Captain; but afterward he would be Dan Tierney, Honor Man at Basic School, who did all right as an infantry platoon commander but couldn't hack it as an Acting CO aboard ship.

Khristy would probably learn of his transfer from her father, who would see his name in the *Gazette*. Maybe she would write him then, knowing he was in trouble. And though he yearned for that letter, he forcefully shook his head, pressed his palms on the desk. If she wrote, it would be with the hope that he was disillusioned and was going to resign. Only for a moment did he consider resigning. If he did that, it was all over: those whisperings of destiny he had heard for seven years, since he first saw the Officer Procurement Officer, a Marine captain in blues, standing near the table and posters in the student union at college. He was not just any man, to sit at a desk or drive around selling things—he had a profession.

His hands were twisting his swagger stick: for three years he would not lead infantry troops in the field. He would not lead anyone. He would watch them work, he would do some paperwork of his own, then go to the BOQ at night and shine his shoes.

He phoned Alex and asked him to go to the wardroom for coffee. Then he went up and waited in the lounge. When Alex came in, Dan caught himself before he averted his eyes. He followed Alex to an empty table and sat beside him, watching a group of junior officers several tables away. He envied their apparent satisfaction.

"You don't understand it," he said, "but you know how I feel about the Corps."

"I understand."

"Wrong word, then. You don't approve."

"I approve of you. I just don't approve of the Marine Corps." Dan shrugged.

"They don't approve of me right now," he said. "I just got a bad set of orders: a service regiment at Camp Lejeune. It's where they put officers so they won't do any more harm. I'm pretty sure I'll get passed over for captain next year and picked up the second time around, in two years. But it's not the promotion I'm worried about: it's doing two or three years in that service regiment, and losing face by getting passed over once."

"I know. I wouldn't say you've acted like a promotion-sweater lately."

Dan remembered how good he had felt when he yelled at Captain Howard and was put under arrest. Still watching the junior officers, he said:

"You become a Marine infantry officer and you think for the rest of your career you'll at least have pride every day. Then they take it away from you." Now he looked at Alex. "For the next two or three years I'll be ashamed of where I work."

"You know that doesn't really matter."

"It does in my world."

"That's the whole trouble."

Dan shook his head.

"No. Listen: I've always been scornful of those guys who aren't line officers. Disbursing, supply, motor transport—I always thought they were just making a living, they weren't really Marines. And now I'm one of them. But I *shouldn't* be: I'm a good Marine. The Marine Corps might not know it right now, but they need me."

He stopped, lifted his hands from the table, and let them fall.

"It's because I *believe. Or* like that general I told you about, what he said: Living the lie and making the lie come true—"

"—We've been doing the first half of that around here for some time."

"Then it's time to start on the last half. I've got to square away at FSR so I can get back to the troops. I'm not going to resign. It's comeback or nothing. Like the Communists say: one step backward and two forward. When I go to that fat happy outfit, I'll have to keep my mouth shut, stop fighting city hall."

"I thought that's what city hall was for."

"Not if you believe in it."

"You can't—not after the past three days on this ship."

"I believe in what it stands for."

"Yes. But what it stands for is—"

Then Alex stopped, put a hand on Dan's shoulder, and squeezed; then his hand was gone.

"All right," he said. "I believe in a few abstract lies too. Like justice. Only thing is, my little beliefs are relatively harmless."

He finished his coffee, frowning as he swallowed, because it had cooled.

"Forget I said that. What about your letter to the Commandant?"

Dan stood up.

"I'll go do that now and see what happens."

For a long while before writing his statements—one for the letter of reprimand and another for the unsatisfactory fitness report—he lay on his bunk, making absolutely sure that his alternatives were simply defined: revenge or his profession. Recalling his fights with Captain Howard he knew he would write to the Commandant and even Magnuson if Freeman were still alive. He had the courage for that. But with Freeman dead, the most he could accomplish with a new fight was revenge, an immediate goal, a thing of the present and therefore almost the past. If he took this revenge, focused his life on one issue right now, he might change the course of his own future. He hoped that after leaving the Force Service Regiment he would command an infantry company. Someday a battalion; then, if he was lucky, a regiment. And he would not get command billets by establishing a reputation as a troublemaker. Already his name was too familiar at Headquarters Marine Corps; it was the wrong time to send a letter accusing Captain Howard of dishonesty, especially when the victim of that dishonesty had become a dead horse.

In a way, he owed it to Freeman to endure as a professional. The dead Freeman did not need avenging; but other Freemans, in junior high schools now all over the United States, would some day need him as their commanding officer, just as he needed them as evidence of his worth. He had something to give them: he could infuse his spirit into training which would make them better men and possibly save their lives as well. That was his final choice; those men who, after two or three years, he would lead.

He left his bunk. Sitting at his desk, he opened his box of stationery. Khristy's letter was there, in its thin blue envelope. He picked it up and read his name and address, then hers. He took two sheets of stationery and dropped Khristy's letter back in the box.

For a while he did not write. He was not hesitating: he had made his decision, and now he was suffering the consequences before his writing made them real, like a man trying a razor blade on his arm before pressing it to his throat. He knew there was more than Freeman involved, that Freeman represented a truth which also needed avenging; yet last night, in his letter to Jan, he had denied that truth. Some part of him as palpable as blood had flowed then; and now he sat, even looking at his right hand, as if he could actually see and feel the blood coursing down his arm to gather in his fingers.

Then he picked up his pen and wrote the first of his statements, using the words which he would repeat in his answer to the letter of reprimand:

I have seen subject fitness report and have no statement to make.

AT EIGHT O'CLOCK next morning, the *Vanguard* was approaching the harbor at Iwakuni. She was too large to moor at the pier, so she would drop anchor, and liberty boats would take the officers and crew ashore. From the sponson deck, where he stood alone, Dan watched

244 • ANDRE DUBUS

the steep green Japanese coast. He knew that Captain Schneider would be waiting at the pier, grinning, quickly returning the salute Dan would give him from the liberty boat, so he could wave. Dan pitied him for having to get all this news at once.

His footlocker and officer's suitcase were packed; his orders were endorsed, and his statements had been typed by Tolleson, who at first had been surprised, then—before Dan could explain—had said:

"That's probably a smart move, sir. Trouble don't raise the dead."

Last night Alex had spent an hour or so with him; Dan had folded uniforms and packed, rarely looking at Alex, who talked about all the possiblities in Hahn's case, finally guessing that Hahn would get the maximum sentence— ten years—and that some of it would be cut by the convening authority. When he asked about the statements, Dan had shrugged and said:

"They're typed and signed, for whatever that's worth."

"Good."

"If they don't follow up on it, we'll know that's the name of the game."

"I wouldn't be surprised at anything," Alex said. "I'll let you know."

Shortly after Taps Alex got up and said he was going to bed.

"We won't sleep tomorrow," he said. "You ready?"

"I'm ready. We'll throw a good one."

So they had not said goodbye, had put it off until to- night when they could drink. But tonight would not be

one of those memorable last drunks with a friend, those
farewells that imitate and foreshadow death. For Dan had
already told him goodbye, yesterday afternoon at his desk,
and it was becoming more difficult for him to look into
Alex's eyes. Now he breathed the salt air and watched the
bright green sunlit hills sliding past. He was having trouble finding something to do with his hands, for he had
packed his swagger stick in its cardboard case where it
would remain until he was a captain with his own infantry
company. Between him and that time, he could foresee
nothing out of the ordinary, no decisions that were not
routine. He would come and go unobtrusively, keeping his
energies dormant until the Corps let him emerge, restored
because forgotten, from the Force Service Regiment.

The *Vanguard* was passing cliffs now, rising straight
from the beach, and he remembered a time when Khristy
had passionately argued that the atomic bombing of Hiroshima and Nagasaki was immoral. Dan had failed to
show her why she was wrong; with tears in her eyes she
angrily shook her head and told him his naiveté was almost as evil as the pragmatic minds of generals and poli-
ticians. On this cruise he had been to Hiroshima, had seen
the museum, the monuments, the ruins at ground zero; he
had looked sorrowfully at children darting through alleys
or urinating on sidewalks. And two months ago, while
he and Alex were drinking one afternoon in a nearly
empty Yokosuka bar, the Japanese bar manager had talked
to them, had a drink with them, and even given them
two rounds. There had been something furtive about the
man, and Dan had assumed that he was going to offer

them women or pornography. So, prepared for that sort of encroachment, he was late understanding what the man actually wanted. Leaning toward Dan's face, he was pointing to the breast pocket of his coat, and saying: *On ship—you have ladiation?* his fingers inserted now into his pocket, an obsequious almost frightened grin on his face, and his eyes blinking and uncertain, as though he might cry—or run away—if he were rebuked. *Have what?* Dan said. Then he knew, an instant before Alex said it: *A dosimeter?* The man nodded excitedly, as if he were relieved, but he was not: he stopped grinning, leaned closer to Dan who was saying: *Tells radiation dosage,* pointing at his own pocket to show that they were talking about the same thing, the man's English was working, and dosimeters did indeed fit in your shirt pocket. Then the man said: *Can you get one? For me?* He was starting to smile again when Dan abruptly shook his head and said: *No, it can't be done,* and now it was Dan who wanted to run away. They had finished their drinks and left.

Now, two months later—and for all his life, he knew—he could vividly recall every nuance of that man's voice, every detail of his face, especially his eyes which must have been forty years old. Yet watching these cliffs from the ship he told Khristy once again: yes, by God, it was terrible; but there had been no other choice, for think of all those young Marines who would have died assaulting the beaches of Japan.

Afterword

IT'S BEEN MORE than forty years since I first read my father's only novel, *The Lieutenant*. I was perhaps nineteen or twenty years old, and I was visiting my father's mother at her small house on the water in Lake Charles, Louisiana. This may have happened in the summer, or it could have been Thanksgiving when I'd taken a bus from Austin, Texas, where I was a student at the university. The chronology here is hazy, but what I remember clearly is the look on my lovely Irish grandmother's face when I told her that I'd never read her son's first book. She was wearing a skirt and blouse, and she pursed her lips and shook her head, then led me to her small library, where she pulled her inscribed copy of *The Lieutenant* off a shelf and pushed it into my hands. I don't fully recall what she said to me then, but she seemed to be implying that it was disrespectful of me not to have read all of my father's work.

The truth is, I had read none of his fiction, or little of any other writer's, for that matter; I grew up in mill-town neighborhoods where if you were a dreamy boy who happily read novels, as I once had, then you tended to get ridiculed and beat up, and so I stopped. Instead, I became overly preoccupied with being as hard and masculine as I could possibly be, and I spent much of my time lifting weights and running and boxing, and so when I opened this novel and found myself reading from the point of view of Dan Tierney, a Marine lieutenant only four or five years older than I, a young officer trying very hard to be as good a leader of men as he possibly could be, I was hooked.

I was immediately drawn to our protagonist having been given "the prestige of being chosen to represent the Marine Corps aboard the largest ship in the Pacific . . ."and that "seagoing Marines are considered elite: traditionally they are at least six feet tall, firm-muscled, and sunburned, the kind who stare at you like your manhood's conscience from recruiting posters." I was even more drawn to the fact that "Dan himself was by no means six feet tall; he was three inches under that and slender (*lean but hard*, he thought, and it was true: he exercised daily) . . . ," for I, too, was about that height (as was my father) and as diligently as I worked out with weights, I could never put on much size so also considered myself merely "lean but hard." As I kept reading, I was taken by the disciplined rituals and routines of Marines aboard ship, of Dan Tierney leading his men in an hour of daily calisthenics on a sponson deck. I could feel Dan's loneliness for his girlfriend, Khristy, back in the States and his disappointment that she did not write to him as often as he wrote to her. But I was especially drawn to Dan's doubts about his competence as a Marine officer. "Then he would become uncertain and on some days he would feel that everything he did was wrong, that he was a totally incompetent misfit." I, too, felt this, that no matter how dramatically I had transformed myself from a victim to a fighter, I was still essentially a weakling and a coward. And as I kept reading one beautifully written page after another, I began to feel Dan's deep devotion to the Marine Corps and found it easy to understand why he covers up the sexual incident with Freeman and McKittrick and Hahn and Jensen, the latter two characters the kind of predatory men I found myself fighting in the streets of my youth.

And so, because I was young, because of my deep need at that time to be a man among men myself, it was through a very narrow emotional lens that I first experienced my father's novel, one he wrote when he was just a few years older than I was then.

I finished reading *The Lieutenant* three or four hours later. The sun was just beginning to sink beyond Lake Charles, and the wonderful smells of my grandmother's crawfish étouffée filled her house. I stood on her front porch and stared out at the water, its surface the color of flames, and I could feel something alight in me, too, for I was still living the dream my father had cast me in with his lean and forward-moving prose; I was feeling the ache of Dan Tierney's girlfriend gone forever from his life; I could feel his abiding love for the Marine Corps despite the bureaucratic corruption that may very well have cost Pfc Freeman his young life; and I was mourning the loss of Freeman, for his family and pregnant girlfriend especially, while also feeling, remarkably, that I, too, had served in the Marine Corps and that I, too, had commanded a detachment of young Marines aboard an aircraft carrier off the coast of Japan.

But more than any of this, standing on my father's mother's porch, I felt moved by the power of my father's writing gifts, and I began to sense that there was an entire part of him I'd never known and how could I possibly truly know my father if I did not know *this*?

NOT LONG AFTER, I read one of my father's short stories for the first time. This is what I wrote about that experience in my memoir, *Townie*: ". . . on a quiet Sunday morning, I took one of his collections off the shelf and read a story called 'Killings.' It was set in a place like Bradford Square and was about a father planning revenge for the murder of his youngest son. The sentences were lean and lyrical and cut deeply into the people Pop was writing about; it was only twenty-one pages long but felt as strong to me as *The Grapes of Wrath*, a novel I'd just read for school and was so moved by I had to go walking after. I had to go walking after reading my father's story, too. The air was cool and smelled like rain, and I walked up the grassy median of Columbia Park. At the base of an oak, I stopped and looked up at its bare branches against the sky. There was the feeling something important had just been revealed to me, that my father had created many stories like the one I'd just read and that's where most of him had been my whole life, in those pages, with people like the father who had lost his son."

I was perhaps twenty years old and had only read *The Lieutenant* and now this devastating short story. I began to read more of my father's stories, each one as beautifully written and often as moving as the next, and soon, much to my surprise, I began to write fiction myself. It was then that I began to learn how very difficult the act of writing fiction is to do well, never mind as artfully as my father had been consistently doing it over the years; and it became abundantly clear that my father had become a master at it. This was an opinion widely held, and in reviews or interviews he was consistently referred to as the "contemporary master of the short story" or as "America's Chekhov."

My father did not read reviews of his work more than once, and he never kept them, even the ones that were raves, but he did share with me once that he certainly did not mind being called "America's Chekhov," for he considered Anton Chekhov to be his artistic mentor, the writer whose work ultimately inspired my father to leave the long form of the novel for the concision of the short story. In a 1994 interview with Kay Bonetti, my father describes reading Chekhov's short story "Peasants" for the first time: "How did he do this? Because it's a thirty-page story that covers one family and its peasant village, and one year, and by doing that also painted a big canvas of what peasant society was like right after the freedom of the serfs, and it's one of the best stories I've ever read. And I finished that and I said, well if he did all that in thirty pages, then he must have used compressed action. So I re-

read it immediately. I said, by God, it is all in scenes. And each scene dramatizes more of his theme. . . . So I finished reading 'Peasants' for the second time, and I said, 'Andre, you're thirty-something years old. I think it's time to learn how to write. I'm going to learn to compress. I'm going to learn to make transitions. I'm gonna restudy Chekhov, and I'm gonna really study him rather than just have read him for pleasure.' And that's what I did. I started working on compressing, and that is why I'm here."

By "here," my father meant his being known not as a novelist but as a short story writer. Not long after this crucial moment in my father's artistic life, he took the pages of his novel-in-progress, held them over the trash basket beside his desk, and dropped them into it. He then rolled a fresh sheet of onionskin paper into his typewriter and began what became a life-long devotion to the short story.

In another interview, my father said of *The Lieutenant*, somewhat dismissively, that he wrote it while he was in his twenties and a student at the Iowa Writers' Workshop. (This was after he retired from the Marines as a captain.) He said years later that if he wrote the novel again, he would cut at least one hundred pages from it.

And yet, what could he have cut?

It has been fifty-five years since *The Lieutenant* was published, in 1967, and as I write this now, I am more than twice the age of my father when he wrote the novel. I have become a writer who works more in the long form than the short, someone who has read hundreds of novels since that long ago afternoon in my grandmother's house, someone who teaches the long form in universities and writers conferences, and I see very little nonessential material here. In fact, *The Lieutenant* strikes me as being a very promising debut for a future novelist.

There is so much my father does right here: he begins in medias res with the action already under way: in the first few pages, we learn that twenty-four-year-old Dan Tierney is leading a detachment of fifty-seven Marines aboard the USS *Vanguard* off the coast of Japan; we learn that he has been away from home for months and writes to his Stateside girlfriend daily; we discover that his commanding officer is being treated on shore for a serious ear infection, which results in young Tierney being given sole command of his troops for the next two weeks; and now, only three pages in, our protagonist is given his first test of leadership when he has to discipline Private First Class Theodore C. Freeman for mouthing off to his immediate superior officer, Corporal McKittrick.

Here, as we experience Lieutenant Tierney consulting the *Manual for Courts-Martial* to view his options for punishing Freeman, a central trait of Dan's character is revealed: he chooses to confine Freeman to the brig for three days on bread and water because "Bread-and-water had an aura of the old and traditional. He had heard about it from Staff NCO's when they spoke of the days when military justice had been revised (and ruined, they believed) . . ." Dan agrees, and we soon see that he "was afraid the Corps might evolve into something totally different from his concept of it." Within this rigid fealty to the old Corps—which includes Dan's insistence on carry-

254 • ANDRE DUBUS III

ing the traditional swagger stick even though his current
commandant has "belittled" it—lie the seeds of Dan Tierney's tragic flaw: an unwavering commitment to the myth
of what it means to be a Marine.

And yet, Lieutenant Tierney has no illusions that this
is a myth. By the beginning of chapter two in *The Lieutenant*, we are given our young protagonist's core belief
that to be a true Marine, one prepared for the sacrifice and
valor of battlegrounds like the Chosin Resevoir, Tarawa,
and Belleau Wood, one must first live the lie of what it
means to be a Marine. It was something he heard a lieutenant-general from Headquarters Marine Corps say in a
speech at a formal dinner, and Dan never forgot it: "The
career of a Marine officer is living the lie and making the
lie come true." And so, in his disciplining of Freeman—
and later McKittrick, Hahn, and Jensen—we watch Dan
Tierney perform the lie of what he believes a Marine officer's leadership should be, an act that leads to his covering
up the sexual assault on Corporal McKittrick, which ultimately leads to the unraveling of it all.

So, again: What could my father have cut? In this already
short novel—just 199 pages in its original hardcover—he
delivers to the reader a living, breathing *world*. Here, we are
given the felt experience of living aboard an aircraft carrier in the mid-twentieth century as a member of the U.S.
military; we are introduced to the blood-soaked history
of past wars and the ghosts that float through the myth
that continues to call young men to duty; we live through
drunken bouts in seaside bars in Japan and, as we descend
into Freeman's point of view and most notably into Dan

Tierney's letters to and from his girlfriend, Khristy, we are exposed to the sexual mores of the 1950s and 1960s, as well as the patriarchal and narrowly defined roles of young men and women of the time; and, perhaps most importantly we are confronted with the era's toxic homophobia.

Readers often make the mistake of confusing a novel's main character with his or her author, and as I read *The Lieutenant* again in the spring of 2022, I could feel myself doing that very thing, for I could see so much of my father in the character of Dan Tierney: my dad, too, had commanded a detachment of Marines aboard an aircraft carrier, the USS *Ranger*, off the coast of Japan (I've kept his gear trunk from that tour, his name and rank stenciled on the lid); my father, too, was only five feet nine inches tall and often self-conscious about having weighed just 139 pounds in high school, though over time, through daily exercise, he, too, became "lean and hard"; throughout Dan's dialogue, I see so many of my father's daily expressions and common word choices: *harass, crapping out, good for the soul, chewed me out, by God*; but especially in Dan's relationship to his girlfriend Khristy (and Freeman's with his girlfriend), I see my father's 1940s and 1950s vision that a man's girlfriend or wife should be: attractive and fertile and faithful, not to mention charming and resilient, but above all, her ultimate role should be to support her man in all ways. My father went on to write empathically and deeply about and from the points of view of many female characters over the course of his writing life; and even here, in Khristy's Dear John letter to Dan, we see genuine agency, a woman who will not be made just another Marine officer's wife, with all the subservience that that life would entail. But above all when rereading *The Lieutenant*, I see my father's lifelong love and devotion to the United States Marine Corps. It is a trait that Dan Tierney shares, so much so that he will lie to protect its image, and he will certainly do whatever he can to rid it of "queers." But this is where any semblance of the novel's main character to its author disappears.

For his entire life, my father was a fierce defender of the oppressed. He despised racism and all of its various chains; he hated poverty and imperialism and capitalism; he often tithed almost forty percent of his meager annual income to the poor; and he always defended a person's right to love another human being no matter their gender, a compassion shown beautifully in his essay "Imperiled Men"—this piece was published not long before my father died, in 1999, and its focus is on a decorated Navy pilot my father had known aboard the USS *Ranger*, a closeted gay man who was investigated by Naval Intelligence and told to resign or be court-martialed; the pilot, my father's friend, left that meeting, walked directly to his quarters, and shot himself in the head.

Today, we are fortunate to be living in a time when the U.S. Supreme Court has held that the Fourteenth Amendment requires all states to grant same-sex marriages and recognize same-sex marriages. So how are we to comprehend Lt. Dan Tierney's feelings regarding gay men in the Marine Corps? ("And if they were queer, then by God his first duty was to drum them out of the Corps. . . . There was no place in the Marine Corps for queers") I would argue that by allowing ourselves as readers to inhabit this hateful worldview (and again, one not shared by my father), we are availing ourselves of one of fiction's central gifts, which is the ability of its authors to take readers into private human experiences that they may not share. This, from Eudora Welty: "What I do in writing of any character is to try to enter into the mind, heart and skin of a human being who is not myself. Whether this happens to be a man or a woman, old or young, with skin black or white, the primary challenge lies in making the jump itself. It is the act of a writer's imagination that I set most high."

Of *The Lieutenant*, Richard Yates wrote: "You can read it one sitting and miss none of its power, but it deserves to be studied for the skill of its construction and the complexity of its interlocking ironies." All of which I missed in that first reading when I was nineteen or twenty years old; instead, I saw Dan Tierney in a heroic light, a young Marine officer who risked his career to save Freeman but then lost and so took his licks and continued to serve. But many years later, my father would tell me that when he was writing the scene when Tierney chooses not to resign his commission after Freeman's court-martial and death, my dad left his desk and told my mother later "Tierney just copped out." It was the way my father wrote all of his life, making the jump "into the mind, heart and skin of a human being" who was not himself, the result being that his characters exuded full agency, often surprising him with their thoughts, feelings, and actions.

And this is what makes *The Lieutenant* so successful and so readable all these years later: my father consistently made that jump Welty describes and captured a milieu that no longer exists. Faulkner reminds us that "the aim of every artist is to arrest motion, which is life, by artificial means and hold it fixed so that a hundred years later, when a stranger looks at it, it moves again since it is life. Since man is mortal, the only immortality possible for him is to leave something behind him that is immortal since it will always move. This is the artist's way of scribbling 'Kilroy was here' on the wall of the final and irrevocable oblivion through which he must someday pass."

ON A FRIGID night in February 1999, my father passed through that wall, and when he did he left behind ten books: seven of them contain his masterful short stories, the form for which he will be remembered; two are collections of his essays; and one, his only novel, is the book you hold in your hands. I believe he had all the requisite gifts to go on to write more novels, but it was not the form that called him. And that makes the reissuing of *The Lieutenant* by his longtime publisher, Godine, all the more precious. Despite his devotion to the short story, I am sure my father would be grateful for this. I feel confident that future readers of this fine novel will be too.

Andre Dubus III

2023

ABOUT THE AUTHOR

Andre Dubus was born in Lake Charles, Louisiana to a Cajun-Irish Catholic family. He graduated from the University of Iowa Writers' Workshop, and later settled in Massachusetts, where he lived for the rest of his life. Winner of the prestigious PEN/Malamud and Rea awards, and a finalist for the Pulitzer Prize, Dubus is widely regarded as a modern master of the American short story. He died in 1999.

Andre Dubus III's books include the *New York Times'* bestsellers *House of Sand and Fog*, *The Garden of Last Days*, and his memoir, *Townie*. His books are published in more than twenty-five languages. He lives in Massachusetts with his wife, Fontaine, a modern dancer, and teaches full-time at the University of Massachusetts Lowell.

A NOTE ON THE TYPE

The Lieutenant has been set in Caslon. This modern version is based on the early-eighteenth-century roman designs of British printer William Caslon I, whose typefaces were so popular that they were employed for the first setting of the Declaration of Independence, in 1776. Eric Gill's humanist typeface Gill Sans, from 1928, has been used for display.

Book Design & Composition by Tammy Ackerman